MURDER CREEK

RAINE STOCKTON MYSTERY #14

BY DONNA BALL

Copyright 2020 by Donna Ball, Inc.

ISBN: 978-0-9965610-9-9

Published by Blue Merle Publishing
Drawer H
Mountain City Georgia 30562

www.bluemerlepublishers.com

Cover art **www.bigstock.com**

First Published March, 2020

ONE

Little known fact: my great-great-great-grandfather, William Peter Stockton, was hanged for murder right here in Hanover County. According to legend, he had been at odds with a man by the name of Jeremiah Bowslayer, a Creek Indian whose property bordered Stockton's on the north and east and about which boundaries there was apparently some dispute. One day William Stockton's milk cow wandered across the creek onto Bowslayer's farm, and Bowslayer locked the cow up in his barn. When William came to get the cow, the other man claimed it was his by law, since it had been found fair and square grazing in his pasture. An argument ensued, which my great-great-great-grandfather solved by hitting Mr. Bowslayer over the head with a nearby ax handle and dumping his body in the creek.

"That," I told Melanie, "was the very first murder by a white man in Hanover County. And that's how the creek got its name."

We were on our way to a day of swimming and picnicking

at that very creek—my fiancé's ten-year-old daughter, Melanie, my three-year-old golden retriever, Cisco, Melanie's dog, Pepper, and yours truly, Raine Stockton. My two amazing Australian Shepherds, Mischief and Magic, are not wild about swimming, so they had stayed behind this trip. Besides, I figured I'd have my hands full with the crew I already had onboard.

I like to think that I am living proof that genetics aren't necessarily a determinate of destiny. The progenitor of the Stockton's claim on this little corner of Smoky Mountain paradise might have solved his problems with an ax handle—although family legend insists, of course, that he was completely innocent—but for the past one hundred years at least, our family has come down firmly on the side of law and order.

I am the latest in a long line of lawyers, judges, and cops. Even though I'm not technically any of those things, I came very close to being a game warden once, and I married—and divorced—a sheriff's deputy. Not to mention the fact that my search and rescue golden retriever, Cisco, and I have played a crucial part in bringing more than one bad guy to justice. That's something, right?

My aforementioned fiancé, Miles—also one of the smartest people I've ever known—says I have some kind of compensation complex. Who knows? Maybe he's right. I prefer to think that history doesn't control our destiny. Necessarily.

Melanie was busy fact-checking my story on her phone, two excited golden retrievers in the backseat panting and drooling over her shoulder. "According to Google," she said, "the Creek Indians were removed from North Carolina on the Trail of Tears in 1836."

"And the Stocktons came here in 1769," I replied. "They were some of the first settlers. William Stockton built his cabin here on the creek in 1833."

"Huh," said Melanie. "So, if he'd just waited a couple of years, Mr. Bowslayer would've been gone, and he could have had his cow back."

"Well," I said, wondering if I'd made a mistake in telling her the story.

"Boy, those Indians sure got a bum deal," observed Melanie, reading on.

"No argument there," I agreed.

"Huh," mused Melanie, thumbing a page. "Maybe I'll write about this for my essay in my Human Experience class."

Melanie was enrolled in one of those progressive private schools where History was called The Human Experience, and English class was called Thoughts into Words. It was hard for me not to roll my eyes whenever she talked about it. On the other hand, no one heard me complain when her Culinary Arts homework included homemade cinnamon rolls and pumpkin soufflé. And did I mention Melanie is only ten years old?

I said, "Sounds good to me."

So here's the deal: I know dogs, not kids. Yet somehow I had fallen flat-faced in love with one curly haired, slightly myopic, outrageously sophisticated know-it-all female child by the name of Melanie Young. By happy coincidence, I was also in love with her father. In a matter of months, it appeared, I was going to be a stepmother. And this weekend I had been granted the rare opportunity to test out my mothering skills while Miles was in Myrtle Beach with *his* mother, who was having gall bladder surgery. So far it was going great.

I mean, come on. How hard can it be? Kids need to be fed, exercised, and intellectually stimulated, just like dogs. They need to play, they need to sleep. Don't leave them out in the rain. Stick to a familiar routine. Reward with treats. People make child-raising sound way too hard.

Of course, it helps that Melanie is a great kid, and that we've been friends for a long time. I don't understand what Miles was so worried about.

Melanie said, "So I guess the moral of the story is that sometimes the good guys get it wrong."

I said, "It depends on who you're calling the good guys. If you're talking about Andrew Jackson and the Trail of Tears, then yes, he got it wrong. Absolutely."

"Yeah, but you said your great-great-great-grandfather was innocent. So some judge, way back then, got that wrong too."

I didn't quite know how to respond to that. It was just a family story, after all. I'd never given it that much thought. After a moment, I managed, a little uncertainly, "I'm not sure there were any judges involved."

Melanie gave a decisive nod of her head and tapped another page on her screen. "Mob rule," she pronounced. "Lynching. That's the first sign of the downfall of a civilized society. Did you know that there are more victims of mass incarceration today than there were slaves in the entire history of America?"

"Um ... no." I made the turn off the highway onto the narrow, winding road that led back into Forest Service land, roughly following the path of the creek.

"Somebody got it wrong," she said.

"I guess." I really wished Miles wouldn't let her watch so much television. If she were my daughter ... but then I realized that was exactly what she was about to become. My daughter.

Wow.

"Did you know that last year in America there were fifty-three police shootings of unarmed ..."

"Say, Mel," I interrupted, "will you do me a favor and text Corny to check on Ruffles? She didn't finish her breakfast this morning and I want to make sure she's not coming down with something."

In dog training, when you're faced with an undesirable behavior you have three options: retrain the behavior, change the environment, or substitute an incompatible behavior. For example, if you have a dog who stands at the window and barks at squirrels, you can either try to discourage the barking with some kind of a reward/punishment scenario—which can be a lengthy and often ineffective process—or you can close the curtains so the dog can't see the squirrels, or you can put peanut butter on the roof of the dog's mouth. A dog can't bark and lick peanut butter at the same time, any more than a kid can search Google and text at the same time. Eventually, instead of barking, the dog will start to look to you for a peanut butter treat when he sees a squirrel, and I happen to know that Melanie likes bossing other people around even more than she likes following Google links on her phone. Problem solved.

See? Raising kids is not so different from raising dogs, after all.

"Corny says Ruffles had a long walk, played with Samson and Radar for half an hour, and caught a butterfly," Melanie reported. "Now she's napping."

"Great," I said. "Thanks."

I should explain that Ruffles is a two-year-old Pomeranian who is currently a guest at Dog Daze Boarding and Training facility, which I own. Corny is the head groomer and general manager, and the only way Ruffles could have been in better hands is if those hands had been my own ... and, honestly, maybe not even then. Also, of course, I had never been in the least worried about the Pom; I just needed a way to distract Melanie.

Melanie's phone chimed again, and she added, "He also says Ruffles finished her breakfast after we left."

"Perfect."

Another chime.

"He wants to know if everything is okay."

"Tell him everything's fine." I would have to apologize to Corny later for alarming him. "Just checking."

I turned onto the short dirt trail beside the road sign for Murder Creek while Melanie typed out and sent my message. She looked up, searching the surrounding woodlands with interest.

"So where did it happen?" she asked.

"What's that?" I minded my driving, trying to maneuver my new vehicle around the ruts and potholes. Of course, the SUV was built to go off-road, but new is new, and I was trying to avoid as many dings to the finish as possible.

"The murder," Melanie said, craning her neck to look out the back window.

"I'm not sure. The creek is pretty long, and I think my grandpa told me one time that the log cabin where the Stocktons first lived was on the other side of it."

"Cool," she said, "Can we go see?"

"The cabin fell down a long time ago," I told her. "And someone else owns the property now."

"Oh yeah? Who?"

"Oh, a lot of people. It used to be a big piece of land, but it's been divided up and sold to different folks over the years."

"Like who?" she persisted.

I had a feeling that somewhere in my future lay a long hike across private property to search for the remains of a two-hundred-year-old log cabin.

I said, "Well, Sheriff Becker, for one. He bought a piece of land over there a few years back and built a new house. And Stan Bixby, one of the people who's going to do the program at your school with me on Monday."

"You mean the guy from the animal shelter?" queried Melanie. "Yeah, he's cool. He brought some of the puppies and kittens that are up for adoption to the Harvest Festival last fall."

"He's also a past president of the Historical Society," I said. "He probably knows more about the Stocktons than I do."

But, predictably, Melanie was far more interested in Mr. Bixby's role as an animal advocate. "Do you think he'll bring more puppies to school Monday?"

"Probably," I said. "Either that, or one of his rescue dogs."

This close to the end of the school year, animal welfare education programs were in big demand at all the elementary and middle schools in the area; I think they were probably one of the few ways teachers could keep the kids' attention as they counted down the days to summer break. Cisco and I were scheduled to do a program of tricks that highlighted his "find it" skills and talk about how we'd gotten into search and rescue. Stan did a great speech about the importance of spaying and neutering, and the sheriff's office usually sent the

K-9 team, which was always a big hit, despite the somewhat dour personality of the county's one and only K-9 handler. All in all, it was a great two hours out of the classroom for the kids, and Cisco and I always had a blast.

"Is that it?" Melanie persisted. "Just Sheriff Becker and the animal shelter guy?"

It took me a minute to realize she had changed subjects again. "Well," I remembered, "there are those folks who own the big horse farm. What's their name? Callanwell."

The remainder of the creek-front property, I knew but did not mention, either belonged to or would eventually belong to her own father, Miles Young. Miles is the premier real estate developer in Hanover County, and one of the top three richest men in the southeast. Or maybe the world by now, as far as I know. This is not something I generally brag about, or even like to think about, to be honest. His tendency to look at virgin forest and immediately start doing calculations in his head about how many housing units it would hold is something we still argue about.

"Dad said I can have a horse," Melanie informed me.

"Oh, yeah?" I happened to know that what Miles had really said was that he would think about it. On the other hand, Melanie was probably right: I had never known Miles to ever deny her anything she wanted. It was just a matter of time.

"We'll probably go shopping for one this summer," she said easily. "You can come too. Maybe we'll go to that horse farm. Maybe we'll see the murder place."

"Maybe."

"So why did you move?" she asked as I made the turn toward the primitive parking area and the trail that led to the creek. "They, I mean," she corrected. "The old-timey Stocktons."

I shrugged. "They wanted a nicer house, I guess. One that was closer to town."

The house they had eventually built was a white-columned, two-story farmhouse nestled at the foot of Hawk Mountain, and I still live there. It had been finished in the late 1800s and was old by any standard, but better than a log cabin, I guess.

"So did they take that land from the Indians, too?"

The question was asked completely without judgement, but I gave her a look of dry reprimand anyway. "For your information," I replied, "the Stocktons already owned that land. They owned everything from here to the other side of Hawk Mountain."

Her eyes went big behind her glasses. "Wow," she said. "You used to be rich."

I shrugged. "Not really. Did you ever hear of thing called 'land poor'?"

She started typing on her phone and I said, "Don't Google it. It's when someone has a lot of land but no money to buy groceries. It used to happen a lot in the South, especially in the mountains, where it was hard to grow crops."

"Huh," she said. "Then why did they want to steal even more land from the Indians, if they already had so much land it was making them poor?"

This parenting thing was exhausting. "Sounds like a good question for you to answer in your essay," I said, and eased the SUV into the narrow, graveled parking area across from the Murder Creek trailhead.

There are literally thousands of waterfalls, streams and hiking trails in this part of the Smoky Mountains. Many are well-known tourist spots that welcome throngs of visitors every year. Others are so far off the beaten path that just finding them is an accomplishment in itself, and others, like the Murder Creek Wildlife Preserve, are known mostly to locals. That was why I was surprised—and a little disappointed, I'll admit—to find another vehicle, a Honda CRV with a Florida license plate, already parked in the four-space parking lot beside the wooded trail that led to the creek. It was the week before Memorial Day and tourist season had not officially begun. We tax-paying residents of one of the most beautiful places on earth had a reasonable expectation of keeping paradise to ourselves for a little while longer.

Nonetheless, I tried not to sound too resentful as I said, "Okay, we'll have to keep the dogs on leash while we're on the trail. You can get them out while I check on your grandmother."

But Melanie was already out of the vehicle, scrambling to release Cisco and Pepper from their canine seat belts and get them into their leashes and backpacks. Normally I would not recommend putting a ten-year-old in charge of two big golden retrievers, but Melanie was no ordinary ten-year-old. I had trained her myself. I had also trained Pepper and Cisco. Nonetheless I kept a careful eye on all three of them as I walked around to the back of the SUV, texting Miles, *How is she?*

I opened the back cargo door to retrieve our gear. Miles replied, *She just went into surgery. Spirits good. Drs say it's routine. She'll be fine.*

I could hear the anxiety behind his confident words, and I understood. As far as future mothers-in-law go, Rita was the best, and I was worried too. I texted back, *Give her my love when she wakes up.*

Out of the corner of my eye I saw Cisco bound out of the backseat, his ears already pricked toward the strange car in the parking lot. In Cisco's world, every new thing was a potential adventure, and every new creature—be it human, canine, or skunk—was a new friend. I heard Melanie say in her stern, big-dog-trainer voice, "Cisco! No!" when he started to bolt toward the car, and I was proud of both of them—Melanie and Cisco—when he actually listened to her and resumed his sit. "Treat," I reminded her, and she produced two from her pocket, one for Cisco and one for Pepper, who was sitting like a champion and whose devoted eyes had never left her mistress.

Miles replied, *Will do. What are you girls up to today?*

I replied to Miles, *Swimming and a picnic at Murder Creek. Afterwards, a little tracking practice.*

He replied, *Too cold to swim,* with a frowny face.

Conventional wisdom has it that no one goes swimming in

the mountains before the Fourth of July. One of the things Melanie and I have in common is a delight in defying conventional wisdom. I typed back, *I know*. Smiley face.

There was a pause while he counted to three. I couldn't help grinning.

His better nature surfaced, and he replied, *Have fun. Love you. Call you later.*

And then ... wait for it ... *Be careful.*

Miles can be a little overprotective. It was something I was learning to live with, just like he was learning to live with the fact, I suppose, that there was a lot I needed protecting from. Or at least that was probably the way it seemed to him.

I typed back, *I will.* I added a heart emoji and a pawprint, and tucked my phone back into my pocket.

"Good job, Mel," I said of the two golden retrievers sitting more-or-less attentively at her feet. I reached inside the car to drag out our backpacks. "Your dad says your grandmother just went into surgery. The doctors say she's going to be fine."

"Probably," agreed Melanie sanguinely. "Unless they nick a bile duct. Then she could die."

I was quick to assure her, "I don't think she's going to die."

"Everyone dies," Melanie returned, holding up a treat for Pepper to follow with her eyes. "And Grandma's pretty old."

I hate it when she talks like that, mostly because I never know how to respond. But Melanie's mother had died violently less than a year ago, and the counselor Miles took her to said that this assumed air of nonchalance toward death was a coping mechanism she would eventually outgrow. I hoped she was right. Because, as I mentioned, I never know what to say.

I slipped my arms into my backpack, which held the majority of our supplies, and passed two sets of canine saddlebags to Melanie. "Here you go," I said. "Get the dogs buckled up."

One of my rules is that everyone carries his or her own gear when we're hiking, even dogs—or I should probably say, especially dogs. If I had filled my own pack with enough bottles of water for two dogs and two people there wouldn't have been room for anything else, so each dog's saddlebags were packed with a collapsible bowl, enough water to last the day, a micro-fiber towel, and a supply of treats. I'd also packed a couple of floating balls because the point, after all, was to have fun.

I waited while Melanie struggled with the buckles of Pepper's brand-new, leather-trimmed designer backpack. I didn't offer to help because Melanie preferred to do things herself, and because I had told her not to get leather. Now she knew why. Cisco's well-worn red canvas backpack, frayed at the edges and scuffed with the charcoal of a campfire or two, lay on the ground at his feet, where he nosed it impatiently. I gave him a small apologetic shrug of my shoulders. I had told Melanie to take care of it, and he would just have to wait.

But waiting, for a three-year-old golden retriever, is a relative term. In his mind, he had already waited longer than any dog should be required to do without a treat. And while Pepper, who was almost two years younger, patiently endured the fumbling of Melanie's chubby fingers with her backpack, Cisco had been charged and ready to go since the minute the car stopped. I could see in his eyes what he was about to do, and I reached for his leash even before we both heard the sound that caused him to bolt.

"Hey!" Melanie cried as Cisco leapt past her with a bark, trailing his leash.

"Cisco, halt!" I shouted, and he halted—as soon as he reached his destination.

He flung his paws up onto the window of the car on the opposite side of the parking lot, barking triumphantly. Melanie, abandoning Pepper, chased after him. Pepper raced after Melanie but only got a few steps before her backpack fell off. I went to untangle Pepper from her backpack before she hurt herself, and Melanie called, "Raine, come here!"

I glanced up long enough to make sure Melanie had Cisco's leash, but before I could command Cisco to get his paws off the stranger's car, Melanie cried again, urgently, "Raine, hurry!

I think there's a dog in here!"

I let Pepper's backpack drop, caught her leash, and trotted over to the other vehicle. "Cisco, quiet!" I commanded, and he looked at me with tongue lolling. The minute he stopped his barking, I could hear it too: the high-pitched, half yelp/half whine of a trapped dog.

I said to Cisco, "Off!" and he could tell by the expression on my face that I meant business. Dogs usually can.

Cisco dropped to all fours and I passed Pepper's leash to Melanie. I went around the car quickly, checking the doors. They were all locked. I cupped my hands against the back window, where the cries seemed to be the loudest, and tried to peer inside. But the windows were tinted and the outside light created a glare, and all I could make out was a shape of indeterminate size on the floorboard. The pathetic cries were growing more desperate, but the animal was either too afraid or too weak to come to the window. "Damn it," I muttered. Who *does* that? Who leaves a dog locked in the car in May— or any time, for that matter—while they go on a hike?

Melanie said anxiously, "Do you want me to call 911?"

I straightened up, looking around. "Hey!" I shouted, as loudly as I could. "Hey, is anybody there?"

I'm not at all sure what I was hoping for—that the owners of the vehicle would have just stepped into the woods for a moment and would come bursting through at the sound of our voices; that they were even now coming down the trail toward their car? It was foolish, of course. Whoever had left this poor animal locked in a car without even cracking the windows on a summer day—even if the car was parked in the shade— would have heard us drive up if he or she was even remotely nearby.

I said, "No. It'll take the police too long to get here." The whimpers were already growing weaker.

I turned back toward the trail and called again, "Hello!"
Nothing.

There is a law in North Carolina against leaving an animal in a car under dangerous conditions—"dangerous conditions" being widely left open to interpretation. There is also a law against breaking into a car to rescue said animal unless you are a law officer, fireman, or other first responder. I was hereby designating myself a first responder.

I dropped my backpack and ran back to my car, trying to remember where the emergency tools were. Even though I'd paid careful attention when the salesman went over all of my new car's features, I had not yet had cause to use the jack. I finally found the tool bag in a compartment on the left-hand side of the cargo area and extricated the jack handle. I ran back to the abandoned vehicle and checked the backseat to make sure the dog hadn't moved to the front.

"Take the dogs over there away from the car," I told Melanie, gesturing toward the far end of the parking lot. "Stand on the other side of my car so they don't get hit by flying glass."

While she hurried away, I put on my sunglasses to protect my own eyes and double-checked to make sure both dogs and one child were out of range. It took three of my hardest swings with the jack handle before the driver's side window shattered, scattering safety glass all over the front seat. I don't know how car thieves make it look so easy. By then the car alarm was blaring and the lights were flashing, and still no one came. I reached inside and popped the automatic door locks.

"It's okay, big guy," I told the poor terrified creature inside. "I'm coming."

Melanie was already running back toward the car, trailing a tangle of dogs and leashes behind her. Cisco lunged ahead, pulling the leash out of her hand. She cried indignantly. "Hey!" but he didn't even look around.

I ran around to the passenger-side back door, where there was less glass, and yanked it open. Cisco reached me just as a big black blur of fur burst out of the car with such desperate force that it knocked me back. I gripped the door handle to keep from being swept off my feet, and the dog took off down the trail toward the creek with Cisco in hot pursuit.

"Cisco!" cried Melanie, running after him.

13

I caught her arm. "Wrong," I said firmly, breathing hard. "You stay here. Hold on to Pepper. I'll get him."

"But—"

I gave her a look that had been known to send a full-grown Rottweiler slinking to his crate without my having to utter a word and had even stopped her father in mid-sentence on more than one occasion. "Here," I repeated darkly, pointing to a spot on the ground.

Pepper sat immediately, but Melanie didn't even blink. "You can't leave me alone," she pointed out. "That's child endangerment."

I continued to try to stare her down.

"Dad will be mad."

Damn it. She was right. Meanwhile, Cisco was getting farther and farther away.

"I just don't want you to get in trouble," she explained innocently.

"Oh, all right!" I started toward the trail at a trot. "Just keep up."

She grinned and took up another loop in Pepper's leash, following fast on my heels. "Come on, Pepper, track Cisco!"

Cisco is a certified therapy dog, a Canine Good Citizen, an obedience competitor, an agility champion and an accomplished wilderness search and rescue dog. He knows dozens of tricks and can even put a basketball through a hoop nine times out of ten. He's been through countless obedience courses and almost always graduates at the top of his class. He is in practically every way an amazing dog. He just has a teensy, tiny problem with impulse control.

He has humiliated me in the obedience ring by completing the long down without twitching a muscle, and, immediately upon being released, dashing across the ring and knocking the judge flat on her back. He has humiliated me in the agility ring by breaking out of his crate and running the course all by himself—when it wasn't even his turn. He has humiliated me at tracking class by taking me on a two-hour chase through poison-ivy infested woods trailing a deer. And he humiliates me every single time he sees my ex-husband, Buck Lawson, by abandoning whatever task he was supposed to be focused on and flinging himself with puppy-like exuberance into Buck's arms.

This behavior used to upset and frustrate me. Now it's become par for the course. What Cisco wants, Cisco goes after. The good news is, he almost always comes back. And for those trainers out there who are smugly looking down their noses at me and saying, "There are no bad dogs, only bad trainers," I wish you, at least once in your life, had a dog just like Cisco.

The trail stopped at the creek about fifty feet away from the parking area, then made a sharp uphill left, following the creek to a wide, shallow waterfall. There were jumping rocks and clear, sandy wading pools, and the waterfall had worn down a big, sloping rock formation into the perfect waterslide. At the bottom of the slide was a pond deep enough to swim in, and surrounding it was a smooth grassy glade that was perfect for picnics. This was where Melanie and I had planned to spend the day, and we would have had a great time, too, despite what Miles said about the cold. I just hoped that some of our fun could still be salvaged.

If I knew Cisco, and I did, he had headed straight for the creek—and so, probably, had the terrified, overheated and probably dehydrated black dog. I could hear them thrashing through the undergrowth beside the trail ahead of us, so I wasn't too worried. But when the trail widened and spread out along the gentle slope of the creek bank, all that changed.

I stopped abruptly, flinging out my arm to keep Melanie back, and I stared. There was a man floating facedown in the creek only a few steps away.

He was wearing khaki pants and a summer plaid shirt with brown loafers and a gold wristwatch. He was a big man, maybe two hundred pounds, and thin strands of wet, grayish hair clung to the back of his skull. All of this I took in with one breath, and all of it registered as something being very, very wrong. I said hoarsely to Melanie, "Stay back."

She said, too close beside me, "What is that?" She tried to peer around me. "Is that a person?"

I slid the few steps down the creek bank into the icy water, wading over to the figure. I slipped a couple of times on hidden rocks and fell to one knee, soaking my jeans. When I reached the man I grabbed his shoulder and almost recoiled in horror. It was cold and hard, unmalleable and rigid, more like a mannequin's arm than a human's. I made myself press my fingers against his neck, searching for a pulse, but I knew it was futile. His skin was like ice, but so were my fingers by then. Gasping and trying to keep my teeth from chattering, I steeled myself and grasped both his shoulders, trying to turn him over. But I couldn't budge him. It was probably just as well. I was beginning to suspect he had been in the water for a while.

This was not my first dead body. In search and rescue, the outcome is not always a happy one. But it never, ever gets any easier.

I staggered back a few steps, heading toward the bank, clawing for my phone with fingers that felt like dead wood. I heard Melanie cry, "Cisco!"

I turned to see Cisco splashing down the creek toward us, followed closely by the big, shaggy, wet, black dog. I surged forward to grab Cisco's leash and ward off the dogs before they could disturb the body. And that was when I got my first good look at the dog we had rescued from the car, and my second shock of the day.

I knew that dog. The last time I had seen him had been on a poster with a missing child. His name was Mozart, and he had disappeared with a little girl named Kylie from their bedroom one night six years ago while Kylie's parents slept only a few dozen feet away. We searched for weeks, but no sign of either of them had ever been found.

Until now.

TWO

Six years ago I was still working for the Forest Service, and volunteering in Search and Rescue with my brilliant, beloved golden retriever, Cassidy, may she rest in peace. Dog Daze Boarding and Training was barely the glimmer of an idea in the back of my head, but I taught beginner obedience classes in my backyard on Saturday afternoons during the spring and summer. Every dog who completed the six-week course and demonstrated a reasonable competence with the four basic commands—sit, stay, down and come—got to march down the aisle to "Pomp and Circumstance" wearing a cardboard mortarboard, where he received a snazzy red-and-gold graduation certificate with a goofy-looking cartoon hound dog logo that announced his accomplishment to the world. The logo, and the certificate, are still the ones I use today.

I don't pretend to remember every dog who's been through one of my obedience courses, particularly the ones from that long ago. But Mozart was hard to forget. His family lived just across the state line in South Carolina, about a thirty-minute drive from me, but they were more than willing to make the trip every Saturday. It didn't take me long to figure out why.

Mozart was a black Lab-Newfie mix with a thick, rough coat and a white starburst blaze right between his eyes, as though he'd been spattered with white paint. One floppy ear was set a little higher than the other, giving him a permanently quizzical look. He was eight months old and already weighed ninety pounds, which, given his build, made him look like a lean, shaggy bear. The first day of class he pulled the leash out of his dad's hand and thundered into me, slamming his front paws onto my shoulders and knocking me flat on my butt. I am 5'5", and when he stood on his hind legs, he was drooling into my hair. And he wasn't yet full grown.

He had been kicked out of three obedience classes before mine. He had pulled his first trainer down and broken her collarbone. He had jumped through a plate glass window to get at a squirrel. A lot of dogs chew up the garage-door opener; Mozart chewed up the garage door. There wasn't a mean bone in his great big, clumsy, grinning, slobbering body, but he was completely out of control. And like most dog owners, his family waited too long to realize it.

I'm a pretty good dog trainer, but I'm no miracle worker. By the end of the first class I suspected I might be the fourth dog trainer who gently suggested that Mozart might not be suited for a group-class setting. And then I noticed something interesting.

As a general rule, I don't allow children under twelve in my classes, and it states as much very clearly on the class application form. But what was I supposed to do when Jason Goodwin showed up for class with his blond-haired, pig-tailed three-year-old daughter in tow, claiming a babysitting emergency? He promised she wouldn't be any trouble, and he was as good as his word. Kylie Goodwin had sat obediently on a camp chair her dad brought, quietly sucking her thumb throughout the class while her dad worked up a sweat trying to keep Mozart from squashing a chihuahua with his paw or taking off half his handler's arm when he tried to offer him a treat.

I remember thinking that if only Goodwin's dog was as well behaved as his child, the class would have gone much more smoothly for everyone.

Mozart lunged this way and that, chasing the other dogs, trying to snatch bumblebees from the air, tangling himself and others up in the leash. Where Mozart went, whoever was attached to the other end of the leash followed. If I'd had the entire class hour to concentrate on nothing but Mozart, I might have been able to teach him to sit for a treat. But I didn't think there was a trainer in the world who could have brought that shaggy-haired monster under reliable leash control in a mere six weeks.

But as they were leaving, a weary, irritable dad holding on to the leash with both hands and assuming the stance of a skier on a tow rope, little Kylie started bouncing up and down, begging to take the leash from her dad's hands. I started to call out a warning as the vision of a perfect disaster unfolded before my eyes, but too late. The dad, who apparently knew what he was doing, handed the leash over to his little girl and, to my astonishment, the big dog fell into step beside her. It looked like one of those memes you see on the internet: the little girl barely came up to his shoulder, but the dog pranced along beside her on a loose leash, as proud as he could be.

Thus began the education of Mozart. I decided to break my policy about having children in an obedience class, and when Kylie returned the next week, I showed her how to feed her dog treats out of the palm of her hand, how to hold the leash, and how to speak to her dog so that he could understand. I've never seen a dog more devoted to a child, nor a child more in love with her dog—not even Melanie, who is convinced that Pepper could teach at Harvard while piloting the space shuttle if given half a chance. Long story short, it was Kylie who walked Mozart down the aisle to a recording of "Pomp and Circumstance," and Kylie who proudly accepted his graduation certificate six weeks later. The first time I ever met Kylie's mother was at that graduation, and I remember being surprised because up until then I'd thought Jason Goodwin was a single dad. I remember her as a wan, absent-looking woman who had to be shown how to operate the video camera her husband had brought to memorialize the occasion. Of course, I always encourage photographs at graduation, and the little girl posing with the big dog in front of my red-and-gold graduation certificate was so cute I even took a picture for myself.

That was in July. In October, that photograph of Mozart and a grinning, gap-toothed Kylie Goodwin holding up their diploma from my obedience school was plastered across every media outlet from Asheville to Miami.

Do you really think I could forget something like that?

Apparently, both Kylie and her dog disappeared during the night from her family's home in South Carolina. At first, the parents thought Kylie had gotten up early and wandered off with her dog. I could see that. The two were inseparable, and where Kylie went, Mozart would follow. Maybe she'd decided to take him for a walk and had gotten lost. Or maybe Mozart had somehow escaped the yard, and Kylie tried to chase him down. At any rate, one cold night passed, and then another. Even though the South Carolina border is usually beyond my territory, when the call went out for experienced search teams, Cassidy and I didn't hesitate about joining.

It was a nightmare, as these things always are. It turned out that Carol Goodwin came from money, and there was a suspicion that Kylie might have been kidnapped for ransom. Jason Goodwin went on television and pleaded for her safe return, but it was days before Carol made a public appearance. Even then, she was so distraught that her pleas dissolved into sobs after the first couple of words.

Meantime, we searched the surrounding woods, neighborhoods and back roads for over a week. I think we all knew it was futile even before they started to drag the lake that was a little over a mile away. The temperatures dropped below 40 degrees, and I kept remembering stories about dogs who had kept lost children warm at night during much worse conditions. Then I reminded myself that Mozart was a water dog, so even if Kylie had somehow made it as far as the lake, there was still a chance. But ten days after her disappearance, the water team found a pair of little girl's pajamas tangled in the weeds at the bottom of the lake, and a near-hysterical Carol Goodwin confirmed they were the ones her daughter was wearing the last time she had seen her. The ground search was called off, and even though they continued to drag the lake for another week, Kylie's body was never found.

The police turned their attention to the father, Jason Goodwin, who had apparently been their prime suspect all along. I had trouble believing there was any foundation to their suspicions, but once law enforcement fixed on him as a suspect, the investigation—and the search—was virtually over. I guess there was some trouble in the marriage, because some neighbors reported raised voices and slammed doors. They even questioned me about whether or not I had noticed anything, but all I knew was what I had seen in obedience class: a patient and devoted father who drove an hour round-trip to get training for the family pet, and who doted on his daughter.

Eventually the authorities, lacking evidence, abandoned their case against Jason Goodwin. The Goodwin family, broken forever, faded into obscurity. Kylie Goodwin's disappearance blended into an endless collage of missing children and was virtually forgotten by the public. But all it took was the sight of one big, shaggy black dog to bring it all back for me.

THREE

"It's the same dog," I insisted in an urgent undertone to Deputy Jolene Smith, who was taking my report. I kept an eye on Melanie, a few dozen yards away, not wanting her to overhear. "It's the same dog from the Kylie Goodwin case. I know it is!"

I had tied Mozart to the back bumper of my car with the spare leash I kept in the glove compartment, and returned Cisco and Pepper to the backseat, safely buckled into their canine seat belts, to keep them out of the way while police cars and rescue trucks swarmed the tiny parking area. Melanie kept all three dogs occupied with bits of the ham sandwiches I'd brought for our lunch.

The clearing was crowded with six deputies, radios crackling, and the red rescue truck. Two more deputies had accompanied the EMTs down the trail to the creek. The coroner's van was the last to arrive. Light bars strobed and swirled. The peaceful little hideaway in the middle of nowhere was neither peaceful nor hidden any longer.

Jolene, jotting down notes in her field book, glanced at me skeptically. "You last saw that dog six years ago? As a puppy?"

"Yes, but—"

"There are a lot of big black dogs in the world, Stockton," she replied, unimpressed.

Jolene was ex-military, ex-Homeland, and ex-Jersey girl. She was the Sheriff Office's only African American deputy, and the fact that she had recently been promoted to chief deputy over men who had been there much longer than she probably hadn't done much to increase her popularity among the guys. Not that she was the easiest person to like under the best of circumstances, and not that she gave any appearance of caring one way or the other what people thought of her, but Jolene and I had our issues—none of which were my fault.

"This one was different," I insisted. "I wouldn't forget him. The man—the drowning victim—has to be connected with the case somehow. He might even be the killer!"

Jolene replied, without looking up from her notebook, "I doubt it. His ID says he's a retired cop from Jacksonville, Florida. James Carlton Rutherford, age sixty-nine."

That took me aback for just a minute. "I wonder what he was doing down here." I also wondered what he could possibly be doing with Mozart, but decided not to press that subject further with Jolene—not until I had more information, anyway.

"No idea." She glanced around. "This place is pretty remote. Any other way to get in?"

I had spent a lifetime exploring the woods of Hanover County, and even Jolene had to respect my expertise in that area. I shook my head. "Not with a car. And that guy sure didn't hike in, not dressed like that." I hesitated, glancing again at Melanie. "What do you think happened? Could he have fallen, maybe from the waterfall?"

She shrugged. "So how long would you say you were here before you heard the dog barking?"

"I don't know, maybe five minutes. But the guy, he'd been in the water for a while. He was, you know, really cold. Maybe a heart attack?"

"Maybe." She glanced across the way at Melanie. "Is that Young's daughter?"

"Yes," I said, trying to disguise my irritation. Jolene knew perfectly well who Melanie was. They had met on at least five separate occasions, not including the one in which the three of us had been held captive by a band of heavily armed militia for an entire day. You'd think something like that would be a bonding experience, but I guess not.

"Where's her father?"

"In Myrtle Beach," I replied. "Why?"

"He doesn't hang around home much, does he?" she observed.

I didn't see what that had to do with anything, but I replied evenly, "That's why we get along so well."

She almost looked amused. "I can understand that. Do you have a temporary order of custody?"

"Of course," I replied without blinking. Some time ago Miles had given me a paper to sign that allowed me to make emergency decisions on Melanie's behalf if he couldn't be reached. I only hoped Jolene didn't ask to see it, because I had no idea where it was.

She jerked her head toward my car, indicating that I should follow as she walked over.

Melanie snatched her hand away just in time to prevent Mozart from swallowing her fist as she tried to coax him into a sit with a bit of ham. She gave me an annoyed look. "This dog," she informed me, "is not very well trained."

Jolene slid me a look, but refrained from comment. She bent down to look at his collar, expertly blocking the dog's head with her opposite arm as she did so. Jolene is the county's only K-9 officer, and with her munitions-detection dog, Nike, has made a few notable saves. I have to admit, she knows what she's doing when it comes to dogs.

"It says here the dog's name is Buzz," she said, turning the tag toward me. "There's a phone number, but I can't make it out." She straightened up. "We'll notify the deceased's next of kin to come pick him up."

I set my teeth but said nothing. What could I say?

Jolene turned to Melanie. "Miss Melanie Young?" she inquired.

Melanie stuffed the remainder of the ham-and-cheese treats into her pocket and straightened her shoulders importantly. Mozart regarded her fixedly, a long strand of drool stretching from his chops toward the ground.

"That's right," she said. "My address is 49 Eagle's Landing Boulevard, Hansonville, North Carolina. My phone number is …"

"That's all right," Jolene interrupted, keeping a straight face. "We have it on file. Just tell me what happened from the time you and Miss Stockton arrived."

"We arrived on the scene at 11:42 a.m.," reported Melanie. "I know because I was looking something up on my phone at the time." She peered at Jolene suspiciously. "You probably want to write this down. It might be important."

Now it was my turn to fight a smile. Jolene put pen to paper.

"Go on," she said.

"I proceeded to get the dogs out of the car while Raine texted my dad," Melanie went on. "You should check her phone to get an exact timeline."

"We'll do that," murmured Jolene.

"That all took about two minutes," Melanie said, "then Cisco got away and ran toward that car over there." She pointed to the vehicle that two deputies were even now searching. "I ran after him and heard a dog barking inside."

Jolene said, "That was the first time you heard the dog barking?"

Melanie said decisively, "Yes."

I added, "I think Cisco might have heard something when we first pulled in. He was anxious to get to the car."

Melanie gave me a dark look. She did not like to have her judgement questioned.

Melanie went on, "As I said, I ran after Cisco, who had put his paws on the back window of the car." Again she pointed. "I could hear the dog barking really clearly then, and I called for Raine."

"Who broke out the front window," said Jolene, trying to move things along.

But Melanie was a stickler. I always did think she'd make a great prosecutor. "First she ran to the vehicle and determined there was a distressed animal inside. Then she called out. Twice. When no one came, she ran back to her car and got a jack handle. I'd say the whole thing took about, oh, three minutes."

Jolene nodded, taking notes. "Go on."

"I took the dogs to the other side of the parking lot, so they wouldn't get hurt," Melanie said. "Then Raine smashed the window. She reached inside and unlocked the door. Then she ran around to the back-passenger door and opened it. The big dog jumped out and ran away. Cisco pulled the leash out of my hand and ran after him."

She proceeded to relate, in infinite detail, how we had tracked the dogs down the narrow trail to the creek, and found the drowned man. "I couldn't see much," she concluded, "but I knew he was dead. If he hadn't been, Raine would've tried to revive him."

I appreciated the vote of confidence, but I could tell Jolene was not impressed. She asked a few more questions, and Melanie was a faithful reporter, taking us up to the time the first sheriff's deputy had arrived. Jolene took careful notes. She said, "Thank you, Miss Young. We'll be in touch if we have further questions."

Melanie said, "I'm planning a career in law enforcement. Do you have any advice for me?"

Jolene did not look up from the last few notes she was jotting in her field book. "Stay in school. Don't do drugs."

Melanie's eyebrows shot up in a mixture of scorn and disappointment. "That's it?"

Jolene closed her notebook and met Melanie's gaze, deadpan. Then she jerked her head toward me. "Listen to everything this one says," she advised. Just as I was starting to soften toward her, she added, "And then do the opposite."

She walked away, and I swear this time she grinned.

I turned to Melanie. "You start packing up," I said. "I need to check with Deputy Smith about something."

"What about our picnic?"

"You fed it to the dogs," I reminded her. "We'll stop for burgers on the way home."

"Maybe," she suggested hopefully, "we could hike down the creek and look for arrow heads and pottery shards."

The expression on my face must have suggested I had no idea what she was talking about, because she reminded me, "You said Mr. Bowslayer lived here, remember?"

"Right," I agreed. "But I don't think he used arrowheads. And we don't want to get in the way of the police. Just get our gear back in the car, and buckle up."

"What about him?" She pointed to the big black dog.

I hesitated. Jolene and I had recently had a dispute about the disposition of a dog whose owner had been taken into custody. She had wanted to follow procedure and turn him over to the animal shelter; I had wanted to take him home with me. I had won that round, but I didn't think she would let me get away with it again. On the other hand, if this *was* Mozart—and nothing that I'd learned so far convinced me otherwise—there was no way I was letting him out of my sight.

I said, "I'll let you know. I'll be right back." I trotted after Jolene.

She was taking a report from one of the deputies who had searched the car, but looked up immediately when I reached her. "Stockton," she demanded, "were the keys in the car when you broke in?"

I didn't like the way she put that: *broke in.* But I replied, "I don't know. I didn't see them, but I wasn't looking."

I added to the deputy, "Hey, Carl." I know all the deputies on the force, and most of them know me from the time my uncle and, more recently, my ex-husband were their bosses. It's only polite to say hello.

He replied, "Hey, Raine. Looks like tourist season is here early, huh?"

I sighed. "Yeah, I guess. I just can't figure out what he was doing out here, can you? Hardly anybody knows about this place, and no one comes out this time of year."

He said, "The state patrol is working a big wreck on I-26, closed down about four miles of it. A lot of traffic was diverted onto 81. Maybe he got lost."

"Boy, you'd have to be really lost to end up in Murder Creek," I said.

He started to answer, but Jolene instructed him impatiently, "You and Briscoe search the woods on either side of the trail and the streambed. He might have dropped them."

"The car keys weren't in his pocket?" I said as Carl moved off to do as she ordered.

Jolene said, "What do you want, Stockton?"

"All four doors were locked," I pointed out. "He had to have the keys with him when he left."

She started to turn away.

"Wait," I said.

She looked back.

"Can we go?" I asked. "I don't think Melanie needs to be here when they bring the body out."

She glanced back toward Melanie, then gave a curt nod. "Go on. I guess we know where to find you."

"I'm blocked in," I pointed out. "You need to get someone to move those cars."

I could tell she was trying not to roll her eyes as she turned and called, "Sweeney! Lambert! Back those units out of the way so we can let our witness go."

Two deputies hurried to comply, and I added, "Also, I'm taking the dog home with me. I'll keep him until somebody claims him. Just so you know."

I braced myself for an argument, but she had turned her attention to whatever she was writing in her field book. "Noted," she said.

I frowned a little, taken aback. Jolene had never conceded to one of my demands so easily before. "Not the animal shelter," I pointed out, just to be clear. "To Dog Daze. My kennel. Which I own."

"I'll let the next of kin know," she said.

She tore out a sheet of paper and handed it to me. I stared at it for a moment before I realized it was from her ticket book.

"What is this?" I demanded, baffled.

"It's a citation for misdemeanor property damage," she informed me. "You'll be notified of your court date."

I gaped at her. "You're giving me a *citation* for rescuing a trapped dog?"

"I'm giving you a citation," she corrected with exaggerated patience, "for breaking the window of a parked vehicle. I could have taken you in for breaking and entering, but I'm feeling generous. Next time, call 911."

"The dog could have been dead by the time you got here!" I objected.

"Tell it to the judge. Also ..." She barely glanced at me as she added, "your kennel has been designated a county-authorized rescue shelter, which is why we're turning over the dog to you in the absence of next of kin. I'm sure you're aware of the consequences should you fail to deliver proper care and security. You're welcome."

I looked from the paper in my hand to her retreating back for one more incredulous moment, but I had clearly been dismissed. I spun on my heel and stalked back to my car.

And that was when I realized that the black dog—and Melanie—were gone.

FOUR

I don't think I can be blamed for panicking. There was a dead man less than five hundred yards away, I was surrounded by emergency vehicles, and I had just lost my soon-to-be stepdaughter ... not to mention the dog who could be a major clue in a long-ago crime. I had a bizarre flash of connection: Mozart and Kylie disappearing from their bedroom six years earlier, and now Mozart and Melanie disappearing from a public parking lot. It was only a moment, but it seemed like an eternity that my heart was stuck in my throat, as I dashed around the car, checking front and back, even though all the doors were open and I could see perfectly well they weren't inside. Cisco and Pepper were just where I had left them, safely buckled into the backseat, panting and looking excitedly around, but no Melanie. I called out for her. I turned in full circle.

All of this took, as Miss Melanie Young would have reported, about 10.5 seconds. Then I heard her call, "It's okay! I got him!"

In the following 10.5 seconds—the approximate time it took me to run from my car to the sound of her voice—my emotions went from, *Thank you, Jesus!* to *I'm going to wring her neck!* and back again. If this was what parenting was all about, it sucked.

I found Melanie with Mozart behind the victim's car, just out of my sight. She had his leash firmly wrapped around her hand and was feeding him smushed-up ham and cheese from her pocket. "He got away," she informed me, "but I lured him back with treats. Pretty good, huh?"

I wanted to yell at her. I wanted to take her by the shoulders and shake her. But as anyone with even a modicum of dog training experience knows, it's useless to correct a dog after the fact for a crime he doesn't even know he's committed. I assume the same is true of children. So I deliberately quieted the slamming of my heart and said, as reasonably as possible, "What have I told you about handling dogs over thirty-five pounds by yourself?"

"Um, don't do it?" she suggested innocently. "Of course, I wasn't actually handling him, I was ..."

I interrupted, "How much do you think this dog weighs?"

"If I had to guess ..."

"More than thirty-five pounds," I informed her firmly, and before she could move too far into smart-aleck territory, I took the leash from her. "Don't do it."

I could have gone on and on about the whys and wherefores, and about how rules were never arbitrary, especially when it comes to safety. No doubt that's what her father would have done. But kids hate that kind of thing, and to be honest, I'm not wild about it myself. Besides, I wanted to be the cool stepmom.

"Yes, ma'am," Melanie replied, looking just chastened enough to cause a small swell of satisfaction to form in my chest.

How to Raise Dogs and Kids by Raine Stockton. I was totally going to write that book someday.

I tugged Mozart's leash and he reluctantly turned his head away from Melanie and her fist full of ham sandwich. "Come on, let's go. I'm starving and we need to call your dad."

"Are we taking Buzz home with us?"

It took me a moment to realize she was referring to Mozart. "For the time being," I said.

"Good. I hope it's long enough for you to whip him into shape. He definitely needs somebody to teach him some manners."

"Well," I said, feeling the need to make excuses, "we don't know what he's been through. Maybe he didn't have the advantages you and Pepper had."

She gave a decisive bob of her curly head, walking ahead of me. "Right," she said. "Like the Indians."

I wasn't entirely sure how that related, but before I could question, her phone rang. She pulled it out of her pocket and looked at the ID. "It's Dad," she declared happily.

I have the most understanding fiancé in the world. That's a good thing, because, otherwise, we would have broken up a long time ago ... and that breakup probably would have involved violence. Miles is just as opinionated, as stubborn, and as loud as I am, and we are on the opposite sides of issues with alarming frequency. But what I love about him—and I mean this sincerely—is that he never lets the need to be right get in the way of what he values: namely me and Melanie.

All this is by way of saying that Miles and I have an ongoing issue about my tendency to get involved with things that don't necessarily concern me, and about the fact that that propensity almost always lands me in trouble. He never would say so, but I know he was worried about leaving Melanie alone with me for exactly that reason. His last words before kissing me goodbye had been, "No drama, okay? It's less than a week. Just keep your head down and stay out of trouble."

I was pretty sure he would consider a dead body in a creek drama. And despite the fact that it had absolutely nothing to do with me—beyond the Mozart connection, of course—I really thought I should think carefully about how I was going to explain this to him.

"Melanie," I said quickly, struggling to hold back an excited Mozart as we approached the car, "your dad has a lot on his mind. Maybe we shouldn't mention ..."

"Hey, Dad," Melanie said, ignoring me. "You won't believe what happened. We found a drowned man!"

How to Raise Dogs and Kids by Raine Stockton, *Chapter One: Don't Be Afraid to Use the Choke Chain.*

I'm kidding, of course. I would never use a choke chain on a dog.

By the time Melanie had related the events of the morning to her dad—in all their glorified detail, of course—I had finished loading the car and secured Mozart into the back cargo area. He took up the entire space, and his hot breath fogged up the back window so quickly that I had to turn on the air-conditioning. Melanie handed me the phone as I got behind the wheel.

"Dad wants to talk to you," she said.

"I'll just bet he does," I murmured, but forced a more cheerful tone as I took the phone. "Hey," I said. "How's your mom?"

"Surgery went well," he replied. "The doctors expect a full recovery. She should go home by Wednesday."

"Oh, I'm so glad," I said, sincerely. "Tell her I'm thinking about her."

"I will." There was a pause, and his voice was tinged with indulgent affection as he added, "So. Always an adventure with you, huh?"

I returned lightly, "You're not exactly a walking advertisement for the retirement home, yourself."

He chuckled. "Which is why we're such a perfect match. I'm glad everything is okay. And sorry your day was ruined."

That was a bit more understanding of him than I had expected. On the other hand, it wasn't as though I *planned* to find a dead body in the creek. "Well," I said, "it's too cold for swimming, anyway."

"I hear you have a new dog," he said.

"Temporarily," I assured him. "The thing is …"

I glanced in the rearview mirror. A deputy was motioning us out of the parking space. I waved back at him. "I'll tell you about it later," I said. "I have to go. The deputies are trying to clear the area. Can we video chat tonight?"

"There's a crabmeat etouffee in your freezer for dinner," he reminded me. "All you have to do is heat it up." Miles never left town without stocking my freezer with enough gourmet meals to last until he got back. He was an excellent cook. Without him, most of my meals would have come from a can.

"Aunt Mart invited us for dinner," I told him, starting the engine.

"Even better." He sounded relieved. "Have a good time, and thank her for the flowers. Mom got them this morning."

Flowers, I thought with a stab of guilt. *Rats*. I'd forgotten to send any.

"I will," I said. I put the car into gear. "We'll call you about 8:00."

"Love you, sugar."

"Me, too," I replied, and handed the phone back to Melanie.

"That went better than I thought," I observed to myself as I backed out of the parking space and made my way back down the gravel road.

"Yeah," agreed Melanie, misunderstanding. "Good thing Buzz likes riding in a car. It would've taken two or three people to get him in the back if he didn't. Say, Raine," she added, twisting in her seat to look over her shoulder, back toward the scene we'd just left, "how to do suppose a grown man fell into the creek, anyway? The bank wasn't that slippery, and the water wasn't that deep."

"I don't know," I admitted. "He might have had a heart attack and fallen in the water."

"Which is why you should never hike alone," she acknowledged sagely.

"Right." I had to smile. I had taught her that.

"If only he hadn't locked his dog in the car," she pointed out, "Buzz might have saved him."

"Maybe," I agreed. It wasn't completely out of the question. After all, he was a water-rescue dog. Mostly.

"Why would anybody do that?" she wondered, frowning. "Lock his dog in the car?"

"Good question," I said. But then, there were a lot of questions about this man's death I'd like to have the answers to. Like, why did a person dressed in slick-soled loafers and khakis go hiking beside a creek? What had brought him to Murder Creek from Jacksonville, Florida, anyway? And ...

"Maybe," suggested Melanie, "he was afraid Buzz would get away from him, just like he did from me."

"Could be," I agreed, and, in fact, that wasn't a bad idea. A big dog like that would be hard to handle on a narrow trail, and if he only planned to walk down to the creek and back it might have seemed logical to leave the dog in the car.

Which only left one important question: How did a

retired cop from Florida end up with Mozart in the first place, and what brought both of them here?

Okay, that's two questions. And the way things were looking at the moment, I wasn't likely to get the answers to either of them any time soon.

FIVE

To say chaos greeted our return would be an understatement, but then it always did. The minute they heard the crunch of gravel under the tires, Cisco and Pepper started panting their hot breath onto the windows and pressing their noses against the glass with excitement. Dogs always know when they're home; don't ask me how. All this anticipation agitated the big fellow in back, who stood up, bumped his head on the roof, and started barking. He had a booming bark, which not only caused me to wince and Melanie to cover her ears, but excited all the dogs in the kennel.

I drove around the circular drive to the back of the house and stopped in front of the picket fence with the arched sign over the gate that announced Dog Daze Boarding and Training. The door to the front office opened and Mischief and Magic, the Australian Shepherd twins, spilled out, wagging their tailless butts as they raced toward the gate. Since it was several seconds before Corny, who manages the kennel for me and also lives on site, appeared, I suspected one of the Aussies of opening the door herself. They are extremely clever.

There followed several moments of dedicated confusion while Melanie and Corny tried to shoo two bouncing Aussies and two playful goldens inside the building and I tried simply to hold on to the leash as Mozart lunged after them. Corny is not a large man, but he is incredibly efficient. The moment he saw us, he dashed from behind the reception counter, swept Mozart's leash from me, and ushered him into an oversized holding kennel in the grooming room in a motion so fluid it was practically a dance. Mozart was safely behind bars before he even knew what had happened. Mischief and Magic, having sniffed all they needed to sniff and learned all they needed to know, went back to their beds and their chew bones in the office, while Pepper and Cisco, with typical golden retriever curiosity, continued to check out the lingering scents of all that had happened since they left.

Corny's eyes grew bigger and bigger behind his thick-lensed, white-framed glasses as Melanie filled him in on the details of the morning. I couldn't be entirely sure whether this was due to the drama of her tale, or the sheer size of the beast who had galloped through the doors of Dog Daze, pulling me behind like the tail on a kite. His gaze kept darting between Melanie, me, and the shaggy black dog in the extra-large kennel, trying to put all the players in the drama into place.

"And then the police came," Melanie said, trying her best to sound worldly and matter of fact, "and the coroner, and the deputies went down the trail with a body bag. It was all pretty exciting. Of course," she added, "I was responsible for keeping the dogs out of the way during the investigation, even the big guy."

"And you did a great job," I assured her. I took a couple of dog biscuits from the jar on the counter and waited until Pepper and Cisco, who had lost interest in sniffing the floor and had turned their hopeful attention to me in anticipation of just such a moment, sat. I tossed them each a biscuit. "I don't know how I would have managed without you."

"Well, it sounds just awful!" declared Corny, pressing a hand to his throat. "I think I would have *died*!"

Corny was what you might call a bit theatrical. With

tufts of bright orange hair poking out on either side of a sequined baseball cap, his bright red overalls and yellow grooming apron hand-appliqued and bedazzled with paisley dogs in every color known to man, a person could certainly be forgiven for thinking he would be more suited to a Broadway stage than a rural dog kennel. "Can you just imagine?" he went on, eyes growing, if possible, even wider. "I mean, you don't have to, of course, you were there, but for heaven's sake, you go on a nice picnic on a beautiful spring day, never expecting for one moment that you'd find ..." He finished the sentence with a dramatic shudder, and then spun back to Mozart. "And the poor dog! Not only has he lost his daddy, but all that trauma! Locked in a hot car! I can barely think about what would have happened if you hadn't come along."

"Well," pointed out Melanie, who hated to have attention diverted from her, "it was me, mostly. And Cisco. He's the one who found the dog in the car."

Corny said, "The whole thing sounds dreadful. Just dreadful. I simply can't imagine."

"It wasn't something that happens every day," admitted Melanie, still trying to sound nonchalant. "But I guess I'd better get used to it, if I'm going to be a homicide detective."

Last week, she had her sights set on becoming a forensic anthropologist.

She added, "I took pictures with my phone. You know, since it was my first real dead body."

Now it was my turn to stare at her. "Melanie, you did not!"

"Of course I did." She pulled her phone out of her pocket to show me. "I posted it on my Insta story. Don't you follow me?"

Terrific. As if I didn't have enough to worry about, now I had to monitor the child's social media. I snatched the phone from her. "You can't post photos of a death scene on Instagram!" I started to thumb through her gallery.

"Why not?" she reached to take the phone from me.

"Because ..." I struggled to come up with something more meaningful—and less humiliating—than *because I said so*. "Because it's not respectful," I said.

"It's not like I posted anything gross," she pointed out. "I didn't really even *see* the corpse. Just police cars and stuff."

She was right, of course. There was nothing to be seen on her phone except some blurry photos of deputies moving back and forth and a close up of the coroner's van, along with multiple pictures of Mozart. Still, I did not think Miles would approve. I knew I didn't. The problem was, I didn't know exactly why.

I said, "Melanie, you can't just ..." Frustrated, I stumbled, took a breath, and tried again, this time more firmly. "It's not right, okay? And I don't want you posting anything else like this on social media without asking your father or me first."

She did not look at all convinced, or in the least chagrined. "Okay," she said, and held out her hand again for her phone. Reluctantly, I turned it over.

"So," said Corny, turning back to Mozart, who was panting and drooling inside the kennel, his massive head brushing the top of his enclosure. "What will happen to the poor thing?"

"The police are trying to locate the man's next of kin," I explained. "They'll take custody of the dog if they want him. Otherwise ..." I shrugged. We all knew the story. That was how dogs ended up in rescue, after all.

Corny's sweet, expressive face softened with compassion. "What's his name?"

"Buzz," said Melanie.

"Mozart," I said at the same time.

Corny lifted a quizzical eyebrow.

I sighed. "Actually," I explained, glancing at Melanie, "the thing is ... I think I might know this dog. He's a dead ringer for a dog I trained six years ago. He, well, disappeared not long after graduation, but I could swear this is the same dog."

"Wow," said Melanie, moving toward the kennel for a closer look. "How weird would that be?"

She was right, of course. Too weird. But I wasn't wrong ... was I?

Corny frowned. "I don't understand. So you know the, um, deceased?"

I shook my head. "Mozart had a different owner when I knew him."

"Wow," said Corny, staring at Mozart. "That's, like, Fate or something."

"Yeah," I agreed unhappily. "Or something." I didn't see any reason to go into the whole thing about Kylie Goodwin, at least not yet. At least not until I was sure.

Corny went over to the kennel, bending down to look closer. With all the attention, Mozart started snuffling and pawing the bars. Pepper and Cisco came over to see what all the fuss was about. Mozart gave a big, resounding—and no doubt amiable—bark. Both Corny and Melanie took a stumbling step backwards.

"He's wearing a tag," Corny pointed out, recovering. "Did you look at it?"

"I tried to, when I was putting him in the car," I said. "It's one of those cheap mail-order things, and the phone number is all worn away. No rabies tag." That didn't mean anything. The law requires that dogs wear their rabies tags, but dogs lose them all the time, and sometimes owners don't even bother putting them on the collar. Just a word to the wise: put the rabies tag on your dog's collar, even if he already has other ID. It never hurts to have a backup.

"Well," declared Melanie, surveying the dog with hands on hips. "I think Mozart is a better name. You know, like that movie, *Beethoven.*"

I couldn't help smiling. That was exactly what Kylie's father had told me inspired the big guy's name.

"Buzz sounds more like a name for a terrier," I agreed.

Corny knelt down next to the kennel again, letting Mozart slurp at a treat between his fingers as he reached through the bars to unsnap the big dog's collar. "Hold on a sec," he said, rising. "I've got an idea."

He went over to the desk and grabbed a pencil and a sheet of printer paper. Melanie and I watched as he placed the paper over the dog's ID tag and started to rub the graphite pencil over the paper until an image appeared.

Melanie said, "I should have thought of that."

I peered over his shoulder. "Anything?"

He took the paper away and we all examined it together. Inside the circle that was the dog's tag, the name was perfectly clear: Buzz. Beneath the name three numbers were readable, and after that nothing but squiggles.

"Eight two six," I read out loud. "That's probably the area code."

"The next one might be a seven," Melanie said, standing on tiptoe to see.

"Or a one," Corny said.

"That could be another eight," I said pointing.

"Or a zero," said Corny.

I sighed.

"Maybe he has a microchip," Corny suggested.

Melanie ran over to the cabinet where we kept the microchip scanner and brought it back. I had debated for a long time about buying one—after all, I ran a kennel, not an animal shelter—but it had paid for itself the first time I had been able to reunite a lost dog with its owner, a tourist who'd stopped at a campground less than a mile away. Most people around here call me first and the animal shelter second when they find a stray.

Corny and I got Mozart on the grooming table— not without some struggle, I admit—and I ran the scanner slowly over his body, head to tail, side to side, up and down his legs and belly. I did two full scans, but no microchip. I gave a helpless little shrug and stepped back.

Corny brushed his hands together, squared his shoulders, and declared, "Well, whether it's Buzz or Mozart, this young gentleman is in need of a bath." He looked meaningfully at Melanie. "It's clearly a two-man job."

"I'll help," Melanie volunteered cheerfully. She never missed an opportunity to insert herself into the daily business of the kennel. "I've still got my swimsuit on under my shorts."

"Sounds like a plan," I said, turning for the office. I have to admit, I was glad to have her occupied for a while. "I need to do some work on the computer, and when I'm finished we'll take the dogs through the Rally course, okay?" Rally obedience is something of a cross between agility and obedience, except that instead of obstacles set up around the course, there are a series of stations with obedience commands the dog is required to perform. It's a lot of fun, and a great way to keep both kids and dogs interested in obedience training.

"Cool," she said. "I've been practicing Pepper's flip finish. I think she's going to be ready for her first competition next month."

"I wouldn't be a bit surprised," I assured her, and hurried toward my office. What I really wanted from the computer was a copy of that graduation photo of Kylie and Mozart, just to check my memory. And if I couldn't find it, I was sure there was an article featuring the Missing Child poster from back then somewhere on the internet.

Just as I was settling down behind the desk, I heard Melanie add, "Say, Corny, do you have anything to eat around here? All I had for breakfast was an apple, and I'm starving."

Once again I smothered a groan. I had forgotten to stop for lunch. "I can make you a sandwich," I called back.

She hesitated just long enough to be insulting. As it happens, I make a perfectly respectable peanut butter and jelly sandwich ... assuming, of course, that I have either peanut butter or jelly on hand, which I wasn't entirely sure I did. And I was pretty sure I'd used the last of the bread making the ham sandwiches that Melanie had fed to the dogs.

"Um, that's okay," she called back. "Maybe I'll just have another apple."

I wrinkled up my nose and turned back to the computer. "Suit yourself."

How to Raise Dogs and Kids by Raine Stockton, *Chapter Two: Don't Forget to Feed Them.*

SIX

Melanie and I shared a bag of corn chips, sent her grandmother a bouquet of yellow daisies and a get-well teddy bear from an online flower shop, and spent an hour on the Rally course with all four dogs. The problem with Mischief and Magic is that they're so smart they almost take the fun out of training, and obedience has never been Cisco's forte. He kept getting distracted by the traffic cones that held the rally signs, and when I took off his leash for the recall he galloped around the course like it was a racetrack, stopping only to snatch up one of the cones and carry it around in his mouth like a prize. Sweet Pepper, on the other hand, never took her eyes off Melanie, and even though she was a little sloppy on her 270-degree turn, it occurred to me that if our two dogs ever did go up against each other in competition, Melanie's dog would win. I wasn't sure how I felt about that.

Mozart, bathed, fluffed and shiny-coated, gobbled his dinner and settled down in one of the oversized runs which were usually reserved for two dogs in one family who needed to stay together. When I stopped by to snap his picture, he had a chew bone between his massive paws and seemed perfectly content.

We were an hour early for dinner at my aunt and uncle's house, mostly because we were both starving and I knew Aunt Mart wouldn't mind, but also because I was hoping to get some time to talk to my uncle alone. I should have called first.

The first thing I noticed when I pulled into the driveway of the neat red-brick ranch was my ex-husband's

Silverado pickup truck there before me. Of course, it was too late to retreat by then, and even as I was trying to come up with a plan to sneak into the house without having to talk to him, Buck came out of the workshop with Uncle Ro.

"Hey," said Melanie, "there's Sheriff Buck! Only," she corrected herself, "he's not sheriff anymore. I wonder what I'm supposed to call him?"

"Not sure," I replied, trying to sound casual as I parked the car. "Why don't you ask?"

From the front porch, a beautiful sable-and-white collie got up, stretched, and barked a greeting.

"Hey, Majesty!" Melanie called out the window, and Majesty trotted down the steps to meet us. Majesty had come to me several years ago from a family who could no longer afford to keep her, and I still thought of her as my dog, even though she had chosen to live with my aunt, who adored her. At my house, she had also been adored, but at Aunt Mart's that affection was demonstrated with designer dog beds, expensive toys, and hand-prepared meals. I think we all had come to agree that Majesty had made the right choice.

Melanie unfastened her seat belt and scrambled out of the car, running to greet Majesty. Buck and Uncle Ro watched her, smiling. Buck looked back at me and I waved weakly. I took my time getting out of the car.

It really wasn't all that strange, running into my ex at my relatives' house. Buck had been a part of our lives since he and I were kids; he had worked for Uncle Ro for ten years and had taken over for him as sheriff when he retired. Sometimes Aunt Mart still forgot the potential for awkwardness and invited him over for birthdays and holiday dinners. As far as she was concerned, once family, always family.

Buck had married someone else last summer, but was now divorced from her, too. Despite this—and despite the fact that his multiple infidelities were the reason we had split in the first place—we had remained on more-or-less good terms. Except when it came to Miles. And this would be the first time the two of us had been together since Miles and I officially became engaged.

Oh, yes. I could definitely expect some awkwardness.

Melanie had made a sufficient fuss over Majesty and skipped over to greet Uncle Ro and Buck, so I postponed the inevitable uncomfortable moment by kneeling to hug my collie, burying my face in her sweet-smelling fur. I dug a treat from my pocket and she responded by sitting and putting her paw on my shoulder. I grinned, tossing the treat to her. "What a good girl!"

I went over to hug Uncle Ro and explained, unnecessarily, "We're early."

"Never too early for me, sweetheart." He grinned, returning my hug. He turned to Melanie, eyes twinkling. "And who's this little cutie you brought with you?"

Melanie stifled a giggle. "You know me! I'm Miss Melanie Young, and I've been to your house lots of times."

He feigned remembering. "Why, now that you mention it, you do look familiar. How've you been, Miss Young?"

"I'm fine," she said. "Can I call you Uncle Ro?"

"Miss Melanie Young," he replied, smiling, "I'd be honored."

She turned to Buck, who was also smiling. "What about you? You're not the sheriff anymore, so what do I call you?"

Buck pretended to ponder this. I was so accustomed to seeing him in uniform that I'd almost forgotten how nice he looked in civvies: worn jeans and a faded sweatshirt, hair tousled by the spring breeze, eyes crinkled with smile lines as he regarded Melanie.

"How about 'Handsome'?" he suggested, and she giggled. "'Hey, good looking'? Or, I've always answered to, 'You, there.'"

Buck was great with kids, and there wasn't a female alive who didn't eventually fall for his charm. Melanie was no exception.

She put her hands on her hips, eyes dancing with pleasure, and demanded, "You know what I mean. A real name."

He nodded and pursed his lips thoughtfully. "You've got a point. How about 'Uncle Remus'? Or 'Captain America'? Oh, here's one I've always liked. Maybe you could call me just plain old Buck."

"Okay, Just Plain Old Buck," she replied, and he laughed.

"Maybe Buck for short."

She looked doubtful. "My dad says I shouldn't call adults by their first names without permission. He says it's disrespectful."

Buck bent down to her confidentially. "You have my permission," he assured her. "And I promise I won't feel disrespected. Deal?"

He extended his hand to her and she shook it firmly. "Deal," she agreed. Then, "So, Buck, did you hear about the drowned man we found today?"

Buck's brows shot up and he looked at me. So did Uncle Ro.

"I did not," Buck said, deadpan.

"Melanie," I interrupted firmly, "it's not nice to come to someone's house for dinner without saying hello to the hostess. Why don't you go tell Aunt Mart we're here and see what you can to do help in the kitchen?"

"But," Melanie protested.

"And if she offers you a cookie …" I said, and I could tell by the way her expression fell that she expected me to say something like "don't spoil your dinner." I therefore finished, "Bring me one."

"Okay." She grinned and turned to Majesty, who was sniffing the ground for more treats. "Majesty, come on! Race you to the house!"

Cool stepmom. Oh, yeah.

We watched the two of them go, and then Uncle Ro said, "Was she talking about the drowning victim at Murder Creek? I heard about it on the scanner." Uncle Ro kept his police scanner going day and night; it was a point of constant contention between my aunt and him. "A tourist, right?"

I nodded. "Jolene said he was from Florida. A retired cop."

Uncle Ro grunted. "Wonder what he was doing out there all by himself."

"Actually," I said, "he wasn't entirely by himself." I dug into my jeans pocket for the printout of the photo I had found in my archives. I unfolded it and showed it to both men. "Remember this?"

Uncle Ro frowned a little, but Buck, who had been married to me at the time and no doubt remembered how upsetting the whole thing had been, was a little quicker to recognize the picture. "Oh yeah," he said. "That's the little girl who disappeared. You trained her dog. What was her name?"

"Kylie Goodwin," I supplied. "The dog's name was Mozart."

"That's right," said Uncle Ro, his frown deepening. "I remember now. Tragic case. Across the border in South

Carolina, wasn't it? They arrested the father."

"I don't think they actually arrested him," I said.

"They never found a body," Buck added. "But I know they questioned the father more than once."

Uncle Ro shook his head sadly. "What kind of man does something like that to his own child?"

Buck had told me over and over again that in law enforcement, a cop's instinct was his most valuable tool, and that the first suspect was usually the guilty one. It would not occur to either Uncle Ro or to Buck that Kylie's father might, in fact, be innocent.

Buck looked at me curiously. "So what does this have to do with the man who drowned this afternoon?"

"I'm not sure," I said. I reached back into my jeans pocket and took out another printout, this one a photo of the freshly bathed and blown-out Mozart. I unfolded it and held it up for comparison. "This dog was in his car."

Buck took the photograph and studied it, then handed it to Uncle Ro. "So you think this is the same dog?" Buck said. "Kylie Goodwin's dog?"

"This one has gray on his muzzle," Uncle Ro pointed out.

"He'd be seven years old by now," I said.

"So you have a positive ID?" Buck said.

"Well, no," I admitted. "His collar tag has a different name, and we weren't able to read the phone number. We scanned for a microchip, but he doesn't have one."

"So you're *not* sure," Buck said.

I met Buck's gaze firmly and said, with confidence, "It's the same dog. I know it. The question is, what was he doing with that man?"

Buck glanced at Ro. Ro folded both papers and returned them to me. "Come on up to the porch and sit down, Raine," he said. "Let's get us a glass of iced tea."

"Well," said Buck, "I'd better get going. Thanks for the loan of the tiller, Ro."

"Wait a minute!" I protested, looking from one to the other of them. "This could be important. Kylie and Mozart were inseparable. They disappeared together. Now he's back. This could be a lead on what happened to Kylie all those years ago. Don't you think somebody should look into it?"

Buck and Uncle Ro exchanged a glance. Uncle Ro said simply, "Look into what? Even if it is the same dog—"

"It's the same dog," I interrupted. I was starting to get a little impatient now.

"Okay, say it is," Uncle Ro conceded. "The most likely scenario is that the dog was picked up as a stray and adopted by this fellow, this policeman, some time ago. It doesn't really give us any new information about the case."

"It might," I insisted, "if we had more details. Like how Mozart got from South Carolina to Jacksonville, Florida. And what he—and his owner—were doing here. Murder Creek is not that far from where Kylie disappeared, you know."

"Only if you call thirty miles 'not far,'" put in Buck dryly. "And come on, Raine, don't you think the whole thing is a little coincidental?"

Well, of course I did. That was really the only thing that bothered me. Well, maybe not the only thing, but the main thing. Still, I felt compelled to defend my theory. "Not if this guy was investigating the Kylie Goodwin case. Maybe he realized Mozart was her dog and ..." But that was where my theory more or less petered out, and I faltered to a halt.

"And what?" Buck prompted. "I don't see how a pet

dog could have any evidence that would have a bearing on the case, do you, Ro?"

"Not even a case," Ro said. "A closed case."

"It wasn't closed if there wasn't a conviction or a resolution," I told my uncle, proud of my small triumph. "And aren't you a member of Mountain Regional Cold Case Squad? A region that includes the part of South Carolina where Kylie Goodwin lived?"

Buck smothered a grin. "She's got you there, Ro."

My uncle had been instrumental in establishing the regional cold case squad as a way to keep busy after he retired. It had started with a handful of other retired cops, all of them volunteers, and over the past year had grown to a force to be reckoned with. So far they had laid to rest upwards of thirty-five previously unsolved cases, most of them related to DNA or other forensic evidence that technology had only recently been able to decipher.

Uncle Ro looked doubtful. "Ah, honey, I don't know. We have a twenty-year backlog of cases we might actually be able to solve. We don't have the resources to go knocking on doors over a case with no new evidence."

"But," I began.

From the front porch, Melanie called, "Hey, Just Plain Old Buck! Aunt Mart wants to know if you're staying for dinner."

Buck turned toward the porch. "Tell her thanks, Pumpkin. But I've got to get home."

She grinned. "I'm not a pumpkin!" She trotted back to the front door and we heard her call inside, "He says no!"

Buck watched her, smiling. "She's a cutie pie, isn't she?"

"Most of the time," I agreed. "But listen, Buck ..."

I was interrupted by the chirping of a cell phone.

Uncle Ro patted his pockets and found his phone. "That's me," he said. "I've been expecting that insurance guy to call back. Excuse me a minute."

He walked away to take the call, leaving Buck and me temporarily alone. I said, "You should stay for dinner."

"Nah." He shrugged a little. "I just came by to return Ro's tiller."

From the porch, Melanie called, "She said don't leave without your to-go bag!"

"Okay," Buck called back, and we both smiled. No one ever came to Aunt Mart's house without taking home a brown paper sack of something edible.

"I'll bring it!" Melanie called, and Uncle Ro covered his ear with his hand as he tried to listen to his phone conversation. "Stay there!"

Melanie dashed back into the house, and Buck and I smiled at each other a little awkwardly.

"So," I said after a moment, searching for something to say, "you're putting in a garden this year."

He looked blank until I reminded him, "The tiller?"

"Oh. Right. Yeah, now that I'm working regular hours I have more time to look after it. Thought I'd give it a try."

After he'd taken his name off the ballot for sheriff, virtually conceding the election to Marshal Becker, Buck had taken a job as county investigator, which was mostly five days a week. There had been a time, shortly before his divorce, when he wasn't even sure he'd stay in the county. I supposed a garden was a way of saying he was now sure.

Almost as though reading my mind, he added, "I guess you won't bother. Not knowing where you'll be living by harvest time, and all."

I was confused, and then he dropped his gaze to my

engagement ring. It wasn't particularly ostentatious, but it was gorgeous—a marquis-cut white diamond surrounded by tiny chocolate diamonds—and it was hard to miss. At first I had been self-conscious about wearing it, and terrified I was going to lose it washing the dogs or roaming the woods, but now it felt like part of me. I often forgot I was even wearing it ... except, of course when the sparkle caught my eye, and then it made me smile. I like pretty things just as much as the next woman.

Now, however, following the direction of Buck's gaze, I was self-conscious again, and I instinctively closed my hand, as though that could hide the ring. Buck said, "Have you set a date yet?"

"No," I replied. I can't tell you how many times I've been asked that question, nor how uncomfortable it made me. That was one of the reasons, in fact, that I was in no hurry to go inside and greet Aunt Mart. "Not yet. But ..." Then I understood the implication of his words. He assumed, once Miles and I were married, that I'd be leaving my creaky old farmhouse with the kennel out back to move into Miles's brand-new mansion on the mountain. I'd never even considered that. Did Miles assume the same thing? We'd never talked about it. Now, thinking about this unexpected complication, I felt uneasy.

Before I could think of how to finish that sentence, the screen door slammed and Melanie came down the steps, Majesty at her heels. Melanie proudly carried a grocery sack that was filled with Tupperware containers. "This is Chinese chicken casserole," Melanie informed Buck as she handed it over, "with toasted cashews on top, and homemade rolls fresh from the oven, and Asian coleslaw. And strawberry pie for dessert. Bake at 350 for thirty minutes. The casserole, that is. Everything else is cooked."

My mouth watered and my stomach growled.

"Well, Miss Melanie," declared Buck, pretending to stagger under the weight of the bag. "I'll eat like a king tonight. Thank you kindly. And thank Miss Mart for me."

"Okay, welcome." She turned to me excitedly. "Hey, Raine, did you know Aunt Mart knows everything about William Stockton and Adam Bowslayer? She even has a picture of him—William Stockton, I mean—in a book, but she says you have to go up in the attic and get it. Can we do that now? I'm supposed to have illustrations."

I said, "Sure. Be right there."

She and Majesty raced off again and I turned back to Buck, still feeling awkward. "Well," I said. "See you."

"Right. You all take care." He turned and called to my uncle, "See you later! Thanks again."

Uncle Ro covered his phone with one hand and waved, then turned back to his conversation. Buck walked a few steps toward his truck and I went toward the house.

He said, "Hey, Raine."

I looked back.

"Listen," he said. "I can ask one of the boys to talk to the deceased's next of kin about the dog, okay? Maybe find out how long they've had it, where it came from, that kind of thing. Will that help?"

I couldn't help smiling with relief. "Yeah, it would. Thanks, Buck."

He smiled back, though it seemed a little strained. "Hey, you know I never could refuse you anything. I'll let you know what I find out."

He put his hand on the door handle of the truck and I heard the word come out of my mouth without ever having planned to speak it. "Buck."

He looked at me curiously.

I felt ridiculous. All I could think to say was, "I appreciate it. Really."

He nodded and got into the truck, and I watched him drive away.

Marriage. Divorce. Friendship. Family. It's complicated.

Kids and dogs don't know how easy they have it.

SEVEN

Buck Lawson was not good at living alone. He didn't like eating alone, or sleeping alone, or waking up alone. He didn't know what to do with himself at night. He dreaded his days off. He was afraid he was starting to wear out his welcome with his friends, and hanging out in bars was not an option. So most of the time, he ended up working.

This time of year, there was plenty to do. People were coming back to their vacation homes after a winter away to find televisions missing and windows broken. Shoplifting was on the rise, as were reports of packages being stolen from doorsteps. Three cars had been broken into over the past week, but Buck was pretty sure he knew the boys who were responsible. Most of his job was routine; he did interviews over the phone, filled out a report, and turned it into Hank Dawson, the county prosecutor. He didn't mind the routine aspects of the job. It was when things *weren't* routine that he got worried. And if he ever got bored, there was always the forum.

He had decided to swing by the office on his way home from Ro's and look over the file on the drowning victim because Raine had gotten his curiosity up. He didn't think there was much of a possibility that the cop from Florida was in any way related to a child who'd gone missing six years ago, but what *was* he doing here, anyway? And in an out-of-the-way place like Murder Creek? There was no harm in glancing over what the deputies had put together so far, so he stopped by

Jolene's office to request the file. She wasn't there, so he texted her instead. She replied she had a few things to finish up before she left for the day, but she'd bring the file by his office on her way out. While he waited, Buck checked out the forum.

The name of the site was "Carolina Free" and it was a closed group that had spun off of a local shooting club's website. The members lived, as far as Buck could tell, mostly within a hundred miles of Hanover County, and the moderator, who Buck had already identified, was careful to keep it that way. The official description was "An open discussion forum for patriots and defenders of the Bill of Rights." It was, in fact, like so many of its ilk, an online place for loud-mouths and discontents to vent their anger about everything from the price of gas to politics and everything in between. Buck knew that people who spent all their time talking rarely did anything else, and most of their rants, though alarming, were harmless. But he also knew all too well how very, very badly things could go when it stopped being just talk.

The furor of the day had apparently begun when Whiplash863 had posted a news article about a politician who proposed a voluntary buy-back of assault weapons in his home state of New Hampshire after a shooting at a shopping mall had killed six people. This was hardly a surprising move on the part of the politician, and neither was the reaction from the members of the discussion group. There was a lot of the usual "from my cold dead fingers" and "I'd like to see them try" and "I'll give up my guns when the criminals give up theirs" until PartyAnimal1850 pointed out, "This isn't even in Carolina, you A-holes. We've got our own way of dealing with liberal jerk-offs that get in our faces about how to run our lives." And that's where it got interesting.

RedneckDaddy32: I say let the government confiscate ever damn gun north of the Mason-Dixon, and California too. Them bleeding heart liberals'll find out soon enough why we're holding on to ours!

MountainMan904: Preach it, brother! I got 1200 rounds stockpiled in my safe room. Ready for the CW.

*Remmington1976:*1200? That'll take you through half a day when the liberals arm the damn Mexicans with all those AR-15s they've been confiscating. I've got 8000. Bring it on!

MischiefMaker18: Build the wall!

StraightShooter: Screw the wall. Walls can be climbed. Walls can be torn down. Walls are worthless when they come for your wife and kids.

MaskedMan113: You want to protect what's yours, you've got to have a plan. Where I come from, we've got a plan. Am I right, SS?

StraightShooter: You know it, brother.

MountainMan904: What kind of plan?

MaskedMan: Seven bridges.

StraightShooter: We got enough ammo stored to blow them ever one.

Buck leaned forward, his interest quickening. For as long as he could remember, he'd been hearing stories about a group of men whose plan to protect Hanover County against invasion by "enemies foreign and domestic" was to strategically blow up each of the seven bridges that connected the mountainous terrain of their county to the outside world. Ro had heard the stories too, he claimed, for most of his life, and so had his daddy, which meant the rumor probably dated from World War II. Who knew? Back then, it might not have been so far-fetched. But these days it was mostly used as a joking threat to stop the onslaught of tourists.

MischiefMaker18: What the hell are you talking about? What bridges?

Remmington1976: Shut up, kid. This is men's business.

MischiefMaker18: I ain't no GD kid!

StraightShooter: Back in the day, when the Creek Indians held this country, long before the white man stuck his nose in, this right here was prime hunting grounds. High, defensible, plenty of water, and when it came time to send out the hunting parties, all they had to do was drive the elk herd or whatever right over the cliff into the gorge, then haul the meat up on a sledge. All the neighboring tribes wanted this place, and they tried to take it too. But the best thing about it was there was only one way in: across the gorge. So this Creek chief, he had his boys build a bridge across the gorge out of tree limbs and stuff, kind of an invitation for the other tribes to send their war parties across. But as soon as those fine painted warriors got about halfway across, ol' Chief, he lit the bridge on fire. Problem solved.

Masked Man: Used to be 1 bridge. Now 7. We got 'em covered.

MischiefMaker18: Sorry, dudes. I gotta call BS. Do you know how much ordinance it would take to blow up 7 bridges??? Where the hell would you store it all?

StraightShooter: I know exactly how much it would take.

So did Buck. He had seen it hidden beneath a tarp behind an abandoned country store in his own county barely a year ago, right before the Feds confiscated it and arrested everyone involved. Or so he'd thought.

MischiefMaker18: So what?? So you blow up the GD bridges, what about air support, satellites? What are you, living in the 1800s? What a bunch of idiots. You better hope somebody does take the GD liberals' guns, because when they come for you your ass is toast. If you can even find it.

Remmington1976: What are you, some kind of little pussy? You better hope I don't run into you on the street, you F-ing ...

There was a tap on his door, which was open, and Buck turned quickly, and a little guiltily. Jolene came in, file folder in hand, and he felt a ridiculous urge to hide the screen.

"Hey," she said, handing the folder to him. "Didn't expect you to be working today."

"I'm not, really." He took the file from her and flipped it open, glancing briefly at the contents. "I just stopped by on my way home."

Jolene said, "It looks like an accidental drowning to me. Did something else come to your attention?"

He shook his head. "Just doing a favor for a friend."

Jolene and Buck had not always gotten along, and most of that was Buck's fault. He had resolved to make an effort to change that, and he could tell she was trying to meet him halfway. They had to work together, after all, and there was no point in making things more difficult than they had to be. She was still a little stiff around him, though, wary in the way a person might be around a dog who's already bitten once. The awkwardness relaxed into a wry half-smile, though, when he mentioned his "friend."

"Right," she said. "Stockton told me her theory about the dog. Well, you can put her mind at ease. I spoke to the wife, and they don't even have a dog. She didn't have any idea what I was talking about when I told her we were holding it for her."

He glanced at her with a mild grunt of surprise. "That's odd."

"Actually, I felt kind of bad," Jolene admitted. "When I mentioned the dog, she got her hopes up that maybe I had the wrong man."

"Any chance of that?"

She shook her head. "Description, car, license plate all check out. And the fingerprints are a match. Not to mention I got the wife's phone number from his own phone, so there's not much chance of a mistake. She's coming down tomorrow to claim the body."

"Is he at Sutter's?"

Jolene nodded. "Didn't seem any reason to move him to Asheville, since they can't start the examination until Monday anyway. I asked the wife if she knew what he was doing here, but she was pretty upset. She said he was only supposed to be gone overnight, had somebody he wanted to talk to here. She didn't know who."

Buck turned one of the photos over. He had seen enough photos of drowning victims to expect the worst, but this one wasn't too bad. The water had been cold enough to preserve his features, and bloat had not yet set in. A male in his late sixties, broad features, thinning grey hair, a little overweight. There was a cut on his forehead, probably from the fall, but no other obvious injuries. He was dressed like a man with an appointment, not someone out for a hike in the woods.

An appointment, on Saturday.

Buck glanced through the inventory of belongings: a leather satchel containing a shaving kit, a couple of pairs of underwear, socks, clean shirts, a pair of slacks. He almost smiled, because that was exactly the way a wife would pack—extra socks, more shirts than you needed. But the smile wouldn't come. He read on, then looked up.

"No keys?"

While he'd been reading, Jolene's attention had wandered to his computer screen. He shifted slightly, blocking it with his shoulder.

She replied, "We didn't find them. The theory is that he had them in his hand when he went in the water, and they're buried under silt downstream by now."

He nodded, looking back at the folder. "Time of death is pretty vague."

"The coroner said he couldn't be sure, with the water temperature and all. Two to three hours was the best he could do."

"Still," murmured Buck, "that's a long time for a dog to be locked in a hot car."

"He could be wrong. The medical examiner's report will give us a better idea."

Buck looked up and noticed that she was peering around him to read the computer screen. Her expression was crinkled with puzzlement and distaste. "What *is* that?"

He hesitated, trying to appear casual. "Just some crazy-ass internet group I'm keeping an eye on."

She stepped in closer, reading. "Jesus. Sounds like some of them should be standing in a park somewhere wearing sandwich signs and preaching about the end days. What's the CW?"

"Civil War," Buck said. "They've got this whole scenario worked out where the liberals and the conservatives—or the blacks and the whites or the immigrants and the natural citizens—grab their rifles and attack each other. They're planning to win, of course."

"Huh." She shook her head, still reading. "Crazy times we live in."

"You don't know the half of it." He turned back to the file.

"Do you know who these loonies are?"

"Most of them." He glanced up again and flicked a casual finger toward the screen. "That's Warner Beale, he moderates the discussion. Pretty good old boy, even if he is a little on the radical side of defending the Bill of Rights. At least he keeps the language clean." He pointed to another name. "That's Tony Wilder, I went to school with him, and Jack Parsons, he's a volunteer firefighter. And this guy Remington, he's out of Black Mountain, I think. A game warden. And Straight Shooter? He's none other than the former Deputy Deke Williams."

She gave him a look that was part astonishment and part revulsion. "The man Sheriff Becker fired last month?"

"The same."

"The man just lost his job, his brother is sitting in county jail waiting trial for assaulting a police officer, conspiracy to commit a felony, and plotting an act of terrorism, and he's hanging out on forums like this, spouting the kind of crap that could get him arrested if he said it out loud in a public place." She gave a disgusted shake of her head as she straightened up. "And to think I thought this would be a good place to raise my kid."

"Ah, most of these boys are all right," Buck said with a shrug. He turned another page in the folder. "Like to shoot off their mouths, is all, sitting safe at home where they don't have to shoot anything else."

She replied, "So why are you monitoring this site?"

"Well, you know what they say. It's never the thing you see coming that gets you." He closed the folder. "Do me a favor, will you? Try to find out what Mr. Rutherford was doing down here when you talk to the wife tomorrow. And what in God's name might have possessed him to pick up a stray dog this far from home. Neither one of us is going to hear the end of it until Raine gets an answer to that question."

She said, "Actually, I'm off tomorrow. I told Mrs. Rutherford to ask for Jacobson when she got in."

"Hey, that's right." He smiled. "Your mom and little boy were coming in this weekend. They settling in okay?"

Jolene's six-year-old had been living with her mother while he finished out the school year in Raleigh. Now that Jolene had decided to stay with the Hanover County Sheriff's Office, she was moving them both to Hansonville, which meant moving them all to a bigger house.

"Yeah," she said. "I meant to thank you for the tip on the house. It didn't make sense to keep two places, especially since I need Mama close in case I get called out on an emergency. So that place on Green Street is going to work out just fine. Three bedrooms, fenced yard for Nike. And not that much more than I was paying for the double-wide."

"Glad it worked out," Buck said. "When are y'all moving?"

She said, "Mama and Willis drove in last night. Mama's furniture won't get here till tomorrow, so I'm taking a couple of days off for the move. She's staying with me in the meantime." She glanced at her watch. "Matter of fact, she's probably taking the chicken out of the oven right now. I need to get going."

Buck said, "Damn, that reminds me, I've got food in

the car. Hold on, I'll walk you out." He turned to close down his computer. "You need any help moving?"

She replied, "The last time I needed a man's help with anything, I ended up with Willis."

She seemed surprised at her own joke, and Buck suppressed a grin. "Well, let me know if you do. I'll bet I could round up a couple of deputies that wouldn't mind getting in good with the chief. And don't worry about meeting Rutherford's wife tomorrow. I'll take care of it."

Jolene glanced back at the computer, the faintest trace of a frown marring her brow. "Is this thing Sheriff Becker's idea? Because I don't remember hearing about any operation ..."

"Marshal knows about it," Buck said. He wasn't being entirely evasive. "After what happened last year, it's a good idea to keep these fringe groups under tight surveillance."

She said, still frowning, "We broke up the Patriots. We got the ringleaders, we got their money, we got their armament. Half of them are sitting in county jail right now, waiting trial. The other half will be going before judges in other jurisdictions. But they're done. It's over."

Buck shook his head sadly. "You can put people in jail, but you can't lock up ideas. They're still out there, and always will be."

She looked at him speculatively, then nodded toward the computer. "So which one of these jerk-offs are you?"

He chuckled, reaching around her to close out the program. "Nah, I don't post anything. I just observe and report."

"Because," she pointed out, "anything more would be entrapment."

"Exactly." He clicked the mouse and the screen went dark. He gestured with the file folder toward the door.

"So, how do you think your little boy's going to like living in the mountains?"

They left the building and crossed the parking lot in the hazy light of the late spring afternoon, talking easily, moving unhurriedly, making themselves perfect targets for the person who watched them, fifty yards away across the courthouse square. He sat at ease behind the tinted windows of the closed car, squinting through the sites of his pistol with the same relaxed stance he employed in front of the video game console, leading the target, squeezing off his shots. First the man, then the black bitch walking beside him, then the man again.

"Pow," he said softly, squeezing the trigger, feigning the recoil. "Pow, pow, pow, *pow.*"

But the safety was on. This time.

EIGHT

All four dogs piled on the sofa with Melanie and me that evening to video chat with Miles. It was a little chaotic—Pepper kept trying to lick the screen and the Aussies got bored and made a game of knocking the phone off its stand on the coffee table, but Miles was used to it. Eventually I banished Mischief and Magic to the kitchen and settled Pepper down with a bone, which left only Cisco, who had never met a camera he didn't like, sitting between us, his ears pricked forward as he tried to figure out how this person that he knew got into the tiny phone.

"So Mel," Miles said, when things were a little calmer, "I've been following your story on Instagram."

Of course he had. I leaned back out of camera range to hide a wince.

"Pretty cool, huh?" Melanie said. "I got lots of good pictures of the cops and the ambulance, but we had to leave before they brought the body out."

Miles was sitting in front of the big window that overlooked the ocean at his mother's house. The last of the sunset was still visible in indigo stripes against a twilight sky, and his face was illuminated by the soft light of a lamp on the table at his side. He was a good-looking man with short-cropped hair and gray eyes that I could look at forever. I wished I had put on lipstick before the call.

He agreed, "They were good pictures. But how do

you think this man's family would feel if they saw your post before they even knew he was dead?"

She hesitated. "Not good, I guess. But I didn't mention any names."

"Doesn't matter. It was careless and disrespectful. We've talked about this. Once it's on the internet it's out of your control. Be more thoughtful next time, okay?"

Her expression fell, exaggerating her contrition, and she mumbled, "Okay."

He gave that a beat, then said, "So how was dinner at Aunt Mart's house?"

She cheered immediately. "Say, Dad, did you know Raine used to be rich? I mean not her, but her family. They owned practically *everything* around here."

He looked amused. "Is that a fact?"

Melanie went on to tell him all about the murder of Adam Bowslayer and the family history of the Stocktons—with which Aunt Mart had so generously provided her—and the essay she was going to write on the subject. "It counts for one third of my quarterly grade," she concluded, "so it has to be good."

"When's it due?" Miles asked, which was something I hadn't thought about.

"I have to turn in the outline Monday."

"*This* Monday?" I stared at her. "That's the day after tomorrow. You're cutting it a little close, aren't you?"

She shrugged. "I'm pretty fast."

Her father said sternly, "You'd better be pretty good, too."

She grinned back at him impudently. "I am."

"Okay, Miss Good-and-Fast," he replied, "go get ready for bed, then come back down to say good night. And—"

"Don't forget to take Pepper out," we both said at the

same time, and couldn't help grinning at each other. Co-parenting via the internet. Not too shabby.

"I *never* forget," Melanie said with an eye roll as she got up. "Come on, Pepper. Later, Dad."

"Later, kiddo."

Cisco stretched out into the seat on the sofa she had vacated, resting his head on his paws while still managing to keep an alert eye on the phone. When she was gone, I said, "Sorry about the Instagram thing. I should have been paying attention."

"That's okay," he said. "I deleted the pictures."

"Oh." I was surprised. "I didn't know you could do that." But I felt as though I should have.

"So," he said, settling back in his chair with a glass of iced tea. "Tell me the rest of the story."

I stretched out a hand to stroke Cisco's fur while I told him about Kylie Goodwin and Mozart, and how I was convinced that the dog who had been locked in the drowning victim's car was the same dog who'd disappeared with little Kylie six years ago. I even pulled out the same two printed out photographs I'd shown Uncle Ro and Buck: the before, six years ago, and the after, today.

"And you think this cop who drowned in Murder Creek today might have been investigating the case, and that's how he ended up with the dog?"

It was uncanny, how much Miles and I thought alike. Or maybe it was just that he had learned, with exposure, how *I* thought.

"It's not such a leap," I said. "Retired policemen investigate cold cases all the time. Just look at Uncle Ro."

"And," he said, trying to help me out, "just because he came here from Florida doesn't mean he's always lived there. He might have been involved in the original case in South Carolina."

As he spoke, he was busily typing on a keypad just out of my sight. This used to make me crazy, but over time I'd learned to ignore it. Miles was one of the few men I knew who actually *could* multitask, as opposed to just thinking he could.

"Exactly," I said. "It can't be a coincidence that they ended up here."

"Unfortunately," Miles said, "there's no record that a James Carlton Rutherford worked in any South Carolina law enforcement agency in the past twenty years."

I shouldn't have been surprised. Miles was something of a techno-geek, and he was always investing in software companies and AI companies and who-knows-what-else that were lightyears ahead of anything you or I have ever heard of. Accessing a state's employment records would be child's play for him.

"What about Federal?" I suggested, trying not to be disappointed. "I know the FBI was called in."

"Beyond my level of expertise," he admitted, and then winked. "For the moment. I'll look into it if you want me to and call you back."

I sighed. "No, that's okay. I'll find out what Rutherford was doing here as soon as the sheriff's office talks to the next of kin. It's just … frustrating, you know? I don't think Uncle Ro or Buck even believe it's the same dog, and I know Jolene doesn't."

"Well," he said, "like you said, it is a coincidence."

I frowned thoughtfully. "I wonder what happened to the Goodwins. The parents, I mean."

"They divorced a year after the incident," Miles said, glancing again at a screen outside my view. "She still lived in the same house as of January of this year, and he apparently moved out of state." And just as I was about to question, he explained, "Property tax records. Available to anyone online."

I said, "Hampton Crossing, right? That's where Carol Goodwin still lives?"

He replied simply, "Don't do it."

I couldn't help being annoyed. Nonetheless, I answered innocently, "I don't know what you're talking about."

"Don't contact that poor woman and tell her you've found her missing daughter's dog."

"Miles," I said, "she has a right to know. This could mean a break in the case, the first one in years. We might finally have a chance to find out what happened to Kylie, and if nothing else that will mean closure for the family. She needs to know."

But with every word I spoke he shook his head. "In the first place, you don't know anything. There is absolutely no way to prove that the dog you have is Kylie Goodwin's dog, and without proof, anything you say to the family would be cruel. Do you remember that case a couple of years ago where the police found a boy who claimed to have been kidnapped thirteen years earlier? They notified the family that they had found their missing child, but a DNA test proved it wasn't the same boy at all. I saw an interview with the father afterward. I'll never forget the look in his eyes when he said that thinking they had found his son and then finding out they were wrong was worse than losing the child in the first place." Again he shook his head. "Don't do it."

He was right. He usually was. Until I had more to go on, there was no point in contacting the family.

He changed the subject. "So," he said, "I'm texting you a copy of Melanie's schedule for next week. Don't forget she has junior debate club on Wednesday and a violin lesson after that. You'll have to pick her up at 5:00 at the school. On Thursday …"

"I know, I know," I said. "You posted a schedule on my refrigerator and on the bulletin board at Dog Daze and I've got two copies on my computer. Relax."

He gave me a wry grin. "Right. I forgot you were Wonder Woman. So, Wonder Woman," he went on easily, "have you given any thought to a date yet? Inquiring minds want to know."

I literally squirmed in my seat. "I don't know, Miles. Do we really have to decide now?"

"No pressure," he assured me with exaggerated casualness, "but Mom was asking."

Way not to apply pressure, by bringing up his hospitalized seventy-year-old mother. I said, "It's just that I was hoping to keep this low key. I mean, we've both been married before …"

"Correction." He lifted a mild admonishing finger. "We've both *tried* to be married before. This time it's the real thing. This time we do it right. That deserves a celebration."

I've got to hand it to him, the man knows how to melt my heart, and I'm not usually one to fall for the sappy stuff. I looked at him for a moment, trying to keep my smile from taking over my whole face. "You're really something," I said. "You know that?"

"I do," he assured me with a wink. "And, honey, I want you to know that whatever you want to do, that's what I want, okay? If you want to get married in the woods in Smokey Bear costumes, I'm onboard with that. Vera Wang dress and rose petal carpets, slightly more onboard. I want this day to be about you, and letting the whole world know how lucky I am that you're going to be my wife."

I tightened my lips against a grin. "Laying on the mushy stuff a little thick, aren't you, cowboy?"

"Hey," he protested, "mushy stuff is one of the things I do best. It's my trademark." He winked at me. "Just a heads-up, though. Mom says if we're going to book St. Paul's Cathedral, we're going to have to give some notice, so the sooner you settle on a date, the better."

It took me a beat—a very heart-stopping beat, I might add—to realize he was joking. "That's a hard pass on St. Paul's," I said, "but I will look into those Smokey Bear costumes, thanks." Then, more seriously, I said, "Miles, I need to ask you something."

"What's that?"

I took a breath. "After we're, you know, married … where do you picture us living?"

He was thoughtful for a moment. "Rome? Monaco? I've always liked Hong Kong."

My alarm must have shown on my face because he laughed. "Come on, sugar, you know I told you a long time ago I'd found the place I want to spend the rest of my life. Why do you think I built my house there?"

"That's the point," I replied, not bothering to conceal my annoyance now. "Your house. So is that what you're thinking? That we'll live there?"

He shrugged. "I guess. It makes sense. I hadn't really thought about it."

I said, "Well, don't you think we should talk about it? Because …"

But I never got to finish that sentence. There was a clatter of feet and paws on the stairs, Cisco leapt off the sofa to greet Pepper, and Melanie bounced into her seat beside me, throwing kisses at the phone screen with both hands. "'Night, Daddy!" she declared. "Talk to you tomorrow!"

"You bet you will, sweetie." He threw kisses back. "And you know what we're going to talk about? The outline for your essay that you're going to e-mail me before 4:00 p.m."

She made a face. "Aww, Dad ..."

"Life is a series of deadlines, sweetheart. Better learn to meet them now."

"But I'm supposed to go to a pizza party after church tomorrow," she protested. "My whole class will be there! It won't even be over until 3:00."

He said, unmoved, "That's a shame."

I don't always agree with Miles's parenting philosophy, but I am smart enough not to say so in front of Melanie. For example, I think kids should be allowed time to be kids, especially when there is only a week left before Dad comes home.

I said, trying my best to be supportive, "Homework comes first."

She glared at me.

I blew my own kiss to Miles. "Good night," I said. "Give Rita my love. I'll talk to you tomorrow."

We disconnected, and Melanie, still pouting, stomped her way toward the stairs. I said mildly, "You've still got an hour before bed. You could work on your outline tonight."

She grumbled, "What's the point? I won't get it done in time to go to the party." Then she looked at me hopefully. "I could skip church."

When I was her age, that would have been my first choice too. But Miles, who wasn't particularly religious, was a big believer in keeping commitments, and Melanie had promised Aunt Mart some time ago that she would attend Sunday School every week. I said, "Probably not a good option. Besides, you said you were fast. You'd probably be even faster if I helped. Maybe over a bowl of ice cream?"

The storm clouds that had begun to reform in her eyes were slowly replaced by a smile, and she bounded up the stairs. "I'll get my laptop," she called back.

How to Raise Dogs and Kids by Raine Stockton, *Chapter Four: Never Underestimate the Power of a Bribe.*

NINE

Elizabeth Rutherford was a well-kept woman in her early sixties, slender, with shoulder-length brown hair lightly streaked with gray. She was dressed in a dark pantsuit that was a little rumpled from the trip, but she had made the effort to apply lipstick to her cracked, dry lips. Had it not been for the swollen eyes and pale, puffy face, she would have been an attractive woman for her age. She looked like someone who, generally speaking, made an effort.

She was escorted by her son, George, who bore a recognizable resemblance to his father. He had the same slightly square build and thinning hairline, and he wore a navy blazer and khaki slacks for the trip, which for some reason made Buck think of the way his father had been dressed when they found him. Businesslike.

Buck met them at Sutter's Funeral Home, whose back room also served as the county morgue when needed. The building was a stately, columned Greek revival that sat on a hill just at the edge of town, and had once served as the Sutter family's home. Now it was completely dedicated to the business of death, and Buck supposed if there was a good place for a family to face the grisly task the Rutherfords now had before them, this was it.

Lee Sutter was with the family when Buck arrived, serving them coffee in the elegant, tall-ceilinged reception room with its elaborate mill work and subdued decor. There was a crystal chandelier that wasn't too bright, dark leather wing chairs and wine velvet sofas. Reproductions of classic paintings hung on the walls. Organ music played softly through the speakers. The room was designed to be reassuring, solid, evocative of things that endured forever. But every time Buck walked in there he was reminded of the last day of his boyhood, when he had stood over his father's casket in this very room. It hadn't been the first funeral he had attended, nor would it be the last. But it had been the worst.

Lee Sutter was both the county coroner and its only funeral director, and he had a natural instinct for knowing just what a grieving family needed at a time like this. When Buck came in, he was sitting quietly beside the widow, patting Elizabeth Rutherford's hand while she talked nervously about how healthy her husband had been, how stubborn and independent, and how you never expected something like this to happen. Her son sat grimly in the wing chair opposite her and sipped coffee from a porcelain cup.

Buck approached with his hand extended. "Mrs. Rutherford," he said. "I'm Buck Lawson, an investigator with the county. I'm so sorry for your loss."

The woman stood and shook his hand uncertainly. She said in a small voice, "Investigator? I don't understand. I thought ... I thought it was a drowning. What's to investigate?"

"It's just routine with an unattended death," Buck assured her. He turned to the son, who shook his hand.

"George Rutherford," he said briefly. "What can you tell us?"

Buck replied gently, "It looks as though your dad might have slipped and fallen from one of the waterfalls. They can be treacherous if you're not familiar with the terrain. But right now ..." His gaze shifted to the widow, and he gave her an encouraging, compassionate smile. "I know this will be hard, Mrs. Rutherford, but we'll need you to identify the body for the records. I'll go in with you, and so will Mr. Sutter. You just tell us when you're ready."

The woman took a deep breath, and let it out shakily. Her son put a hand on her shoulder. "Mama?" he inquired softly.

She straightened her shoulders. Her misty gaze steadied. "Now," she said. "I'm ready now."

Lee Sutter took them into one of the private parlors, where the body had been laid out on one of the wheeled tables and covered with a sheet. The table was skirted with a pleated cloth, and even though Buck knew the body had been stripped and enclosed in a body bag below the neck, the sheet disguised the fact. Sutter was thoughtful that way.

The coroner drew back the sheet to the chin, and Mrs. Rutherford looked at the face that was revealed for a long time. So did Buck, focusing particularly on the cut on the man's forehead. The water would have washed away the blood, but why was there no bruising?

George Rutherford put a hand on his mother's shoulder. "That's him," he said hoarsely. "That's Daddy."

Buck looked at the widow, and she nodded, tight-lipped. Sutter pulled the sheet back over the face, and she turned away.

George said, "What do we do now? I mean, about transporting him … and his car …" He trailed off, his square face sagging, looking completely baffled.

Buck said, "Let me buy you and your mother a cup of coffee. I'll explain everything to you, and there are just a few questions I need to ask you for our records." He nodded back toward the reception room. "I'm going to have a word with Mr. Sutter first, and I'll meet you outside."

When they were gone, Buck said, "Your preliminary report put the time of death at between 9:00 and 10:00 yesterday morning?"

"You know that's just a guess, what with the temperature of the water and all. But I'd be surprised if it was any earlier than that. The medical examiner will have the final say."

"So you're saying he'd been dead at least an hour and a half before he was found."

"That's my estimate," agreed Sutter.

Buck nodded, frowning thoughtfully. "Can you tell for sure whether the cause of death was drowning? I mean, could he have had a heart attack or stroke before he went in the water?"

Sutter replied, "The ME will be able to tell for sure by whether or not there's any water in his lungs, but if I had to guess I'd say blood flow stopped before he went in the water. Did you notice that cut on his forehead? If it had been caused by the fall, and he was still alive, you'd expect a bruise."

"Yeah," Buck said, his tone preoccupied. "Can I have a look at his clothes?"

"I already bagged them up to send to Asheville with the body."

"Unbag them," Buck said.

Sutter retrieved the sealed mylar bag and cut it open, laying out the articles of clothing on the credenza that would have held the guest book and vases of flowers in the event of an ordinary viewing. Buck gave only a cursory examination of the shirt, pants, belt, socks and underwear, but he looked carefully at the shoes. He even took out his phone and snapped some close-up shots before turning back to Sutter. His expression was somber.

"You're sending him up to Asheville today?" he said.

Sutter nodded. "I was just waiting for the family to get here."

"Do me a favor," Buck said. "Make sure the medical examiner knows this is a priority."

"I'll call the office as soon as you all leave," replied Sutter, looking puzzled. "Anything in particular you want me to mention?"

Buck hesitated, still frowning. "It's just … his shoes. They have scuff marks on them."

Sutter looked back at the man's brown leather loafers. "I'm not sure I follow you. I have a few pairs of shoes at home myself that could use a good polishing."

"Yeah, me too," Buck agreed. "But these scuff marks are on top."

I stared in amazement at the wreck of what once had been a state-of-the-art kennel enclosure. A chew-proof dog bed had been completely shredded, filling the six-foot space with a sea of puffy white polyester fiber fill that covered the floor like snow and still drifted in flakes from the ceiling with every random current of air. The tamper-proof bolt lock that secured the kennel door had been twisted just enough to loosen the screws that secured it, and the door stood wide open. At the end of the corridor the latch on the storage room, which wasn't nearly as secure, had given way to what was apparently the weight of a one-hundred-twenty-pound dog being repeatedly thrown against it, and trails of dog food and empty bags littered the corridor from one end to the other.

Corny had called me as soon as he'd discovered the wreckage, and Melanie and I were still in our pajamas. Corny had clearly tried to mitigate the damage before I saw it; he had tufts of polyester fluff in his hair and a distressed look on his face as he quickly put aside the broom and dustpan he was holding.

"Holy cow," said Melanie in a small, awed voice behind me. "It looks like Bigfoot broke in here."

"Oh, Miss Stockton, I'm so sorry," said Corny, wringing his hands. "I never imagined ... who would have thought ... I could hardly believe it when I came to feed him this morning and saw, well, this!"

I answered absently, still trying to take it all in, "Don't be silly, Corny, it's not your fault."

The culprit was now ensconced in a kennel more suited for a dog half his size, panting genially at us from a few rows down, apparently none the worse for wear after his midnight adventures. The expression on his face suggested he was only remaining inside the enclosure to humor us.

Melanie went forward to examine the lock. "Wow," she said. "He must be as strong as a dinosaur!"

I have known dogs to do incredible things under stress: chew through wooden doors, jump through plate glass windows, climb twelve-foot-tall fences. I should not have been surprised that a dog of Mozart's size, left unattended for eight hours, could wreak this much havoc. As it happened, Mozart had been the only occupant of the big dog area of the kennel, so there had been no barking dogs to alert Corny to his misadventures. I was just glad that Mozart had been unable to break through the fire doors that separated the big dog kennels from the rest of the building. Who knows how much damage he might have done otherwise?

Corny ventured, "He probably has a touch of separation anxiety."

"A touch?" I repeated, still dazed. "A *touch?*"

"Maybe if I let him sleep in my quarters tonight," Corny went on hopefully.

I blew out a long breath, took a breath, and squared my shoulders. One thing at a time. "We'll figure that out later," I said. "For now, let's put him in the playroom where there's nothing for him to break." The only equipment that wasn't put in storage when not in use were the big, colorfully painted truck tires that were mounted to the floor for puppies to run through and climb on, and if Mozart wanted to have a go at chewing those up he was welcome to try. Likewise, the padded floor was made of woven recycled tires, and the walls were concrete block. On the other hand, hadn't there been a movie about a prisoner tunneling through a reinforced concrete wall with a spoon? I supposed anything was possible if you're desperate enough to escape, whether you're a dog or a human.

I couldn't help remembering how devotedly Mozart used to follow Kylie with his eyes when they were in my class. I had even joked with Kylie's father about what might happen if anyone ever tried to keep Mozart away from Kylie. In my mind, the scene had looked something like this.

"I'll take him!" Melanie volunteered eagerly and started toward Mozart. Mozart stood, thumping his tail again the bars of the kennel.

I caught her arm. "You," I told her firmly, "most certainly will not. Go get ready for church."

"But we were going to make pancakes!"

"Get a bowl of cereal."

"But I wanted …"

I held up a hand, staring her down. Generally, I am the very soul of patience, as you've probably noticed, but it wasn't even 9:00 in the morning and I was already having a bad day. "Go," I repeated sternly. "Eat cereal. Get dressed. We're leaving in half an hour."

She glared at me for a couple of seconds, just to make sure I knew she was not happy about this decision, then she spun on her heel and stomped off, her tangled curls bouncing angrily. I gave a nod of satisfaction and turned back to Corny, when she declared, pushing open the metal fire door, "I'm not going to wash my cereal bowl!"

"And don't forget to put your bowl in the dishwasher!" I shouted to her retreating back.

She let the door slam shut with a clang.

How to Raise Dogs and Kids by Raine Stockton, *Chapter Five: There Can Only Be One Boss. Make Sure it's You.*

TEN

Buck took the Rutherfords to the only place that was open in town on a Sunday morning, a little coffee shop/bakery on the corner of Elm and Valley Street that served hot donuts in the morning and pie and cake in the afternoon. The donuts were some of the best he'd ever had, and he encouraged the Rutherfords to order one. They didn't, so neither did he.

Buck had explained to them about transporting the body to the medical examiner's office on the drive over, and he could tell neither of them were happy about it. But George Rutherford waited until the coffee was served to say, "Look, you said this was a drowning. I don't see why we need to have this delay. All we want to do is make arrangements to have my father …" He paused a moment to clear his throat and gain his composure, and then went on, "To have my father sent home."

Buck assured him, "The delay will be minimal. A day at most, maybe two. You can leave instructions with Mr. Sutter about transporting your father, and he'll take care of it. It's the law that the medical examiner has to be notified in the case of an unattended death, and since this county is too small to have its own ME, we share one with the region. That's why we have to send him to Asheville."

"It's just," said Mrs. Rutherford in a small voice, "it's just so far from home."

"Yes, ma'am," agreed Buck. He waited a respectful moment before adding, "Do you mind telling me what brought your husband to Hanover County? Did he have business here?"

She shook her head and cast a helpless look toward her son. "Jim has been retired for almost ten years. He was head of the major crimes division with the Jacksonville Police Department," she added with an unmistakable note of pride. "He did that job for twenty years, and he was good at it too. Who knows how many criminals are off the streets because of him?"

Buck took out his notebook, figuring he might as well get a head start on the paperwork that would accompany the body to the ME's office. "Did your husband have any health problems?"

"He just had a physical last week," she asserted. "His cholesterol was a little high, but everything else was perfect. That's why it was such a shock ... I mean, after a certain age you expect it will be cancer, or a heart attack, but ... falling into a creek?" Again she shook her head in a display of disbelief. "It just doesn't seem right."

Buck knew there was nothing to say to that. In a moment he went on, "How did he seem to you these last few days? Was he worried about anything, or depressed?"

"No," she insisted. "No, just the opposite. He was excited about what he was researching, spent hours in his office, on the computer and on the phone, and then he couldn't wait to get on the road to get up here. I haven't seen him that enthusiastic about anything since he retired. He loves solving problems." A shadow crossed her face and she dropped her gaze to her coffee cup. "Loved."

Her son covered her hand with his own and picked up the story. "One of the things that kept Dad busy after he retired was looking into old cases. Never anything official, you know, just more of a hobby. Some people do crossword puzzles, he'd look at old crime scene photos." He shrugged. "Every once in a while he'd take off on a road trip to"—he put his fingers up, enclosing the next phrase in air quotes—"look into something. A lot of the time one of his buddies from the department would go with him, and I think they did a lot more fishing and drinking than investigating. It was just a way to keep his hand in, you know, and have a good time with his friends at the same time."

Buck nodded. "But nobody came with him this time?"

Mrs. Rutherford looked up from contemplating her coffee cup, and she shook her head. "It wasn't that kind of trip. He said he had found something that might be important and he needed to see a man in North Carolina. He was only going to be gone a couple of days. He likes to drive at night, so he left while I was still sleeping. He called me yesterday morning when he stopped for breakfast in Atlanta. He sounded ..." she swallowed hard. "He sounded fine."

Buck said, "About what time was that?"

"About 6:00. He knows I'm an early riser. We both are. We like to ... used to like to ... take our coffee out to the deck and watch the sun rise."

Buck said, "It's about a three, three-and-a-half-hour drive from Atlanta to here. So he got here maybe 9:30?"

She shook her head. "I don't know. I didn't talk to him again. He usually calls me morning and evening when he's away from home, so I didn't think anything was wrong."

Buck said, "He never mentioned the name of the person he came here to talk to? Or maybe wrote it down somewhere?"

She shook her head, but looked uncertain. "Not that I

recall. Why? Is that important?"

Buck made an effort to keep his voice reassuring. "I'm just trying to put together a picture of what happened. The place where your husband died isn't a very well-known spot, and I wondered why he was there. Maybe he was supposed to meet someone there."

He waited to see if that speculation sparked recognition with either of them, but their expressions registered nothing. He went on, "Do you have any idea what he found that he thought was important?"

"I'm sorry," she said, looking distressed. "I don't. I didn't take much interest in his work, I'm afraid, even when it was actual work and not just a hobby. I think he appreciated that. It was a part of his life he liked to keep to himself."

Buck glanced at the son. "Did he ever talk to you about the cases he was working on?"

"Sometimes," George said. "We'd play golf with some of his buddies from the force once a week and now and then they'd talk about old cases. I didn't pay a lot of attention. I really couldn't tell you what he was looking into now. But I could give you the names of some guys who might know."

"That would be helpful," Buck said. He looked from one to the other of them. "Did you ever hear him mention the Kylie Goodwin case?" They looked blank so he prompted, "A little girl who disappeared in South Carolina about six years back."

One by one they shook their heads. "I honestly can't remember," said Mrs. Rutherford, and added sadly, "So many awful things happen to children these days." Her voice faded as she repeated, "So many awful things."

Buck persisted, "And he never worked in South Carolina?"

Again, Mrs. Rutherford shook her head. "We were there on vacation once, right after we got married. But that was almost forty years ago, and as far as I know he never went back. I can't think of a reason why he should."

George looked concerned. "Mr. Lawson, I thought my father's death was accidental. But you're asking an awful lot of questions about his work. Do you think the two could be related somehow?"

Buck glanced at the widow, with her wet, bloodshot eyes and the expression of shocked dread that seemed to be permanently stamped on her features, and he knew that if it had just been George and himself he might have been more forthcoming. As it was, he merely returned a reassuring smile and said, "I'm just trying to gather as much information as I can. The more I can do on this end, the sooner the medical examiner can complete his report, and you can take your father home."

That seemed to satisfy the other man, at least for the moment. He glanced at his mother and said, "Well, of course we want to help, but my mother is exhausted. We saw a hotel just outside of town. I thought we'd try to get a couple of rooms for the night. "

Buck nodded agreement. "It's a nice place, good breakfast buffet. You should check in and get settled, and I'll have some papers for you to sign in a couple of hours. You can talk to Mr. Sutter about arrangements for transporting your father back to Florida in the morning before you head home. We'll handle everything else from here."

Mrs. Rutherford looked dazed. She picked up her coffee cup, looked at the contents, and put it back down, untouched. She said in a wavery voice, "You've been very kind."

George put his hand on his mother's arm in preparation for helping her to her feet.

Buck said, "There was just one more thing." He had genuinely almost forgotten.

George looked back at him.

"The dog that was found in your husband's car," he said to the wife. "The officer who talked to you on the phone yesterday said he didn't belong to you?"

Mrs. Rutherford said, "No. We don't have a dog."

"This was a big dog," Buck persisted, "black, long-coated, about seven years old. Does that sound familiar? Maybe he belongs to someone your husband knew?"

"No." She couldn't have sounded more certain.

"I wonder what he was doing in your husband's car," Buck said. "Was he the kind of man to pick up a stray?" He glanced at George. "Maybe as a surprise for his grandkids?"

"Both of my kids are in college," George said, "and my dad didn't even like dogs."

"Jim was allergic to dogs," his mother explained. "There's simply no way he ever would have allowed one in his car. No way at all."

Of all the things Buck had learned that day, that one was the most puzzling.

ELEVEN

There was no way I was leaving Corny to clean up the mess by himself, so I decided to drop Melanie off at church and go home to help out. The good news is that by then Melanie was completely over her snit and couldn't wait to regale her friends—and Aunt Mart—with the morning's adventures. The bad news is I got a very disappointed look from my aunt, who stood on the church steps and waited for me to come in.

Uncle Ro was standing on the lawn with a group of other men, catching up on the week's gossip, and he came over to the car when he saw me. "Not staying for services, Rainbow?" he said with a twinkle in his eye. "Your aunt's not going to like that."

"Yeah, I can tell." I waggled my fingers toward Aunt Mart with an apologetic smile as Melanie ran up and gave her a hug. "I have to go home and clean up a mess at the kennel. Will you explain it to her?"

"I'll do my best." His smile faded a little as he bent down and rested an elbow on my open car window. He was dressed for church in a suit and tie, which might have made his expression seem more somber than he intended. He said, "This is probably not the place to bring it up, but you got my curiosity up about the Kylie Goodwin case, and I spent a little time digging up the old reports last night. From what I can tell, the investigating officers had their eye on the father even before the little girl's pj's were found in the lake. When forty-eight hours passed without a ransom demand, the kidnapping theory was all but dropped, and the whole thing always looked fishy to the men on the scene. I mean, the kid disappears from her own bedroom with her mother sleeping next door, no sign of a break-in, not a bark from the dog, nobody even noticed the girl missing until the next morning. Jason Goodwin had decided to replace their security system only that day, so the old one was completely disconnected. Carol Goodwin suspected her husband was having an affair for some time, but refused to divorce him because of Kylie. It sounded like a pretty troubled marriage to me. She's the one who kept insisting that the police investigate her husband, that he was doing this to punish her, that he knew what had happened to Kylie. She says when she woke up that night around two, he wasn't in bed beside her. He claims he was downstairs in the den watching television. But investigators noticed mud on his shoes and on a pair of sweatpants they found in the hamper, which he claimed came from his morning jog around the lake. You probably remember some of this."

I nodded. "Wasn't there something about the doors being locked?"

"There were chain locks on all the doors, and the mother claimed they were still in place when she got up and saw Kylie was missing. The father said she was mistaken. He accused her of drinking too much, and of being passed out drunk the night Kylie disappeared. Anyway, that's when they started to suspect foul play."

I said, "They thought Mozart escaped when the intruder took Kylie. Then they thought it wasn't an intruder after all, but that the father had gone out to dispose of the body and then locked the doors when he came back inside out of habit. But Mozart never came back. If he had just run through an open door he would have still been out there somewhere, all the time we were searching. A big dog like that is hard to miss."

Uncle Ro nodded soberly. "That was a puzzle, all right. Somebody even floated a theory that the dog and the girl might have been taken together, but it was shot down pretty quick. I mean, the little girl might have slipped through the Amber alert, but a little girl traveling with a big black dog? No chance. Then they thought Goodwin might have killed the dog, too. There was blood in the back of his car that they thought might have come from Kylie, but it turned out to be canine. Goodwin claimed the dog had gotten into a fight with another dog a week earlier, and that's where the blood came from. They didn't take him to a vet, so no way to prove it."

I shuddered. "No offense, Uncle Ro, but this is a really depressing conversation."

"Sorry, honey." He tapped the doorframe and started to straighten up. "I just thought you'd want to know. The chances of that dog you found yesterday having anything to do with the Goodwin case are pretty slim."

I was far from convinced of that. I said, "I just don't see Jason Goodwin as the kind of man who'd murder his own daughter—or dog, either, for that matter. I told the police back then that he seemed crazy about her, as far as I could tell. And he was a wimpy little guy. He could barely handle Mozart on a leash, much less ..." I trailed off, unable to vocalize what I could barely envision. "Anyway," I went on firmly, "it doesn't make sense. Why would he kill his child and dog but not his wife? That wouldn't get him anything."

Uncle Ro nodded. "For a while they thought Carol might be involved somehow, trying to cover up an accident or working some kind of insurance scam, but none of it panned out. Then there was a theory that Goodwin had planned to kill his wife, too, but ran out of time or guts." He shook his head. "Who knows, honey? I gave up on trying to figure out how psychopaths think a long time ago. Anyway, they were never able to get enough evidence to make an arrest, and eventually the case went cold."

"What about Jason Goodwin's girlfriend?" I said. "I mean, the woman his wife thought he was having the affair with. Did they interview her?"

He shook his head. "I was curious about that, too. Lots of times in cases like this the girlfriend is the weak link—you know, she's ready to stand by her man through thick and thin, until you show her prison time. But in this case, they never even found the girlfriend, and it wasn't for lack of trying. So it looks like the wife was wrong."

"And the police just stopped investigating?"

"These things have a natural timeline to them, Rainbow," he said. "They would've kept an eye on Goodwin for a while, but if nothing turned up ..." He lifted a shoulder. "Sometimes a trail just goes stone cold, and you have to close the file."

"Still," I persisted, "if we could find out where Mozart's been these past six years, and how Mr. Rutherford came to have him in his car, that might shed some light on what really happened that night, wouldn't it? Maybe enough to reopen the case?"

Uncle Ro looked skeptical. "I don't see how. Even if it is the same dog—and like I said, that's highly unlikely—it doesn't prove anything. All the evidence points to the fact that little Kylie is dead, and the dog's not talking. Sorry to be the bearer of bad news."

I sighed. "Well, thanks for checking into it, Uncle Ro. I've got to get back. Tell Aunt Mart I'm sorry about services. I'll be back for Melanie at noon."

I gave my aunt one more small wave as I drove off, but it was an absent gesture; my mind was preoccupied with other things.

The next bad news came in the form of a text from Buck that arrived just as I was sweeping the last of the spilled dog food into an oversized dustpan. I leaned the broom against the wall and left the dustpan on the floor as I dug my phone out of my pocket to read it.

Rutherfords say they don't own a dog. Victim allergic. No idea who he belongs to. Sorry, guess it's your problem now.

I tried to repress my dismay as I looked around my wrecked kennel. That was *not* what I needed to hear right now. I started to text him back when I heard the fire door open behind me and Corny said, "Miss Stockton, I wondered if ..."

Before he could finish the sentence, a golden blur squeezed passed him through the door, tail spinning and claws scrabbling on the polished concrete floor. He made a beeline for the dustpan filled with dog kibble but couldn't quite brake in time. I shouted, "Cisco!" but he didn't even look around. He skidded into the dustpan and kernels of premium dog food exploded across the room. I grabbed for his collar but slipped on dog food and flung out a hand to catch myself. My phone flew from my grip. "Damn it, Cisco!" I cried and scrambled for my phone.

Cisco, who was gobbling food from the floor as though he had never, in all his life, even begun to imagine anything so miraculous, only wagged his tail faster and did not spare me a glance.

Corny clapped his hands together sharply and strode

into the room. The door clattered closed behind him. "Mr. Cisco! What are you thinking?"

Cisco stopped gobbling and cast him a baleful look over his shoulder. Corny said, "Shame on you! That is *not* the behavior of a gentleman."

Cisco licked is lips guiltily and sat down, his tail swishing a slow apologetic arc through the carpet of dog food on the floor.

I have no idea how Corny does that, and I have long since given up trying to figure it out. His power over dogs—all dogs, not just Cisco—is nothing short of miraculous, and that's only one of the reasons I'm lucky to have him.

I grabbed my phone, then Cisco's collar, checking my phone for damage. Fortunately there was none. "Thanks, Corny," I said. "I guess I forgot to close the office door." I turned Cisco toward the door with a firm grip on his collar and pointed sternly. "Go," I commanded him.

Corny held open the door and I released Cisco's collar. Tail hanging low, he moved obediently toward the door. But he couldn't resist snatching one last crumb off the floor just before he scooted through. "Hey!" I scolded him, but Pepper was waiting on the other side of the door and he bounced playfully toward her, having already forgotten his transgression.

Kids and dogs. They just can't resist pushing the limits.

Corny picked up the broom and started sweeping up the mess. "I've finished exercising the boarders," he said, "and I wondered if you wanted me to let Mozart outside. I'll stay with him, of course."

The kennel exercise yard is surrounded by an eight-foot-tall chain-link fence with a two-foot, 45-degree chain-link panel on top to foil jumpers and climbers. Eighteen inches of fencing are buried beneath the ground and topped with concrete, so digging under is not an option. Like I said, I've seen it all, and I take my responsibility toward my clients very seriously. My boarding kennel is virtually escape-proof. Nonetheless, after last night, there was no way I would leave Mozart outside unsupervised.

"Thanks, Corny." I tucked my phone back in my pocket and took the broom from him. "How's he doing?"

"I just checked on him in the playroom and he seemed a little depressed," Corny said. "He was just lying there with his head on his paws. I thought some fresh air would do him good. Do you think his family will come for him today?"

The last was said with hope underscored by just the slightest note of desperation. I was sorry to shake my head. "It turns out the Rutherford family doesn't know him," I said.

"How odd," Corny said. The overhead fluorescents glinted off his big glasses, emphasizing his puzzled frown. "Do you suppose poor Mr. Rutherford picked him up along the road?"

"Probably not. Apparently he was allergic to dogs." At least I assumed that was what Buck had meant when he typed "victim allergic." Buck was not one to waste words when it came to texting.

"Well, how in the world did he get in the man's car?"

That, of course, was the question of the hour. "No idea," I said. "But I'll start making some phone calls, see if anyone has reported him missing. Meanwhile, go ahead and take him out, but keep your eye on him."

I finished sweeping up and checked my watch. I still

had over an hour before I had to pick up Melanie. I hurried to the office, where Cisco and Pepper were playing tug of war with a rope toy, as innocent as you please. They abandoned the toy and bounded over to me, wrestling for first place in my notice, when I came in. I couldn't help smiling.

"You," I told Pepper, taking her face in my hands, "are a good dog." I turned to Cisco and made my expression stern. "You," I said, "not so much."

Unfazed, he bounded over to the rope toy, snatched it up, and gave it a good shake. I went to my desk, kicked off my shoes, and woke up my computer, taking out my phone again. I couldn't help smiling, though, when Cisco came over to me and dropped the rope toy in my lap. He sat down and looked at me with big expectant brown eyes, grinning his happy golden retriever grin. "Oh, all right," I said. I ruffled his ears and dropped a kiss on his nose. "You're a good dog too. Some of the time."

I picked up the toy and tossed it in the air. Pepper scrambled to catch it, but Cisco snatched it from the air before she had a chance. Another tug of war ensued, and I dialed Buck's number.

"Look, Raine," he answered without so much as a how-do-you-do. "I spent over an hour with the Rutherfords. The dog is not theirs, and as far as I've been able to tell the victim had absolutely no interest in the Kylie Goodwin case. Never worked in South Carolina, didn't know anybody who has. No explanation at all for how the dog ended up locked in our victim's car. So, sorry. Looks like your theory is blown."

I said, "Good morning to you, too, Buck. How are you doing on this fine Sunday?"

There was a pause, and he sighed. "You know, the reason I took this job is so I wouldn't have to work weekends. Now it seems like all I do is work weekends. Didn't mean to snap at you."

"That's okay," I said. "And for your information, nothing you just told me blows my theory. It just makes it harder to prove. So you're officially calling the dog a stray?"

"Officially."

"And you're not in the least bit curious about how he ended up locked in a dead man's car?"

"Of course I am." The impatience returned to his voice. "I'm just saying it doesn't have anything to do with a six-year-old missing persons case." He paused. "You were right about one thing, though. Rutherford was working on a cold case. Or cases. Just not the one you thought."

Generally, I would have gloated over that, but I was too surprised—and curious—to do so now. "Seriously? What case?"

"I don't know yet. But it looks like he was down here to interview a witness. Don't know who," he added before I could ask. "That's why I'm working on Sunday."

"Huh," I said thoughtfully. "Interesting."

"You could say that."

"I don't suppose you've got any more information on the cause of death. I mean, was it a drowning, or a stroke, or what?"

"Nah. He goes to the ME tomorrow, we should have a preliminary report pretty soon. It looks like he was dead before he went into the water though. Sutter thinks it happened a couple of hours before you found him."

"No way," I said immediately. "If that dog had been in the car for two hours he would have destroyed it. You should've seen what he did to my kennel this morning." Except for the window that I myself had broken, I couldn't remember noting any real damage to the inside of the car, and Jolene hadn't mentioned any. I couldn't even begin to imagine what that car would have looked like if Mozart had been trapped inside long enough to get desperate. "Not to mention there was absolutely no ventilation in that car," I went on. "And it was close to 80 degrees when Melanie and I got there. I'm not sure he could even have survived that long under those conditions. When we let him out, he was in distress, sure, but he was still in good enough shape to lead Cisco on a chase up the hill, and he was only moderately dehydrated. No way he was locked in a hot car for two hours."

Buck murmured, "Right. That's what I thought too."

"Half an hour at the most," I insisted.

"Yeah."

"So," I speculated, "if the time of death is right, Mr. Rutherford was already dead before Mozart was locked in the car. So ..."

He said, "Bye, Raine."

That was his way of telling me to mind my own business. It hardly ever worked, but today I had my own problems to deal with so I was inclined to let it go. I said, "Okay, whatever. But here's a question for you."

He replied impatiently, "What?"

"If Mr. Rutherford was allergic to dogs, what was so special about this one that would make him put him in his car? And if he didn't, who did?"

The silence went on so long that I thought he had, in fact, hung up. Then he said, heavily, "Yeah. Exactly. Talk to you later, Raine."

TWELVE

MountainMan904:   Did you see this? Just in case you're still thinking cops keep us safe.

Police Chief Convicted of Planting Drugs on Motorists

Police Chief Dwight Cannon of Linville, Texas, was convicted Tuesday of making over two hundred false arrests for drug possession in the past three years.

The arrests typically began with a traffic stop, at which time Cannon would conduct a vehicle search on the pretense of having smelled marijuana or alcohol. The search would yield a small amount of narcotics, drug paraphernalia or marijuana. Revenue generated from the arrests amounted to close to a million dollars in the three-year period.

Linville is a town of approximately two square miles and 1800 people with four full-time police officers. Typically, a town of this size can expect under ten felony convictions a year.

Cannon's scheme was uncovered when one of his victims turned out to be an undercover FBI agent.

MaskedMan: What an idiot! Hope he fries.

StraightShooter: 200 drug arrests by one cop and nobody got curious? In a town of 1800? Jesus H., there was more than one idiot involved.

Remington1976: Some judge had to be in on it. You know these pot-bellied towns. Crooked as a dog's hind leg from the mayor on down.

MountainMan904: If you ask me, a man like that ought to be stood up against a wall and shot. Nothing worse than a cop that breaks his oath of office.

Stonewall: You start shooting all the crooked cops you're gonna run out of ammunition before you run out of cops.

Rebel4Ever: You ask me, the real danger to this nation is the one riding around in a black-and-white thinking he's got unlimited power.

MischiefMaker: They do have unlimited power! Look at all the police shootings of unarmed, innocent citizens. How many of those cops are behind bars, you tell me. They stick together, that's the problem.

Rebel4Ever: This is one innocent citizen that ain't never going to be caught unarmed, I can tell you that much. I'd like to see some Smokey Bear try to pull that sh-t on me.

Stonewall: The only way to take these A-holes out is one by one.

MountainMan904: This country is never going to be safe until the citizens have the same rights as the cops.

Rebel4Ever: You tell 'em, bro! Wonder how they're gonna like it when WE start shooting first and asking questions later.

Remington1976: Okay, you guys realize that there are cops on this list, don't you??

As much as Buck complained about working on weekends, he'd found that Sundays were a surprisingly good time to get things done. For one thing, his office was in the wing of the Public Safety Building that was occupied by the county prosecutor and staff, and they were closed on Sunday. It was as quiet as a tomb in that part of the building: no ringing phones, no mail, no one tapping on his door with "just one quick thing," no one dumping a pile of papers on his desk every five minutes. Without those distractions, he actually had a chance to get some things done.

Secondly, he'd found that Sundays were a great time to do interviews, particularly by phone. For some reason, people were more inclined to pick up the phone on a Sunday; maybe because they thought telemarketers didn't work weekends. They tended to be more genial, off-guard, more willing to answer questions. Maybe they were just in a better mood after a Saturday of rest and relaxation, or maybe the simple fact that a government official was working on a Sunday gave his questions a sense of urgency. Whatever the reason—and despite the fact that Buck had still rather be at home eating microwave nachos and watching baseball—the Sunday strategy hadn't failed him yet. And it didn't now.

He got the names of Jim Rutherford's golfing buddies from his son, George. The first one did not answer; Buck left a brief message and moved on. The second one, Gil Monroe, picked up on the second ring. Buck identified himself, ascertained that Monroe was, in fact, a colleague of the late Jim Rutherford, and broke the news of his demise with as much compassion as possible.

The silence that followed was weighted. Then Monroe said huskily, "Damn it. Damn it all to hell." He cleared his throat and demanded gruffly, "I guess your people notified his wife. Liz."

"She and her son George got here this morning. It will be a day or two before we can release the body, but I think they're going to head back home tomorrow."

"You said you're a county prosecutor?"

"Investigator," Buck corrected.

"What division?" the other man demanded. "Homicide?"

Buck replied carefully, "What makes you think that?"

"You wouldn't be calling me on a Sunday if this was an ordinary drowning," the other man snapped back. "I worked homicide for twenty-two years. Jim is—was— my friend. What're you looking at?"

Buck got straight to the point. "His wife said he was excited about some cold case he had been working on, and that he came here to talk to somebody. Do you have any idea who that might have been?"

There was a long silence, followed by something like a muffled groan. "No," he said wearily. "I don't. He didn't say anything to me about it. I didn't even know he had left town."

"I guess it was a last-minute trip," Buck said. "What about this case he was looking into? Do you know anything about that?"

Again silence. Finally, the other man said, sounding reluctant, "I might. Maybe. I mean, the whole thing sounded kind of hokey to me. Not really a case, more like a theory. Conspiracy theory, if you want to know the truth. I didn't take it seriously, at least not at first. I didn't think he did either. But then … these last few months he started to get, I don't know, obsessed or something. It was all he could think about, talk about."

Buck prompted, "What was?"

Monroe blew out a breath that hissed through the phone. "So, Jim retired a few years back, and we gave him a big send off. Hired a room at the Radisson, catered a dinner, the whole she-bang. People liked the guy, you know? Paid for the whole thing with donations. Anyway, we tried to track down as many of the guys as we could who'd been under his command over the years. You know how it is, folks get transferred, get promoted, move away, leave the force altogether. You hardly ever end up with the same crew you started with. Turns out that eight of the men under Jim's command were dead. Three of them we knew about, they were still with the department when it happened. One died of a heart attack. Another one ran his car off a bridge during a rain storm. The other one was shot, ambushed while he walked to his car to go to work one morning. We arrested a gangbanger for it. The other five moved on over the years, but it bothered Jim when he found out that all of them were dead. None of them were over forty."

"Well," Buck felt compelled to point out, "being a cop in a city the size of Jacksonville isn't exactly a low-risk occupation."

"That's the thing," Monroe said. "That's what Jim couldn't let go. He did the math and it turned out that the percentage of deaths under his command was higher than the casualty rate for the entire department during the same time period. What you call a statistical anomaly. That's what got him started looking into those other deaths."

Buck said, "I'm not sure I follow."

"Yeah, okay, neither did I when he first started talking about it. But I've got to tell you, after a while it started to sound like Jim might be on to something. Those other five guys ... one of them left the force to work for his father-in-law's construction company in Alabama. Six months later, he was killed when a propane storage tank blew up at the job site. He was the only one there at the time. Another guy took a job with the Atlanta PD. He worked there about a year, and was found dead in his garage of carbon monoxide poisoning. They ruled it suicide. Another one died two years after he left here, house fire. The other two—and this is where it gets kinda interesting—died a year apart and three states away, each in a home invasion. The first one was shot through the head while his wife lay sleeping in the next room with a colicky baby. The second one took a shotgun blast to the face point-blank through a plate glass window while he was watching television. His family was out of town. These guys were cops and ex-cops, remember. Somebody had to be pretty smart, and pretty determined, to pull that off."

Buck said, "No arrests in the home invasions?"

"The way I understand it, the Orlando police—that's where the guy with the baby was shot—had a couple of suspects, but no evidence. All of this was back in the nineties, you know, before everybody had security cameras on their doorbells. Not a lot to go on in something like this, with no obvious motive."

Buck rubbed his forehead with his index finger. "So you think this is what Rutherford was doing here in Hanover County? Investigating one of those deaths from the nineties?"

Monroe was silent for a moment. Buck sensed as much thoughtfulness as reluctance in his hesitation. "The thing is," he said, "if you think about it, eight men dead, three of them homicide ... and the other five accidents, that wouldn't have been all that hard to arrange, if you know what I mean."

"Even the heart attack?"

"Sure. A shot of potassium nitrate, an overdose of digitalis ... I was in homicide a long time. I've seen some things."

"Still," said Buck, "it doesn't sound like the profile of your average serial killer."

"Yeah," admitted Monroe heavily, "that's what I kept telling Jim. A serial cop killer was bound to attract some attention from the FBI, even back then. No motive, no MO, no pattern, no evidence, not really. I told him it sounded to me like one of those, what do you call it, unexplainable phenomenon. Like when everybody that messed with King Tut's tomb started keeling over, or when the cast members of that movie *Poltergeist* started dying one by one. And you know what he did? He laughed. He said I'd just cracked the case for him. He said he'd been looking at it all wrong, that instead of trying to figure out what they had in common when they died, he should have been looking at what they had in common when they were alive."

"Any idea what he meant?"

"No." Monroe's tone was grim. "But I'm going to find out, I can promise you that."

Buck picked up his pen and pulled a notepad closer. "Can you give me the names of the men who died?"

"Some of them. But, hell, man, I'm sixty-five years old myself, and that was a long time ago. I know none of them had anything to do with North Carolina."

"You never can tell," Buck said, and proceeded to jot down the names, and the places of death, that Gil Monroe remembered. None of them struck a bell with him, or gave any indication why Jim Rutherford might have come to Hanover County.

He was about to say his goodbyes when Gil Monroe, sensing an end to the interview, said, "Tell me what you're not saying."

Buck hesitated. It was against protocol, not to mention his personal policy, to discuss an ongoing investigation with a civilian. But Gil Monroe was not a typical civilian, and Buck needed him on his side. He said, "The place where Rutherford died, it's not on the tourists' maps. He wasn't dressed for hiking. He had a cut on his forehead, but no bruising, likely post-mortem. And there were scuff marks on the top of his shoes."

"Like he'd been dragged," said Monroe.

Buck said, "Yeah. Like that."

There was another long silence. When he spoke, Monroe's voice was curt. "Yeah. I'll see what I can find out. I'll have to wait until Liz gets home to check Jim's computer. Give me your e-mail and cell."

Buck did so, and Monroe replied shortly, "I'll get back to you."

When he hung up, Buck leaned back in his chair and looked thoughtfully into the distance at nothing at all for a moment. Then, almost absently, he clicked on the forum.

RableRouser1776: What about that woman that called 911 about an intruder and was shot dead in her driveway running away? The cops are idiots! They all need to die!

MrIndependence: The family got a $5 mil settlement, I hear.

RableRouser1776: Like money's going to bring back those kids' mama.

SmokyBandit: Yo, check this out. 20% off ammo at all Dave's Hunting and Fishing Shops this weekend only! Made in America, you know it!

Buck clicked off and sat there for a long time, gazing at the blank screen, thinking.

THIRTEEN

My first call was to the local animal shelter. I knew they wouldn't be open to the public on a Sunday morning, and that the desk probably wouldn't be manned, but I wanted to leave a message just in case someone did call in looking for Mozart. I gave his description and the circumstances under which he had been found, and added that any calls about the dog should be referred to me at the Dog Daze office.

I was surprised when, just as I was about to make my next call, to the local radio station with a "found dog" announcement, the office phone rang. Stan Bixby, the shelter manager, was on the line.

"Hi, Stan," I said. "I didn't think you'd be at work today."

"I'm not," he said. "I just called in to pick up the messages, and got yours. So what kind of dog have you got, again? Newfie, did you say? We sure don't see too many of those around here."

There are some people who are simply born to do this kind of work, and Stan Bixby was one of them. Most people, myself included, burn out pretty quickly when faced day-in and day-out with the kind of human neglect and cruelty that results in lost and abandoned animals. Shelter workers deal with the sick, the maimed, the feral, the carelessly overbred, the completely unadoptable eight hours a day, and the last thing they want to do in their off hours is track down more hapless animals who need their care. But Stan was the exception, which was exactly why, when the local humane society had finally been able to afford a real shelter manager, the only person we'd considered for the job was Stan.

"I think he might have a little Lab mixed in," I said.

"Now you're talking my language," he said with a smile in his voice. He'd been rescuing Labs, and fostering them in his home, as long as I'd known him. "But we haven't gotten any calls about a missing dog that answers that description. The Hunters came and picked up their Irish setter yesterday, somebody found it wandering way over on Bear Gap Road. And Joe Benton's beagle went missing last week, but that's about it. So, what's this guy's story?"

Briefly, I told him about finding the dog locked in the car of the drowning victim whose surviving family members claimed they didn't even own a dog. "But he's well cared for," I concluded. "Not your typical stray. Someone is bound to be missing him."

"Well, I'll be damned," Stan said, and then added, "Pardon me, Raine." He was my uncle's age and had similar old-fashioned manners. "But that's sure not the kind of story you hear every day. So who was this fellow who drowned? Anybody we know?"

"No," I said. "It looks like he was just passing through. From Jacksonville, Florida."

"No kidding. That's a long way from home." Then Stan added, "The dog's all right, though? Did you take him to the vet?"

"No, he was in pretty good shape when we got him out of the car. My guess is he wasn't in there that long." Which again begged the question of how he'd gotten into the car in the first place, if its owner had been dead for two hours. "He splashed in the creek to cool off, drank about a ton of water, and ate two ham sandwiches."

"Thank God," he said fervently, "that you found him." A pause. "What do they think happened to the man in the creek? Slipped and fell?"

"Maybe," I said. "It's a little early to know much of anything yet. The police are investigating, though."

"Lucky for the dog you came along when you did. No ID, I guess."

"He had a collar," I said. "It said his name was Buzz. No phone number, though." I was reminded by the piece of paper on my desk with the rubbing Corny had done of the collar tag that that wasn't entirely true. "Well," I corrected myself, "we got a partial one." I turned the paper around and read the numbers. "It looks like the area code is 826, but we couldn't make out anything else."

"That's not a Jacksonville area code," Stan said. Before I could ask, he explained, "I have a brother-in-law who lives there. You can look up the 826 area code on the internet, though, if it would help."

"Yeah, maybe I'll do that," I said, "if nobody calls about him." I hesitated. "The thing is, he's really suffering from separation anxiety. He tore the lock off of one of my kennel gates last night and broke down the door to a storage room. If there had been a window, I know he would've gone through it. We really need to find his owner." I saw no point in going into the other, much more urgent reason for finding out where he had come from—the fact that he was very likely the only existing evidence in a missing person case. I had been ridiculed enough, and Buck's announcement that the Rutherfords didn't even own a dog had put me back at square one in terms of proving Mozart's identity.

Stan gave a long, low whistle of sympathy. "Sounds like the poor fellow's got some problems, all right. Listen, Raine, I've got some room over here. You want me to take him off your hands while we look for his owner?"

I was tempted, believe me. But I said, somewhat reluctantly, "Let's give it a few days. I think he'll be okay as long as he's not left alone again. Meanwhile, if I e-mail you his picture, can you get it on your website right away?"

"I'll get it done today. We can put his picture on our page in the newspaper, too. It might get more attention than a lost and found ad."

"You're a saint, Stan," I said sincerely.

He chuckled. "Happy to help. Just let me know if you change your mind about needing a place for him."

"I will. Thanks. I'll see you at the school program tomorrow, right?"

"You bet. I wouldn't miss it. Maybe we'll have some good news on your guy by then."

I sighed. "We can only hope."

"Say, Raine," he said just as I was about to hang up, "if worse comes to worst, don't forget about that Newfie Rescue place over in Greensboro. In fact, it might not hurt to give them a call, just in case they hear anything."

"Yeah," I said, sitting up straighter as I remembered what should have sprung to mind earlier, "that's a good idea. Thanks again, Stan. See you tomorrow."

The minute I hung up I went to my filing cabinet and started riffling through my old files again. Stan's comment about Newfie Rescue had reminded me of something, and for the second time in twenty-four hours I dug out the six-year-old file on Mozart Goodwin. I had barely glanced at it yesterday, since I was mostly interested in the graduation photograph. Now I pulled out the Goodwins' application and took it over to my desk to study.

I skipped over the basic information—name, address, phone number—just as I usually did when evaluating a new client, and got straight to the part that interested me: the dog.

Your Dog's Name: Mozart
Dog's Gender: Male
Age: 8 months
Spayed or Neutered: Neutered
Breed: Labrador/ Newfoundland mix
How long have you had this dog? 4 months
Where did you get this dog? *(breeder, rescue, human society, etc.)* 4Ever Paws Newfoundland Rescue, Greensboro South Carolina
How did you hear about us? Jenna at 4Ever Paws

And there it was, just as I thought I remembered. Mozart had come from the same rescue group who'd ended up recommending me as a dog trainer, which is not surprising. Even back then, I went to enough dog shows and trials to know—or at least to know of—pretty much everyone in the dog business around here.

There aren't that many organizations that are dedicated to the larger breeds, and unfortunately there is a great need for them. It's one of Nature's great tricks that the cutest puppies in the world are the St. Bernards, the Great Pyrenees, the Newfoundlands and the Mastiffs. It's hard for a prospective owner to imagine, when that sweet puppy weighs twelve or fifteen pounds, exactly how big a 120-pound dog is. So the pup—now a dog—ends up in rescue.

In Mozart's case, I thought I remembered Kylie's father telling me that he had been part of an unplanned litter that the breeder had tried to sell, but had ended up giving away. Mozart was the last puppy, and had started to lose his cuteness, so she turned him over to rescue. I knew the chances of anyone in the rescue organization remembering one particular puppy among the hundreds they'd placed over the years were slim, but I decided to shoot them an e-mail anyway.

I returned to the application form.

Have you ever trained a dog before? No
Other pets in the family? No
How many hours a day do you spend with your dog? All of them

Here I glanced back up at the "personal information" section of the form. Under "occupation" they had written: Jason, real estate agent, Carol, homemaker. They had sounded then, as now, like the perfect family. I remember seeing their house while we were there searching for Kylie. It was a beautiful brick Tudor on a quiet country road, surrounded by rolling meadow and white pasture fencing, the kind of house you drive by and wonder who's lucky enough to live there. Lucky, of course, is not always what it seems.

I turned back to the application form, and to the two questions that invariably give me the most insight about the relationship between a dog and his owner.

What do you like most about your dog? The way he's devoted to our daughter
What do you like the least? Stubborn, difficult to handle, destructive, doesn't listen, jumps on people, chews up things, raids the trash…

The list went on. I flipped over a page to the waiver, which was a general disclaimer of responsibility in case anyone was hurt—or, God forbid, bitten—while on the premises. Jason Goodwin had signed it, and the handwriting was the same as the person who had filled out the form. Generally, it's the wife who does that kind of thing, especially if she's a full-time homemaker. But Jason Goodwin had been interested enough to enroll his dog in obedience school and fill out the application himself, then drive thirty minutes each way every Saturday for six weeks to see it through. He didn't sound to me like the kind of man who would, six months later, kill the little girl he was obviously so crazy about, much less the dog.

It took me a while to find an e-mail address, but eventually I discovered a business card for 4Ever Paws Newfie Rescue in a box of vendor pamphlets and old trial premiums. I sat down at my computer again and typed.

Hi,

It's Raine Stockton from Purebred Rescue in Hansonville. I think I may have one of your former dogs who was picked up here as a stray. Hoping you might be able to help me find his owner. Could you post his picture on your web site with my contact info? Thanks!

I signed my name with my phone number and attached the photo of Mozart I'd taken yesterday at the kennel. I e-mailed Stan the same photo, then called the radio station and left a description of the lost dog. Even though Stan was going to put Mozart's picture on the shelter's newspaper page, I decided to go ahead and e-mail the newspaper with a lost and found ad. It was free, and there's no such thing as overkill when you're trying to get the word out about a found dog.

Finally, out of nothing more than idle curiosity, I did a Google search for the area code, 826. It turned out it belonged to the Kansas City, Missouri, metropolitan area. Not South Carolina, as I had hoped. Not Jacksonville, Florida. Not even North Carolina where Mozart had been found. This puzzle grew more and more convoluted.

By this time Cisco and Pepper, with that enviable ability of dogs to play full speed and then crash with equal intensity, were sound asleep on the floor in front of my desk, paws touching. I called Miles.

He answered with, "Why aren't you at church?"

"Doesn't anybody say 'Good Morning' anymore?" I complained.

"Good morning, sugar. Why aren't you at church?"

"Kennel emergency," I said. "I dropped Mel off at Sunday School and came back to clean up. Why aren't *you* at church?"

He chuckled. "Touché, baby. I'm on my way to visit Mom. So, listen. About this outline Mel e-mailed me at 11:15 last night."

"Right," I said confidently. Melanie had fallen asleep a little after 9:00, and I had polished the outline and sent it off. "What did you think? Pretty good, huh?"

"Not her best work," Miles replied.

I bristled. "What do you mean?"

"In the first place," he replied, "the format was all wrong. The teacher sent out a template. It's on Melanie's laptop. She should have transferred this to the template before finishing it."

I used to wonder how a man like Miles, who ran multiple corporations, traveled around the world, and supervised hundreds of employees and various enterprises, could find the time to read every e-mail Melanie's teachers sent out, monitor her social media, and check every page of her homework. Now I realized that all of those things were intertwined somehow. It was like some kind of overachiever's syndrome.

"Well," I justified, a little uneasily, "this was just a draft."

"And she used the word 'allegedly' nine times in a two-hundred-word outline. Come on, Raine, what are you, the counsel for the defense?"

I determined it was beneath my dignity to reply to that.

"Don't do Melanie's homework for her, sugar," Miles said. "It's a cutthroat world out there, and she's got to learn to stand on her own two feet."

"She wants to train dogs for the CIA," I pointed out, miffed. "Not as much cutthroat competition as you might imagine."

"Particularly since the CIA doesn't employ canines in its operations," he countered.

"Yet," I snapped back. "Who knows what life will be like by the time Melanie grows up?"

"Exactly," he said. "Don't do Melanie's homework for her. What did you call about?"

At this point, a lot of people would have taken offense and hung up, and, a year ago, I would have been first among them. But Miles and I had come to an understanding: I tolerated a lot from him, and he tolerated a lot more from me. It was worth it. Most of the time.

I said, "Mr. Rutherford, the drowning victim, didn't own a dog. His family says he was allergic and wouldn't have stopped to pick up a stray. Nonetheless, a 120-pound Newfoundland was found locked in his car. And get this—the coroner puts the time of death two hours before I found Mr. Rutherford."

"The dog would have been in bad shape by then, if not dead." Miles got it immediately. "So someone put the dog in the car after Rutherford died. The question is why."

"Exactly," I said. "And I was right about something else, too. Rutherford *was* working on a cold case, and he had a lead that brought him here. Nobody knows exactly what it was, and," I admitted, "the family says he was never involved with the Kylie Goodwin case, but there has to be a connection. That's the only explanation."

"Sweetheart," he said, and sounded mildly amused, "your tenacity amazes me. I've got to go. I'm pulling into the hospital parking lot. Tell Mel she can expect a call from me this afternoon. Oh, and listen, I did a little more research on Jason Goodwin last night, Kylie's father. I was curious about what became of him after he divorced his wife and left."

"Oh, yeah? What did you find out?"

Cisco woke up, stretched out his forepaws and curled his tail over his back, then trotted over to me with his rope toy in his mouth. Pepper watched lazily from the floor as we began a game of tug.

"Not much. He seems to have led a pretty uneventful life. He moved to Kansas City, bounced around from one entry level job to the other until ..."

"What?" I said, sitting up straight. "What did you say?"

"I said he moved to Kansas City."

"Kansas City, Missouri?" I repeated.

"That's right, why?"

I dropped the tug toy, every nerve in my body tingling with excitement. "That's the area code that was on Mozart's collar tag," I said a little breathlessly. "Kansas

120

City, Missouri!"

There was a brief silence. "That's odd," Miles said.

"It's more than odd!" I exclaimed. "Jason Goodwin once owned Mozart. He moved to Kansas City and, according to his tag, Mozart's owner is someone in Kansas City. You *can't* think that's a coincidence."

"No," he admitted. "If the dog you have does turn out to belong to Goodwin, it certainly proves he likes big black dogs. Unfortunately, there are two things you still don't know: that this is the same dog the Goodwin family owned six years ago, and that he belongs to the same Jason Goodwin who moved to Kansas City."

I scowled, trying not to feel deflated. "There's one way to find out," I said. "Do you have a phone number for Jason Goodwin?"

"It won't do you any good."

Now I was starting to lose patience. "Why not?"

"Because he died two years ago in a cancer treatment center in Kansas City."

FOURTEEN

So that, as any sensible person could clearly see, was that. I was back to square one with Mozart, no closer to finding his owner than I'd been when I first rescued him from a dead man's car. It was starting to look as though Mozart, or whoever he was, was destined to become just another statistic in the world of canine rescue, and the mystery of his past would never be solved.

I got Melanie to school without incident on Monday morning—with the revised and updated outline for her essay in hand, as per her father's instructions. I'll admit, I wasn't prepared for the chaos this involved. We have a routine around here: awake by seven, make breakfast for the dogs, make coffee for myself, check on the kennel, take Cisco for a run. Melanie has her own routine, which involves a three-course meal of eggs, fruit, and toast, an endless debate about hair ornaments, lost shoes, lost phone, lost iPad, wrestling with Pepper, changing her outfit, forgetting to brush her teeth, and still somehow making it to school by 7:45. I didn't get coffee, I didn't get to check on the kennel, and the dogs didn't get their breakfast until 8:30. It is safe to say that the morning— not to mention the week—was not off to a very promising start.

How to Raise Kids and Dogs by Raine Stockton, *Chapter Six: The Importance of Maintaining a Routine.*

I called Corny as I was dishing out dog food to four very impatient canines, anxious to know how Mozart had fared during the night. We had agreed that Mozart would stay with Corny in his quarters overnight in hopes that would alleviate his anxiety, but I kept having visions of his small apartment having been reduced to the same shambles as my kennel had been yesterday. I was relieved to hear otherwise.

"He was a little restless at first," Corny admitted, "but he settled down once I let him sleep on my bed."

I stirred chopped roasted chicken into Pepper's kibble and added organic chicken broth and vegetable puree. All four dogs, holding their perfect sits, watched me fixedly. I said, "Your bed?" Corny's twin-sized bed, which was all the room would hold, was barely big enough for him, much less a giant Newfie. "But where did you sleep?"

"Well," he replied, "I do have a sleeping bag, and the floor wasn't that hard."

I started on Cisco's meal: oatmeal, ground turkey, blueberries, broccoli. Miles has often remarked that my dogs eat better than I do, and he's not wrong.

"You slept on the floor while the dog slept on your bed?" I said, only a little incredulously.

He sounded a little abashed as he answered, "It seemed like the simplest solution."

I closed my eyes with a slow shake of my head. This definitely was not going to work. Mozart had to go. "Okay, Corny," I said. "Thanks." I put Cisco's dish aside and poured kibble into the two Aussie's dishes. Cisco shifted his weight impatiently and licked a string of drool from his chops, but did not break his sit. "I'll be down in a minute to help out. Just leave Mozart in the playroom until I get there."

"No hurry," he replied cheerfully. "Slow morning today."

I added canned salmon and raw eggs to the Aussie's dishes, and gave all four dogs a stern warning look as I took the bowls to their feeding stations and set them down. I am very proud of my dogs' table manners; without them, mealtime would be chaos. But I have to be absolutely consistent. If even one dog breaks his or her sit before I release them, all of the dishes go back on the counter and we try again. After I placed all four dishes on their respective place mats, I stood, holding their gazes for another ten seconds or so to give them a chance to exercise their own self-discipline, and then released them. They stampeded to their bowls.

How to Raise Dogs and Kids by Raine Stockton, *Chapter Seven: Consistency, the Key to Success.*

I finally got that cup of coffee and stood sipping it while the dogs scarfed down their breakfast, only occasionally sparing me a reproachful look for the lateness of their meal. They were well-mannered dogs, but they were still dogs who were eating within a foot of each other and I did not like to leave them unsupervised. When my phone rang, I had been trying to decide whether to tackle the pile of dishes in the sink or the pile of bills on my desk, and I was glad of an excuse not to do either.

"Hey, Raine," said the female voice on the other end. "This is Isabel, over at the paper?" She was one of those women who ended every sentence with a question mark, as though seeking approval before going on.

I said, "Hey, Isabel."

"I hope I'm not calling too early, but I was just going over the e-mails that came in over the weekend, you know, the ads and all?"

I sipped my coffee and encouraged, "Hmm-hmm."

"And I saw your lost-and found here, you know, the

124

one about the dog?"

"Right," I said. "Lost and found pet ads are still free, aren't they?"

Cisco, who was always the first to finish any meal, looked despondently into his bowl for a moment, his ears flopping forward comically, and then he seemed to remember there was still food to be had. He cast his eyes toward Mischief's dish and she showed him her canine tooth. I snapped my fingers at both of them. Mischief resumed eating, and Cisco flopped belly-down on the floor, his head between his paws, heaving a huge sigh. It was a familiar routine for all of us.

"Yes, ma'am, that's right," Isabel was saying. "They're free. But I thought you'd want to know there was another ad, came in Friday night? It happens that way, sometimes, somebody loses something and somebody else finds it and their ads cross in the paper?"

I straightened up with my coffee cup halfway to my lips, listening.

"So this other ad, the one I'm talking about?" she went on. "It says, 'Lost dog, black, 120 pounds, blue collar, near Exxon Station on Highway 81'?"

I said eagerly, "Yes?"

"And yours says, '"Found: black dog, Newfoundland mix, 120 pounds, blue collar, name tag reads Buzz,' so I just wondered if it could be the same dog?"

"It is!" I exclaimed. "It's the same dog, it has to be. That Exxon Station is only a couple of miles from Murder Creek if you go through the woods. And how many 120-pound black dogs with blue collars could have gotten lost this weekend? Oh, thank goodness, Isabel! Do you have a phone number?"

"Yes," she admitted, and sounded reluctant. I thought she was about to give me some nonsense about the paper having a policy against releasing phone numbers, in which case John Wilkins, the editor of the paper, and I would be having a serious face to face within the hour. But all she said was, "But it's not local. Is that okay?"

I assured her it was, and I jotted down the number as she read it off. The area code was 826. I dialed as soon as I hung up with Isabel.

I was directed to voice mail, and a terse man's voice said, "This is Scotty. Leave a message."

I was disappointed, because I had a lot of questions that I hoped this Scotty person would be able to answer, and now it looked as though I'd just have to wait. Still, I used my most pleasant voice to leave the message.

"Hi, this is Raine Stockton in Hansonville, North Carolina, and I think I may have found your dog. He looks like a Newfie-Lab mix, black, about 120, blue collar with the name tag 'Buzz.' We found him yesterday in a park not far from where you reported losing your dog. Please call me back." I left my cell phone, the number at Dog Daze, and even my home phone number. I was taking no chances on missing that call.

I gave a nod of satisfaction and lifted my coffee cup in a self-congratulatory salute. "Well, what do you know about that?" I said, and all four dogs, having now finished their breakfast, looked at me expectantly. "You just never know how a day might turn out."

I let the dogs out into the backyard and turned back into the kitchen, wondering if there was any bread left for toast, when my cell phone rang. I snatched it up, expecting the call to be from Mozart's owner. It wasn't.

"Raine!" Melanie exclaimed on the other end of the line. She sounded desperate. "I need pictures!"

"What?" It took me a minute to understand that the note of panic in her voice did not mean that she had been kidnapped or was being chased by a masked man with a knife, and my heart slowly resumed an almost normal rhythm. "What pictures?"

"For my essay! It says right here, 'include at least three illustrations with outline. Examples are maps, graphs, photographs, or original artwork.' Everyone else has pictures! Johnny Markham even went to a museum and photographed a passenger train from the 1800s and, Rebecca drew a cartoon strip of a—"

"Jeez, Melanie," I said, "what grade are you in again? I didn't work this hard in college."

"Raine!"

"Okay, okay." I refilled my coffee cup. "What do you want me to do?"

"Can you take some pictures with your phone and e-mail them to me? Please? My class isn't until 12:30, and as long as I attach them to my outline I don't have to have a hard copy."

"Pictures of what?"

"There was that picture of William Stockton in the book Aunt Mart loaned me," she said. "It's on the coffee table in the living room."

I walked into the living room, kicking aside dog toys, a pair of my sneakers, a plastic bowl Melanie had left on the floor after she'd finished her ice cream for Pepper to lick. I found the book on the coffee table underneath one of her sweaters. "Okay," I said. "Got it."

"There's a map in there too," she went on, a little breathlessly. "Showing what this place looked like back in the olden days."

"Cool." I opened the book to the place she had bookmarked with a coaster—which, in fact, was not a very good way to treat a book she had borrowed—and flipped through the pages. I found the map, and the picture of a very stern-looking William Stockton. According to the caption, he had only been thirty-six when he died, but in this photo he looked at least fifty. Life was hard back then. "Hold on. Sending." I snapped a photo of the map and of my illustrious ancestor, the first man charged with murder in Hanover County, and sent them to her. "Did you get it?"

"But that's only two!" she wailed. "I need three!"

"Melanie ..." It was hard to keep the exasperation out of my voice.

"Do you think Aunt Mart has any more pictures? Maybe there's a picture of Mr. Bowslayer in the library?"

I was beginning to understand why Miles thought it was a bad idea to help Melanie with her homework.

"If Aunt Mart had any more photos she would have given them to you," I told her. "and I don't have time to go to the library. I'm doing that program for your school at 2:00 and have a ton of things to do before then. Besides, aren't you supposed to be in class?"

"I am in class," she replied impatiently. "We get ten minutes of personal time at the top of each hour."

It occurred to me that if Miles was concerned about preparing his daughter for the cutthroat world of real life, he might have chosen the wrong school. The last time I'd had ten minutes of personal time at the top of each hour I'd been in diapers.

"Why don't you just use one of those photos you took at the creek Saturday?" I suggested. "That's what your whole essay is about."

"That's a stupid idea!" she shot back. She sounded as though she was about to cry. "I didn't even get to take any pictures of the creek! All I got were ambulances and policemen!"

As much as I like Melanie, and as much as I want her

to like me back, there is a limit to the amount of abuse I'm willing to take.   I replied coolly, "That's a pity. And sorry, but the only ideas I have are stupid ones."

"Raine!" she pleaded. "I'll get an incomplete!"

"Well, that would be a pity."   I was proud of how mature I sounded.   "But you should have read the instructions and you should have planned ahead."

"You sound just like my dad." I could practically see her pouting.

"Good," I replied firmly.   "Look, I've got to get to work. I'll see you at 2:00. Have a good day at school."

"But—"

I pressed the disconnect button and gave a sharp nod of satisfaction at my own excellent parenting.

Half an hour later Cisco and I were in the car, headed to Murder Creek for a quick photo shoot. *How to Raise Dogs and Kids* by Raine Stockton, *Chapter Eight: Never Let Them Forget That Choices Have Consequences.*

But you don't have to be mean about it.

FIFTEEN

Buck glanced up from the computer at the sound of claws clicking on the linoleum outside his office, and smiled when a regal white golden retriever padded her way inside. "Well, hello, gorgeous," he said, holding out his hand. "To what do I owe the honor?"

Cameo was one of Raine's rescues, now contentedly living with Sheriff Marshal Becker. The sheriff brought her to work with him most days, and between Cameo and Nike, Jolene's highly trained K-9 officer, the public safety building was quickly becoming known as a dog-friendly workplace.

"Just came over for a cup of the good stuff," said Marshal, holding up his coffee mug as he followed Cameo inside. The coffee in the bullpen of the sheriff's office was notoriously bad, possibly because the urn hadn't been cleaned in all the years Buck had worked there. In the prosecutor's office wing, though, the coffee was made twice a day in a glass pot by an administrative assistant who knew how to do it. "You got a minute?"

Marshal was not much older than Buck, an ordinary-looking man with wire-rimmed glasses and a mustache. He wore a short-sleeved, white knit uniform shirt with the sheriff's emblem embroidered on the front pocket, something Buck had never bothered to do when he was sheriff. He didn't even know you could order those shirts. He'd just pinned his name tag above the Hanover County Sheriff's Office logo on the front of his regular khaki uniform shirt.

In most ways, Marshal was a better sheriff than Buck had been, and Buck had been glad to turn the job over to him. But Marshal was a relative newcomer to the county, having lived here less than ten years, and he did not know the people like Buck did. The fact that he recognized this, and wasn't afraid to ask for advice when he needed it, was one of the things Buck liked about him.

Buck said, "Sure thing." He gave Cameo's silky head a final stroke and took a dog biscuit from the stash that he kept in his desk in case Cisco dropped by. These days, Cisco almost never dropped by.

Cameo took the dog biscuit politely and lay down on the floor a few feet away, holding the treat between her paws as she crunched on it. Marshal sat in the chair by the door. "Bring me up to speed on this drowning victim," he said.

Buck pushed his chair back from his desk a little, stretching out his legs. "I guess the most important thing is it might not be a drowning," he said. "Did you make it over to the scene Saturday?"

Marshal shook his head. "I was in Chattanooga this weekend. My niece's wedding. I just heard about it when I got in this morning."

"Yeah, well, you probably could've seen the rescue trucks from your place if you'd been home," said Buck. "It happened right there at the falls. We thought maybe he'd fallen from the top, but now it looks like his injuries might have been post-mortem. I'm hoping to hear something from the ME before the end of the day. I put in a priority request."

"I understand he was a cop?"

"Retired," specified Buck. "But it looks like whatever brought him to this part of the country might have been related to some cold case he was looking into. I'm running down some leads."

Marshal nodded. "Coordinate with Jolene on whatever resources you need from this office. Do I need to talk to the family?"

Buck told him that the family had left town for Florida early that morning, and they chatted for a few more minutes about the details of the case, including the dog that had been found inside the locked car. Marshal didn't think the dog had any more connection to case than Buck did at that point, and agreed it wasn't worth following up on. Marshal finished his coffee, Cameo finished her dog biscuit, and the conversation was winding to a close when Marshal said, "I hear you're still keeping an eye on that Carolina Free forum."

Buck suddenly knew that was the real reason Marshal had stopped by his office. He replied mildly, "Who'd you hear that from?"

He knew the answer, of course, and Marshal did not bother to reply. Instead he said, "We got those guys, Buck. There's no longer an urgent threat."

Buck said nothing.

Marshal leaned forward a little, dangling the empty coffee cup between his knees. "Look," he said. "I know this is personal for you. These idiots held your ex hostage, shot your wife, destroyed your family. Yeah, there may be a few guys still around with similar points of view …" he nodded briefly toward the computer screen, which had defaulted to the HCSO logo. "But the bad actors are in the hands of the Feds now, and you told me yourself you know most of those loud-mouths in that forum and they're harmless. I just don't want this to become an obsession with you. There's no case."

Buck recognized, deep inside, a spark of resentment that he wasn't comfortable with. He didn't like being told how to do his job. He didn't like the fact that a colleague had gone running to the sheriff with a report about the way he was doing his job. And most of all, he didn't like how much that pissed him off.

He thought about eight dead cops. He thought about the retired head of Major Crimes who had come here to investigate those deaths, now dead himself. He thought about the anti-law enforcement thread that had popped up over the weekend. Yeah, he knew most of the boys in the group. But not all.

He said, "You're probably right. No case." He forced a smile. "It's not like I don't have plenty of other things to keep me busy."

"Good enough." Marshal stood, and Cameo came to his side without being summoned. Marshal absently stroked her head. "Let me know what you hear from the medical examiner."

"Will do."

When Marshal was gone, Buck returned to his computer and clicked on the Jacksonville, Florida, Police Department Employment Records database once again. He'd only gotten access to the database a couple of hours ago, and he had spent the time since then inputting various criteria, trying to figure out what the common denominator might be between the dead men and James Rutherford. So far all he'd discovered was that they all had died within three years of each other, which probably what made Rutherford suspicious in the first place. It was slow, frustrating work, and the worst part was that as far as he was concerned, in his role as a criminal investigator for Hanover County, there wasn't even proof of a crime.

Shortly after 11:00 a.m., with his head hurting from hunger as much as eyestrain, he gave up. He was trying to recreate Rutherford's work with only a fraction of the information the other man had had. Maybe Rutherford had left some clue as to what—or whom—he was looking for in Hansonville on his computer, and maybe that fellow Gil Monroe would find it. If worse came to worst, Buck might have to take a trip to Jacksonville himself. The only thing he knew for sure was that he was getting nowhere this way.

It was early for lunch, but he hadn't had breakfast, and all he found in the break room was one stale powdered donut. He called across the street to Miss Meg's Diner and put in an order for a hamburger and fries to go. Sitting behind a desk all day, eating junk food and Aunt Mart's homemade pies, was causing him to put on weight, but he told himself he'd start getting back in shape now that summer was here. Just another thing on his to-do list.

Meg told him he could pick up his order in about twenty minutes, so he leaned back in the chair and absently clicked on the Carolina Free forum.

StraightShooter: You wanna hear something crazy, I got a brother that's been sitting in jail 6 months for trying to poison a police dog. They got no proof he even did it! A dog, for cripes' sake, and they charge him with a felony. You tell me that ain't screwed up.

"Ah, Deke, you idiot," Buck muttered. Everybody in the county knew that Deke's brother was bad news, and that he had poisoned Nike to distract deputies from the bigger, far more important crime that was taking place. If the point on this forum was to keep your identity a secret, Deke was too stupid to realize it.

MountainMan904: I hope he rots there. Killing's too

good for anybody who'd hurt a dog.

Remington1976: You tell 'em, brother. I got a Springer I wouldn't take the world for. Sleeps on my bed every night, chased off a pack of wild boar one time. I don't know what I'd do if anything happened to her.

The phone rang, and it was the medical examiner's office. Buck shut down the page.

"That was quick," he said. "I didn't expect to hear from you guys until tomorrow, late tonight at the earliest."

"You got lucky." The young man on the other end had identified himself as Dr. Braselton's technical assistant, Toby Walker. "We were overstaffed on a slow morning. Also, when a suspicious death comes in from a little town like yours, we know it's priority."

Buck had not said anything about a suspicious death on the paperwork, and he knew Sutter hadn't either, but he did not correct Toby. The conclusions were pretty easy to draw.

"So what do you have?" Buck asked.

"Just so you know, this is preliminary. We haven't completed the full autopsy, but Dr. Braselton wanted me to let you know the cause of death was not drowning. There was no water in the lungs, and the injuries sustained were definitely post-mortem, probably caused by the body being knocked up against the rocks in the creek."

Buck sat up straight, listening intently. "So what was the cause of death?"

"Cardio-respiratory failure secondary to a massive dose of secobarbitol."

"Seco ..." Buck searched his memory. "Seconal, right? I've heard of it, but can't say I know much about it."

"It used to be known on the street as 'reds' or 'red devils,' but you probably wouldn't see much of it where you're from.   It's legitimately used as an injectable pre-anesthetic sedative, and sometimes you hear about in cases of physician-assisted suicide."

"Are you telling me this guy committed suicide?"

"I'm not saying that at all.   I'm saying there was approximately a ten times lethal dose in the blood sample we tested."

"Any other drugs?"

"None."

Buck rubbed the bridge of his nose, but it didn't help his headache. How the hell was he supposed to go to the Rutherford family with a verdict of suicide? Especially since he wasn't sure he believed it himself.   "Yeah, okay. Thanks for keeping me in the loop. When will you have the complete report?"

"Twenty-four hours, latest.   We'll notify the family from here when we release the remains."

Buck thanked him again and hung up.   Seconal. Suicide drug. Was he really supposed to believe that a retired cop from Florida would drive all the way to North Carolina just to take a walk in the woods and overdose on something like that? There were lots of easier ways to kill yourself, especially for a cop. It made no sense.

And he still had no case.

SIXTEEN

At 10:00 on a Monday morning, Murder Creek Park was deserted and, frankly, given what I knew about what had happened here on Saturday, a little spooky. It was a bright blue spring day with just a few puffy clouds in the distance, and I'd been comfortable in my short-sleeved tee shirt on the drive over. But the tree canopy was high here, casting shadows over everything, and the rushing of the creek dropped the temperature significantly. I grabbed a windbreaker from the car and slipped it on.

I released Cisco from his canine seat belt and he bounded out, immediately putting his nose to the ground to sniff out all the many intriguing scents that had accumulated since he'd been here last. I never like to miss an opportunity to practice Cisco's off-leash skills, and this remote area seemed like the perfect place to do so. There was no wild dog for him to chase today, and I was confident that the plastic bag of hot dog pieces in my pocket could compete with any other distractions that might come our way. Nonetheless, I fastened a tab leash to his collar, which is a short loop handle designed to make it easy to grab your dog while in training, and called him into a formal heel position before setting out.

I snapped a photo of the Murder Creek Park sign, and then walked down to the creek. The narrow trail made it easy for Cisco to maintain his heel, and the hot dog slice that I held between my fingers didn't hurt, either. I stopped abruptly a couple of times and Cisco, whose attention never wavered from me, tucked right into a sit each time. I was grinning with pride by the time we reached the water.

For a moment I hesitated, suppressing a shiver as I looked over the spot where James Rutherford's body had been lying facedown, pinned between the rocks and the rushing water. I couldn't stop a flashback of wrestling with the current to try to turn him over, of the cold water soaking into my jeans and numbing my fingers. Then I squeezed my eyes shut and swallowed hard to block out the memory.

"Come on, Cisco," I said, and abruptly turned back onto the trail, following its upward path toward the waterfall.

It wasn't a hard climb, and once there I had a perfect view, not only of the splashing waters below, but of the gorgeous spring day surrounding me. I snapped the perfect picture of Murder Creek, then sent both photographs to Melanie. A moment later I got back a series of heart emojis, smile emojis and hug emojis that made me smile.

Corny had promised to let me know the minute Mozart's owner returned my call, and I checked quickly to make sure I hadn't somehow missed a call or a text from him. There was nothing. I told myself that was okay. Maybe the owner was still on the road, maybe he hadn't gotten my message yet. It was Monday, he was probably at work. He'd call by tonight. I was sure of it.

I sat on a rock overlooking the waterfall and put my arm around Cisco, enjoying the view. To the west I could see a rim of blue mountains and waves of forest in a dozen shades of green. The creek wound on to the east, bounded by rich, flat bottom land and sturdy hardwoods. I caught a glimpse of a red metal roof and white pasture fencing through the leaves, and, when I looked to the south, I recognized the flash of sunlight on metal from the cars that traversed the highway. Even though this place felt a million miles from civilization, I realized we were within walking distance of both a major thoroughfare and some of the best farmland in the county. No wonder the Stocktons—and the Creek Indians before them—had decided to settle here.

I glanced at my phone one more time before putting it away and getting to my feet. I'd promised Corny to have Cisco home in time for a bath and a blow-out before his big appearance at the school, but we still had some time, and it would be crazy to miss a training opportunity as perfect as this.

I called Cisco to heel again and followed the trail a little farther into the woods, away from the waterfall and back down toward the bottom land that bordered the creek. I put Cisco in a down-stay, and reinforced it by clipping the lightweight leash I had in my pocket to his collar, and then looping it around a tree. I might have time for a few "find-it" games, but I most certainly did not have time to chase him through the woods for the rest of the morning.

I had a pair of gloves in my windbreaker pocket that were leftover from winter, and, after repeating my firm "stay" command, I put them on to make sure that were saturated with my scent. I walked about fifty yards into the woods and hid one of them beneath a sprinkling of dried leaves. I took a 45-degree turn, went another ten yards and tucked the other one into the crook of a sweet shrub bush. Then I returned to Cisco, unhooked his leash, and told him excitedly, "Okay, Cisco, find it!"

This was one of Cisco's favorite games, and one we planned on demonstrating for Melanie's class that afternoon. The object was for him to follow my scent trail, and then to find the objects I had hidden. This is not as easy as it sounds, even for a certified wilderness tracker like Cisco. He had no idea what I had hidden, and he had to learn to filter out distractions and focus on the items with my scent. In a public park like this, as in many of our real-life searches, there were plenty of things left by humans that had nothing to do with what he was a searching for, and I had noticed some of them myself: a rusted-out soda can, a soggy matchbook, a foam beer koozie half-buried by a season's worth of snow and shifting soil. People were pigs. But in this case that worked to my advantage.

Cisco took off into the woods, nose to the ground and tail whirling excitedly. I jogged to keep up, checking him with a sharp, "Hey!" when he got too far ahead. He paused, gave me a tongue-lolling grin over his shoulder, and waited until I was only a couple of yards behind him to take off again. A perfect dog would have waited until I was right beside him, but for Cisco, this was as perfect as it got.

He found the first glove with absolutely no trouble, digging it out of the leaves and giving it a couple of shakes for good measure. I put the glove on my hand, thinking to permeate it with my scent and use it for another exercise before we went home, then praised Cisco to the skies. I fed him five or six hotdog slices, one right after another, while exclaiming, "Smart boy! Good guy! Now, go find the other one."

Cisco spun around and took off, nose to the ground, in exactly the direction of the other glove. I thought my face would split with my grin of delight. Cisco had caused me enough frustration over the years that, when he performed as flawlessly as this, I had a right to be proud. I should have remembered that pride always comes before a fall, especially with Cisco.

I took off at an easy trot behind him, grateful that the thickly wooded terrain prevented him from getting too far ahead of me. I caught a glimpse of him plowing through a rhododendron thicket on a slight downward slope that led to the creek ... nowhere near the spot where I'd left the other glove. Sure enough, when I reached him, he was pawing at the ground in full pursuit of the wrong object. I caught the tab leash on his collar, just to make sure he didn't become distracted by something even more interesting, and he looked up at me with his cute, happy-go-lucky grin. It was hard not to ruffle his ears and toss him a hot dog treat, but the object of the game had been to find the matching glove, and he had failed to do that. I didn't want to accidentally reward him for something he hadn't done.

I bent down to see what had caught his attention, expecting a snack wrapper or a soda can or some other piece of discarded detritus that had been washed down from the trail by spring rains. I was surprised. The object I picked up with my gloved hand was a set of keys on a leather fob. There were a couple of brass keys that might have been for door locks, and a larger one with a Honda emblem on it, along with a matching remote car door opener. The fob was shaped like a police shield with "Jacksonville Police Department" embossed in faded gold on the banner at the top and the letters "JCR" in the box at the bottom where an officer's badge number might go. It was the kind of novelty item you might order from a specialty catalogue, or give as a birthday gift to someone in law enforcement who had everything. JCR. James Carlton Rutherford, Jacksonville Police Department.

"Holy Cow," I said. Cisco had found James Rutherford's missing car keys, the ones the deputies were so certain had been lost at the bottom of the creek. But what were they doing out here in the middle of the woods? We were nowhere near the trail, too far away from the creek for sightseeing, and why would Rutherford be wandering around in the woods in the first place? He'd been wearing loafers, not hiking boots, and besides ...

A cracking sound exploded overhead and I whirled around just in time to see a dead branch from the poplar tree next to me sheer off and fall toward us. I grabbed Cisco and dived for cover, but it wasn't until I hit the ground that I realized the sound I'd heard before the branch fell had been a rifle shot.

SEVENTEEN

Miss Meg's Diner was famous for its homestyle country meals, hand-cut French fries, and desserts. From 7:00 until 9:00 in the morning, the businessmen of the town could be found solving the problems of the world over three-egg platters and melt-in-your-mouth sausage biscuits. The hard-working blue-collar fellows descended on the place around 11:00 a.m., loading up on the meat-and-three plates with a slice of pie to get them through the rest of the day. From then until 2:00 it was often standing room only while everybody in town tried to make the most of their lunch hours, and Buck had to edge through the crowd at the door to make his way to the counter. There were three or four people at the register, waiting to pay, but Meg saw him come in and raised her hand in acknowledgement. "With you in a shake, Buck," she called out and disappeared into the kitchen.

He spoke to Ed Hague, who ran the local H&R Block office out of a turn-of-the-century white clapboard house a couple of blocks down, and who was at the counter ahead of him, waiting for his own order. They talked about nothing for a minute or two, and while they did Buck tried to decide whether to speak to Jolene, who was sitting at a table a few feet away, or pretend he hadn't seen her. That was ridiculous, of course, because she had already seen him and nodded in acknowledgement as she lifted her sandwich for a bite. Buck nodded back, and that was when he noticed Dr. Ellory sitting at a table toward the back of the room. Buck excused himself to Ed and went over to him.

It was commonly accepted that Brett Ellory had treated everyone in town, but that probably wasn't true. There were several other medical practitioners in the county, most of them with part-time office hours who worked out of the regional hospital, but Ellory was the oldest, and the most popular. He was finishing up a chicken salad plate when Buck approached, and he waved him over, wiping his lips with a paper napkin.

"How're you doing, Buck?" he greeted him. "I haven't seen you in a while."

"I'm great," Buck returned with a grin. "That's why you haven't seen me."

Ellory chuckled. "Sit down. Let's get you a glass of tea. I'm about to finish up here, but ..."

"That's okay," Buck said, "I've got an order coming up to go, and I'm not going to interrupt your lunch." Nonetheless, he pulled out a chair and sat down, mostly because this was police business and he didn't want to have to shout over the chatter of the crowd. "I just wanted to ask you a quick question, if I could."

"Go ahead." The doctor used his fork to cut a bite of lettuce. "I'll do my best."

Buck said, "Where would I go to get my hands on some Seconal, if I had to?"

If Ellory was surprised by the question, he didn't show it. He was perfectly aware of what line of work Buck was in. "Around here?" He speared the lettuce and a bite of chicken salad. "Not my office, for sure. The pharmacy would have to order it in, and there'd be a clear paper trail. The hospital, maybe, but I wouldn't promise you."

Buck said, "I thought it was used in anesthesia."

"Some places, maybe," Ellory agreed, "but there are better alternatives for most applications. Propofol, for one. My guess is you'd be more likely to find that on hand at the hospital than Seconal." He took a bite of the chicken salad and chewed thoughtfully for a moment. "You know who you might talk to," he said, pointing at the air with his empty fork as the idea occurred to him. "Sam Witherspoon."

"The vet?"

"Sure," said Ellory. "Seems to me I read somewhere Seconal is still used by some veterinarians as a large animal sedative. Don't quote me, but it might be worth checking out."

Buck said thoughtfully, "Yeah, okay. Thanks." He sat there for another moment, mulling it over, then tapped the table lightly as he stood. "I appreciate it, Doc. Talk to you later."

There was no way to avoid going by Jolene's table on his way back to the counter, and there was no way to avoid speaking to her. He had already made up his mind he wasn't even going to try.

"I thought you had the day off," he said, pausing by her table.

"Yeah, I thought so too." She reached for a paper napkin from the table dispenser and gestured for him to sit down. "The sheriff wanted Nike and me to do a PR thing at one of the schools this afternoon, so I figured I might as well put in a half day. Anything new on the Rutherford case?"

"Yeah, a couple of things." Buck remained standing. "I'll send you an e-mail this afternoon." She looked puzzled at his formal posture, but he ignored it. He kept his tone deliberately mild as he went on. "Meantime, do me a favor, will you? The next time you have a question about the way I'm doing my job, talk to me, not the sheriff. I told you before, I've got no patience with spies, and I won't work with somebody I don't trust. It was true then, and it's true now."

She frowned sharply. "What are you—"

Meg called, "Buck, honey, you're up!"

He turned without another word and started toward the counter. He was mad—at her, sure, but also at himself for being mad at her. That was probably why he didn't look up at the clatter of the bell over the door, and he didn't see Deke come in until the other man's shoulder bumped into his, hard. Or maybe it was Buck who bumped into Deke; he didn't know. All he knew was that Deke, scowling, unshaven, and smelling of alcohol, stood his ground in the defiant way of a man looking for a fight and glared at Buck.

"Well, will you look at this," he said, his tone dripping with contempt. "If it ain't the high and mighty officer of the law."

Buck had known Deke all his life, and had worked with him as a Hanover County Deputy just about his entire career—until Marshal Becker had fired Deke a couple of months ago. Deke was a screw-up and always would be, but Buck had learned to put up with him. Marshal's standards were a little higher.

Buck said, "A little early to be hitting the bottle, isn't it, Deke?"

Deke laughed, loudly enough that heads turned, and gave Buck what was supposed to look like a playful punch in the arm. It wasn't playful, and it was hard enough to cause Buck to take a sideways step to maintain his balance. "Hey, that's what's so great about being unemployed, bro! Nobody to tell you what to do." He leaned in, close to Buck's face, his eyes narrowing. "You ain't trying to tell me what to do, are you, Buck? Huh, old *friend*?" He practically spat the last word.

Out of the corner of his eye, Buck saw Jolene put down her sandwich, watching them. Other people were watching too. He held Deke's gaze. "Look, Deke, I don't know what your problem is, but you need to back off. I didn't have anything to do with Marshal firing you, and you know it. You screwed up one time to many, that's all. And if you want to know the God's honest truth, I'm having a hard time feeling sorry for you right now."

He started to move past Deke and then looked back. This time he didn't bother to keep his irritation in check. "You want some free advice, Deke? Stay off the damn internet. You're making a fool of yourself."

This time when Buck started to move forward, Deke grabbed his arm. "Did you hear me asking you for any advice?" he demanded.

Jolene's chair scraped back, her hand near her taser.

Buck looked down at the other man's fingers on his arm. He looked at Deke. He said, "You've got two choices. You can either go sit down, or you can get out of here. Either way, you're going to let go of my arm, and you're going to do it right now, or I swear to God I'll haul you in for public drunkenness."

Deke glared at him for another moment, then released Buck's arm with a snap. "You better watch your back, Buck Lawson," he said angrily. "You'll get yours. You just wait and see if you don't." He turned and stalked away, causing the bell to jangle furiously as he pushed through the door.

The other diners returned to their meals, but Buck's appetite was noticeably diminished. He went to the counter to pick up his take-out box, and Meg said, nodding sharply toward the door, "That man's a pestilence, all right. You want me to pour you a to-go cup of sweet tea to go with that, honey?"

Buck said, "Nah, I'm good. I'll get a Coke back at the office." He took out a twenty to pay for his meal and she waved him away.

"You get on out of here, Buck Lawson, and have yourself a good day."

He smiled as he tucked the bill back into his pocket. "It's looking better already."

Jolene came up behind him, reaching around to lay some bills and change on the counter. "If you're done being a hero," she said, "I just got a call you might be interested in."

"All I'm interested in is lunch," he answered, picking up his box. "You can brief me later."

She pushed open the door and held it for him with her hip. "It's Stockton," she said. "It looks like somebody might've taken a shot at her."

EIGHTEEN

I know Jolene doesn't like it when I call her on her cell, and honestly, I try not to do it unless, well, I need to talk to her. It's not like we're friends or anything, and she made it clear a long time ago that if I was looking for the kind of inside connection to law enforcement that I'd had when Uncle Ro or Buck held the office of sheriff, I could just keep looking.   I was therefore surprised when, instead of responding with her usual sarcasm (*911, Stockton. Three digits. How hard is that for you to remember?*), she listened to my report about finding the keys and about the rifle shot, and she said crisply, "Mark the spot. Go to your car and wait inside. Lock the doors. If you see anybody, leave. I'm on my way."

She arrived fifteen minutes later, and I was even more surprised when Buck pulled into the parking lot behind her.

I may have mentioned that Cisco has absolutely no self-control when it comes to Buck, and of course I had not been waiting inside my locked car as instructed. Cisco pulled the leash out of my hand and barreled toward Buck the minute he opened his car door, and I had learned from long experience how futile it was to try to stop him. Cisco twirled and reared on his hind legs, ducked and dashed and bowed, all of which was his version of a doggie happy dance, then flung himself into Buck's arms.   Buck, in clean Dockers and an open-collared shirt, got down on his knees and wrestled with Cisco, which is one of the main reasons I've given up on trying to modify my dog's overly enthusiastic greeting behavior. Until Buck stops rewarding him for it, I don't have a chance.

Jolene got out of her SUV and strode over to me. She was in the K-9 unit, and I knew by the fact that she left the air-conditioning running that Nike was with her—also by the way that Cisco, cutting short his ecstatic visit with Buck, bounded over to the vehicle and started sniffing the doors. I called to him sharply, and he came to me happily, trailing his leash. I slipped him a hot dog treat and snatched up his leash just as Jolene reached me.

"Tell me what happened," she demanded.

I told her about the training exercise, and how Cisco had found the keys half-hidden by leaf debris in the woods. "Right after I picked them up I heard a rifle shot," I said, "and the tree limb fell. I didn't see anybody," I added, "and neither did Cisco."

I was about to explain what I meant by that, but Jolene interrupted, "What did you do with the keys?"

I reached into the pocket of my windbreaker and took out a dog waste bag, which was the only thing I'd had to wrap them in. "I had a glove on when I picked them up," I said, handing the bag to her, "so my fingerprints shouldn't be on them."

Buck gave a dry lift of his eyebrow as he came up. "Nice to see you're finally catching on," he remarked, and I ignored him. He had lectured me more than once about mishandling evidence, and I did not want to give him the satisfaction of acknowledging the fact.

Jolene took a latex glove from her back pocket and removed the keys from the bag. She examined the fob and the car key, and showed both to Buck. "Looks like these are the missing keys, all right," she said.

Buck nodded. "Bag them as evidence, and get

somebody to try them in the ignition after they're processed." He looked at me. "Show us where you found them."

I led the way up the trail with Cisco at the end of his leash ahead of me, his nose retracing our steps. Buck paused to look back when we passed the waterfall, measuring the distance, and he did the same when we left the trail.

After a few minutes of pushing our way through pine branches and undergrowth, Jolene said, "What happens if you stay on the trail?"

"It's a loop," I explained. "After about three miles, you end up back at the parking lot."

We reached the spot where I had planted the first glove and Cisco sniffed the ground eagerly, no doubt hoping for a morsel of hot dog treat he might have missed. "This is where I left the glove." I pointed to the west. "The keys were over there about ten yards. That's where the branch fell."

We could all see the tree with its branch freshly shorn off about a foot from the trunk. No one needed my guidance to the spot, which I had marked with my glove on a stick for reference.

Neither Jolene nor Buck said anything for a time while they examined the site. Buck took photos with his phone of the tree and the soil that Cisco had disturbed while retrieving the keys, then walked away and took more shots for perspective. Jolene squatted down on her haunches and examined the forest floor, then stood and looked around, moving as little as possible in the way law enforcement officers are trained to do at the scene of a crime. The only problem was that, as far as I knew, there had been no crime.

Jolene said, "Is there another way to get here?"

I shrugged. "Sure. There's more than one way to get anywhere. But if Rutherford was coming from the parking lot, the easiest thing to do is to take the trail, then leave it at some point, probably within a few yards of where we did." If there was one thing I had learned in search and rescue it was that people, like animals, almost always took the easiest route through the wilderness. "If he'd gone any higher, he would have to fight his way back down through blackberry thickets, and if he'd gotten off the trail sooner there's a rock bluff that would've stopped him. You can't get over it without climbing equipment."

She gave me a look that was a mix of skepticism and puzzlement. "Jeez, Stockton, is there anything about these hills you don't know?"

It was the closest thing to a compliment she had ever given me. "Not much," I admitted, trying not to sound smug. "Except maybe why Mr. Rutherford would leave the trail in the first place."

Buck returned to us and handed me my other glove— the one Cisco had failed to find before he took off in search of more interesting things. "So you didn't see or hear any signs of anybody else out here before the branch fell?'

I shook my head. "That's what I was trying to tell you before. We were doing a tracking exercise. If anyone was in the immediate vicinity, or even if somebody had been there in the past couple of hours, Cisco would have followed the scent. But he didn't."

Jolene said, "Are you sure it was a shot? Maybe the branch just fell on its own."

Buck answered that one for me. "Nah, that's fresh wood on the end of the branch, and you can see the slug mark. It sheered right through." He looked around again, then nodded toward the downward slope. "What's down there?'

"The creek," I said, though they could see that for themselves. "Some farms. The highway's about a mile away. That's how Mozart got here," I volunteered. "At least that's what it looks like." When both of them looked at me blankly I reminded them, "The dog that was in the back of Rutherford's car?"

Jolene looked impatient. "Oh for heaven's sake, Stockton, not everything is about a dog."

I ignored her. "His owner put an ad in the paper, saying they lost him at the Exxon Station," I explained, and then I frowned thoughtfully. "Maybe *that's* what took Mr. Rutherford off the trail. Maybe he saw Mozart in the woods and put him in his car while he tried to find the owner."

I saw the flaw in that logic even before Buck pointed out, "Don't know how he could do that without his car keys."

"Still," I said thoughtfully, looking around, "if Mr. Rutherford lost his car keys out here in the woods, that would definitely explain how Mozart got locked in the car."

He turned back toward the creek. "A lot of undergrowth down there. You might not see anybody on the other side. It can't be more than, what? Fifty, seventy-five yards?"

"A .30-.06 might make the shot," suggested Jolene. "I'll take Nike and sweep the area for the shell casing."

Buck nodded. "Take her through that area over there, too, just in case the bullet hit the ground." He gestured north of the place where the tree branch had fallen. "My guess it's embedded in a tree trunk somewhere though, probably fifteen or twenty feet above ground."

Jolene nodded. "Let's hope we don't need to try to

find it. That's a lot of trees to go through."

I said, growing alarmed, "Wait a minute. Why are you treating this like a crime scene? You don't think somebody *deliberately* shot at me? Why would anybody do that?"

Buck squinted upward at the sun that filtered through the leaf canopy. "Abundance of caution, Raine. It was probably just somebody out target shooting. He might not have even seen you. Or ..." He lowered his gaze to me. "He might have been out here looking for the very thing you found."

"The keys?" I stared at him. "But why?"

Jolene frowned. "DNA? Prints?"

"Maybe," replied Buck. "Maybe he just didn't want us to find the car keys where they were."

I still didn't get it. "Why not?"

"Because it proves that Rutherford was somewhere he had no reason to be," Buck explained. "He came to Hanover County to talk to somebody that was connected to a case he was interested in. Maybe they arranged to meet here at the park. Maybe he was lured off the trail by whoever he came here to meet." He gave a short shake of his head. "Just thinking out loud, here. There are a lot of pieces missing."

I said, "Are you saying Mr. Rutherford didn't drown?"

"According to the ME," replied Buck, "he died of a barbiturate overdose."

Jolene said, "Suicide?"

Buck looked thoughtful, but reserved. "I don't think so. Anyway, let me know if Nike hits on anything. I'm going to talk to the neighbors on the other side of the creek, and then I need to have a look at Rutherford's car."

I could tell that Jolene didn't like being kept in the

dark any more than I did, but it was clear Buck had said all he was going to say. I looked at my watch and muffled an exclamation of dismay. It was almost 1:00 p.m., which barely left time to brush Cisco out, put on his Therapy Dog bandanna, and gather the equipment I needed for the school demo. The bath would have to wait, which would not make Corny happy at all.

I said, "Do you need me for anything else? Cisco and I are supposed to do a school program this afternoon, and I need to get going."

Buck gestured back toward the trail. "Go ahead. I'll call you if I have any more questions."

I glanced at Jolene as we all started down the trail together. "Aren't you supposed to be there too?" I asked. "At the school, I mean."

Jolene glanced at Buck, who didn't seem to notice. "I might be late."

In the parking lot, Buck ruffled Cisco's ears one more time before getting into his car, and when he was gone I looked at Jolene. "I never really thought anybody was shooting at me," I said, a little defensively. "If I had, I would've called 911. I just called you because of the keys."

She nodded, her expression thoughtful. "I don't see how anybody could've targeted you from the other side of the creek, not without a telescopic sight."

"It was probably just an accident," I said. "I don't know why Buck would think it's not."

She looked as though she was about to say something, then changed her mind. "Well, it's worth checking out, I guess. Put your dog away so we can get started."

I fastened Cisco into his seat belt in the back while Jolene got Nike out of the car. At least he hadn't gotten muddy. I was going around to the driver's door when

Jolene spoke behind me.

"Say, Stockton, mind if I ask you something?"

She had Nike, her beautiful Malinois, in a regal sit at her side at few feet away from me, and I resisted the urge to reach out and stroke the dog's silky coat. "What's that?" I slid into the seat and pulled on my seat belt.

She frowned a little. "Do you have any idea what's up with your ex?" She nodded her head in the direction in which Buck had gone. "He reamed me out at lunch for something I didn't do, almost got into a fight with Deke Williams in the diner, and it's not like him to hold back on a case we're both working on. Not smart, either."

I was surprised, because I could not remember Jolene ever asking for my opinion on anything before. For that reason alone I wished I could have been more helpful. But I had to shake my head. "Sorry," I said. "We don't talk that much anymore."

"Yeah," she murmured, a little absently "I guess not."

She clucked her tongue to Nike, who came to an immediate heel, and executed a sharp military turn. "See you, Stockton."

"Do you want us to wait for you at the school?" I called after her.

But Jolene and Nike were working, and she did not reply.

NINETEEN

Old Stage Road—which once had been called Stockton Place Road—was the main spur off the highway on the east side of the junction of the Little Tennessee River and Murder Creek. It meandered beside the creek bed for about two miles, dead-ending into the sprawling horse farm called Callanwell Estates. Along the way, the pavement gave way to a narrow gravel lane, which in turn gave birth to a number of dirt roads with names like "Greg's Lane" and "Washboard Road" that were little more than private driveways. Some of those roads had two or three generations of the same family living on them, usually indicated by a single stick-built house with several mobile homes set at various distances from it. A couple of the dirt lanes led to long-deserted farmhouses, and some of them led nowhere at all. Buck had heard that Miles Young was planning to put some kind of upscale community out here along the creek bank, maybe even condos. He hoped he'd heard wrong. Some things you couldn't get back once they were gone, and the peace and quiet of a place like Murder Creek was one of them.

Buck stopped by the homes of everyone on the creek side of the road, bypassing the sheriff's neat, riverside log cabin for obvious reasons. Most people were at work, but those who answered his knock weren't very helpful. Either they had heard nothing at all, or admitted to hearing shooting but didn't think anything of it. Nobody had seen anything unusual, either on this side of the creek or in the woods beyond. One person said he thought the shot might have come from farther down the road, which made sense. The Callanwells had a lot of property at the end of the road, and only part of it was cross-fenced for horses. The rest was wild fields and tangled woodlands, good for hunting rabbit and squirrel—both of which were out of season now, but you couldn't tell a man what to do on his own property.

Buck knew both the Callanwells, and they were good, hard-working people. Their kids were a mess, though. The daughter had gotten pregnant in high school and now had three kids by three different fathers; the last Buck had heard she was living in California. The son, Daniel, had been in drug rehab at least twice and had even done a stint in the Hanover County jail. Buck thought he was still living with his folks despite the fact that he was pushing thirty.

They kept a pretty place, with glossy-coated horses munching grass behind white pasture fencing on either side of the long dirt driveway that led to the main house. Halfway to the house there was a turn-off that led to a gravel parking lot and a long red barn with the sign "Boarding Stable" over the door. Buck pulled in and got out, looking around.

There was a good-sized horse community in Hanover County, which was only natural with so many scenic places to ride, but most people didn't have enough flat pasture land to keep a horse. The Callanwells made a good part of their living boarding other people's horses and giving riding lessons. The boarding stable sat on a knoll just above the creek, with a riding ring on the right side of it and open pasture on the left. Buck walked around to the riding ring and gazed across the creek. From here it probably wasn't more than a couple of hundred yards to the place Raine had found the keys, as the crow flies. Too far to make a clean shot, but if you stood on the creek bank ...

"Help you?" demanded a voice behind him. The question sounded more threatening than welcoming, and that impression was only reinforced when Buck turned and saw that the man was holding a rifle.

Buck didn't know Daniel Callanwell personally, but it wasn't hard to figure out who he was. He had the thin, hollow-eyed look of a career addict. He wore a Callanwell Estates tee shirt that hung on him, and faded jeans that were dirty at the knees. His blond hair was pulled back at the nape of his neck into a stringy ponytail, and he held the rifle far too casually at his side.

Buck said, nodding at the weapon, "Is this the way you greet your customers?"

The other man scowled. "You ain't no customer. You're the law." He turned his gaze pointedly to Buck's car, where the Hanover County Sheriff's Office logo was plainly displayed on the door. "What do you want?"

Buck said easily, "I'm Buck Lawson. I'm out here talking to people about something that happened on the other side of the creek this morning. You must be Daniel. Are your folks home?"

Daniel scowled. "They're in town. And I don't know nothing about anything on the other side of the creek. I been here all morning."

He turned to go back into the stable, but stopped when Buck spoke. "Is that a fact?" Buck said. "You wouldn't happen to have been out doing a little hunting this morning then, huh?"

Daniel turned slowly. Buck noticed then what he had failed to see before: the eyes that burned with a low, frenetic fire, pupils the size of dimes. He was on something, and whatever it was, Buck was one hundred percent certain it did not mix with firearms.

Daniel said, holding steady, "I told you. I been here all morning. You need to move on." He raised the rifle to his chest, not pointing it at Buck, just holding it.

Buck said, careful to keep his voice pleasant, "Your folks've got you mucking out the stables for your rent, huh? Believe me, man, I feel for you. Been there, done that. No law against taking a little walk, though, maybe firing off a few rounds across the creek when you get fed up." He dropped his gaze to the rifle. "Nice piece. I brought down a 9-pointer with a gun like that last fall. Mind if I take a look?"

Buck reached out a hand and Daniel swung the rifle on him, his finger curling around the trigger. "I said," Daniel said in a low, furious voice, "*move on.*"

Buck felt his chest constrict in a way it had done only a few times in his life. He was carrying a Glock in a holster behind his waist; the chances of him drawing it and getting off a shot before that rifle blew a hole in his chest big enough to drive a wagon through were not good. The chances of him talking down a strung-out junkie with a clear chip on his shoulder were even less.

Buck showed Daniel his palms. "No problem," he said, very calmly, very steadily. "I didn't come here for trouble. Just tell your folks I stopped by, okay?" He took a step back. "I'm leaving now."

Daniel screamed, "Go!" He braced the stock against his shoulder and the weapon shook. "Get out of here! I told you once! Go on!"

Buck walked slowly and carefully back to his car, never taking his eyes off the man with the gun. He was acutely aware that the barrel of the rifle followed his every step, but it wasn't until he opened the car door that the first shot cracked. He dived inside and grabbed the radio, leaving the door open in hopes that it would provide a more compelling target than one of the windows. Sure enough, the next shot went right through the door. Another one blew out a headlight.

"This is Lawson in Unit 18 requesting backup at the Callanwell Estates horse farm," he said, breathing hard. "I'm taking fire at the boarding stable. Repeat, I'm taking fire. One assailant, approach with caution."

He heard the beginning of the dispatcher's response, "All available units ..." and then another rifle shot zinged off the roof of the car. He drew his Glock.

"Daniel," he called, "you don't want to do this! I've got no beef with you!"

"I'm not going to jail!" the kid screamed back.

"Put the gun down," Buck shouted. "We can talk."

Another shot cracked, and Buck heard the flasher bar explode on top of the roof. Either Daniel Callanwell was the worst shot in the world or he was too messed up to see what he was shooting at. He had yet to hit the windshield, and he was standing less than ten feet away.

Buck was stretched out over the front seat, putting as much metal as possible between himself and his assailant, and he had absolutely no view of Daniel. He didn't dare try to look through the window, but neither did he want to let Daniel walk right up to the car and put a bullet through his brain.

One of the first things Marshal Becker had done after being sworn in as sheriff was to upgrade the rolling stock with state-of-the-art computer and surveillance systems. The county commissioners had objected to the cost, but the deputies, as susceptible to the lure of new toys as any man, had been one hundred percent in favor. Buck had privately thought the upgrade was overkill for a rural jurisdiction like this. He had never been so glad in his life to be proven wrong.

He reached up and switched on the computer, then activated the three forward facing cameras. The center camera showed nothing but the driveway ahead. The right camera showed a pastoral view of the meadow and two horses, spooked by the gunfire, galloping away. The left camera showed a pair of boots and jeaned legs. Buck pushed a key that moved the camera view slowly upward: torso, gun barrel, the sweaty, wild-eyed face of Daniel Callanwell.

The radio crackled. "Unit 18, what's your status? Buck, are you okay?"

Buck grabbed the microphone. "I'm alive," he said briefly, watching the camera. "Trying to stay that way. Where's my backup?"

"Two units at Highway 81 and Old School Road. Twelve minutes out."

Nothing was easy, fast or close in Hanover County. That's why, when you were in trouble, you learned to fend for yourself.

He called, "Put the rifle down, Daniel. You've fired four shots. I haven't fired one. But I can see you now, and the next time you reload, I'm going to shoot you. Don't make me do that. Hell, man, I don't even know you!"

"You're not taking me in!" On the camera, Daniel swiped sweat off his face with his shoulder. The barrel of the rifle was leveled straight at the front windshield of the car. "You're not!" And on the camera there was something else. A movement from the side of the barn, behind Daniel. Just a shadow, then gone.

Buck called, "Daniel, listen to me! Whatever's going on with you, we can work it out! We can talk! We can—"

From behind the barn a low, black and tan projectile shot forth, ears slicked back, teeth bared. At the same moment Daniel pulled the trigger.

The shot went wild as Deputy Nike slammed into Daniel from behind with all the force in her ninety-two-pound canine body, pinning the man facedown in the dirt with her teeth on his neck. Daniel was screaming. Jolene stood over him, gun pointed at his head, shouting, "Don't move!" Buck bolted from the car, his own weapon covering Daniel from the front, and kicked the rifle aside. Jolene said something to Nike in German, and the dog released the screaming man. Buck planted a knee in Daniel's back, wrestled him into cuffs, hauled him to his feet.

The whole thing took less than sixty seconds, but Buck was sweating and gasping for breath when it was done. This kind of physical exertion was not usually called for in his job, and neither was the adrenaline rush which, now that it was all over, was pounding in his ears. He glanced to Jolene. "Nice takedown," he managed. "How'd you get here so fast?"

She jerked her head toward the creek bank, and he noticed that her uniform pants were wet to the thighs, and Nike's coat was damp. "We were in the neighborhood," she said.

Buck looked back toward the creek, and in the back of his head an idea began to form, a question found its answer. Once the adrenaline cleared it would make sense, but for now it was all he could do to focus on the task at hand.

"So, Daniel," he said, pushing the young man toward the car, "when we search inside that stable, what're going to find?"

TWENTY

Melanie's school is located about twenty minutes from my house in one of the most beautiful valleys in North Carolina. The view alone is worth the outrageous tuition fees, and every time I drive by there I understand why the rich and powerful from all over the country—in fact, all over the world—send their children there.

The school accommodates boarders as well as day students, K through 12, and even though they offer a number of scholarships "to encourage diversity," there aren't that many local kids besides Melanie who can afford to go there. They have an equestrian program, a working farm, and a performing arts theater that's fancier than some of the public theaters I've been to in Asheville. Security is so tight that, whether you're a delivery truck driver or a parent, if your fingerprints aren't on file, you don't get in.

Cisco and I were cleared at the guard gate and drove through the tall, white, arched gates to the west parking lot, where I checked in at the office. I had done this gig a couple of times before and knew the drill, but it never failed to impress me. The tall atrium with a water feature trickling down a three-story marble wall on one side, floor-to-ceiling windows overlooking the majestic Smokies on the other, a fifteen-foot-tall tropical umbrella tree stretching its leaves toward the sunny skylight in the middle of the room, the goldfish pond, the aviary ... it was hard to know where to look. The office staff oohed and ahhed over Cisco in his crisp red bandanna and the plastic ID badge the guard had given us at the gate, and the secretary told me that Stan was already here and setting up outside.

A young man in a blue blazer and yellow tie—a senior who had earned the privilege of acting as one of the school's ambassadors for the week—escorted us to the elevator and asked if I needed any help unloading the car. He was polite and personable, and I suspected he was destined for a career in politics. I told him I had everything I needed in my duffle. Like I said, I've done this before and I knew how far the walk was from the parking lot to the outdoor pavilion where we would do our presentation. I tried to keep the gear to a minimum.

Lydia Crown, Melanie's Learning Facilitator—who would have been called a teacher in my day—was talking to Stan when I crossed the lawn toward the pavilion, still faithfully escorted by the ambassador.

Stan had set up an exercise pen with some darling beagle-mix puppies inside, and some of the older students were setting up a tall cat cage where, judging by the carriers that were waiting in the shade, would soon display at least three felines. By Stan's side was a black Labrador retriever named Regis whom he had rescued after he'd been hit by a car and abandoned by the side of the road. Regis still walked with a limp, but had turned into an excellent therapy dog, and was perfect for events like this—calm, friendly, and the virtual poster-dog for what can become of an animal someone once threw away.

"Miss Lydia," said our escort when we arrived, as formally as the sergeant-at-arms at a state event, "Miss Raine Stockton."

"Raine, Cisco!" exclaimed Lydia warmly, beaming her welcome. "Thanks so much for doing this. The kids have talked about nothing else all week, and I was just telling Stan, this is my favorite day of the year, hands down. Andrew," she added, turning to the ambassador, "help the girls set up the cat habitat, if you don't mind, and then report to the office to wait for our K-9 officer."

"Oh," I said quickly, "they might be a little late. They had a last-minute work thing."

Miss Lydia was a fresh young thing in a flower-print dress that showed off her slim torso before falling casually to mid-calf. Her shoulder length blond hair was caught away from her face with a clip, and, except for a sheen of pink lip gloss, her features required no makeup. I remember teachers being a lot older—and sturdier— when I was in school.

Her face creased with concern at my words. "Oh dear," she said. "Nothing bad, I hope."

"Just routine," I assured her. "I'm sure they'll be here before the end of class."

Her wide, Peter-Pan smile returned, and she clasped her hands together. "Excellent! My para-professional will bring the students out in"—she glanced at her smartwatch—"exactly seven minutes. They'll take their seats under the pavilion …" She gestured to the row of chairs that were set up at one end of the open-sided building. "I'll introduce you and turn the program over to you. They've been studying the social consequences of animal welfare all week, so be prepared for some questions. Do you need any help setting up?"

I said, "Cisco and I will be doing a demo in search and rescue, so I need to place some objects for him to find before the children get here. Also, I usually pick someone to hide for him to find, and it shouldn't be anyone he knows."

"All taken care of," she assured me happily. "I

166

remember from last year. It really is *so* nice of you both to do this!" She beamed at Stan and me once again, and then something caught her eye over my shoulder. "Adrienne," she called, "not there! Closer to the speakers, please, in the shade!" She glanced apologetically at us. "Excuse me," she said, and hurried off.

Stan grinned as he watched her go. "Man, if school had been like this when I was a kid I never would've left," he said.

Stan was a fit man in his sixties, bald and broad shouldered with a big, affable grin. He had the USMC insignia tattooed on his right forearm, which was visible today because the sleeves of his denim shirt were rolled up. He also wore a gold wedding band, even though he told me once that his wife had been dead for over twenty years.

He could wrestle a recalcitrant Akita into a cage one minute and bottle-feed a blind kitten the next, each with the same calm, easy confidence of someone who knew exactly what he was doing and why. By the same token, I'd personally seen him cry when he had to put down an old or sick dog, and I knew he had quietly taken many of them home to spend their last days in peace with him. I don't think I'd ever known anyone with a greater love of animals, and I was always glad to let him take the lead when we did events like these together.

"My thoughts exactly," I agreed. I lowered my duffel bag to the ground and bent to unzip it. "This place is really something."

Cisco strained at the leash to get a sniff of the beagle pups, who yipped and pawed their enclosure in return. Regis yawned and plopped down on the grass.

"So how many dogs do you have at home now, Stan?" I asked, giving Cisco's leash a sharp tug. Cisco came over to me just long enough to see what I wanted, then immediately returned to the puppies.

"It's just me and Regis these days," he said. "I found a home for that sweet little female I took in—a family with two kids in north Georgia. And I had to put poor old Shadow down last week. He stopped eating, and I could tell he was in pain. No dog is going to suffer if I can help it."

I said, meaning it, "I'm so sorry."

He nodded, his expression heavy. "He was a good dog. Sixteen, if he was a day." And then he looked at Regis. "Of course, Regis isn't getting any younger, either. I doubt that he'll make it back here to do the program next year."

This conversation was making me too sad, and Stan must have seen it because he changed the subject.

"So," he said, "do you know what's going on with Deputy Smith? The sheriff—I mean, the former sheriff, Buck—stopped by as I was getting ready to leave, asking if I'd heard gunfire this morning. Does that have something to do with why the deputy is late?"

"Kind of," I said. I pulled Cisco away from the puppies once more, snapped his leash around my waist, and put him in a sit. I resumed unpacking my bag. "Cisco and I found Mr. Rutherford's car keys out in the woods this morning—that's the drowning victim, the one who had the dog locked in his car? Except it turns out he didn't drown after all."

Stan lifted his eyebrows. "What do you mean?"

"I'm not sure. Buck said something about an overdose, but I think he suspects foul play."

I took out a plastic bag containing a set of oversized plush blocks with numbers on them. It was one of Cisco's most popular tricks: I would spill the blocks on the ground, ask Cisco to solve a math question—say, what's two times four—and he would choose the block with "eight" written on it. I just had to make sure that I surreptitiously handled the "eight" block long enough to permeate it with my scent before sending Cisco for the answer. "While we were out there," I went on, "somebody was shooting in the woods and they hit a branch right over my head. Buck's just trying to find out who was out there, so he has Jolene and Nike looking for the shell casing."

Stan drew his brows together, disturbed. "Good Lord," he said. "That must have been terrifying."

"It kind of was," I admitted. "I screamed when I heard the shot, and then I started yelling to let whoever was out there know where I was. But nobody came. I mean, if somebody was out target shooting or squirrel hunting and they heard me yelling at them, you'd think they'd come up and apologize, or at least make sure I was okay." I shrugged. "Buck thinks the shooter might have been across the creek. Maybe he didn't hear me."

"Still." Stan shook his head. "I don't know what this world is coming to. A man dead in the creek, and now they think he was killed? People taking pot shots in the woods? And all this going on in my backyard, mind you. You just don't expect things like that to happen here. And here I am living practically next door to the sheriff."

"Well," I agreed, "like my uncle Ro always used to say, there's meanness all over." I brightened. "Good news, though. I think we found the dog's owner."

For a moment he looked blank, and then relieved. "Did you now? That's wonderful news. Somebody from around here?"

I explained about the ad in the paper, and that I was waiting for him to return my call even now. "But," I pointed out, "we still don't know how he got locked in that poor Mr. Rutherford's car."

"Well," said Stan cheerfully, "it doesn't really matter now, does it? Everything worked out okay. Listen, if it's okay with you, I thought I'd do about ten minutes on the importance of spaying and neutering and keeping your dog on a leash, then turn it over to you and Deputy Smith, if she gets here. Maybe spend the last fifteen minutes letting the kids handle the pups? Those little beagles have some of the best temperaments I've seen in a long time. I wouldn't be surprised if we adopted out every one of them before the week is over."

We finished finalizing the details of our program just as the line of fresh-faced young students in their crisp khaki shorts, white shirts and yellow ties filed out and took their seats. Melanie grinned and waggled her finger at us, and then quickly pulled a neutral face, trying to look professional. Miss Lydia introduced us, gave some statistics about the number of homeless cats and dogs in America today, and Stan took over. He was an entertaining speaker, throwing out math puzzles to the kids about how many kittens one unspayed cat could produce in a lifetime, with the winner receiving a stuffed cat wearing a bandana reminding people to spay or neuter their pets. Regis carried the handle of a basket filled with brochures from the Humane Society in his mouth, moving through the crowd while Stan told the story about how the sweet Lab had almost lost his leg after being hit by a car.

Cisco is a born showman, and when it was our turn he brought out all the stops. He did math. He brought the red ball, not the green one. He tracked down a canvas duck, a wooden dumbbell, and a little boy hiding in the topiary garden at the other end of the manicured lawn. I tied each of his feats into a story about his training or his work as a search and rescue dog, and at the end took him through a set of portable jumps and weave poles to show what he did "to relax." The crowd loved him, not that I ever doubted they would.

At the end of our routine, Miss Lydia came up to announce that she had been in touch with the sheriff's office, and that Deputy Nike was on a call and wouldn't be able to appear today. The kids were disappointed—after all, what ten-year-old doesn't love a police dog in full demo mode?—but I wasn't surprised. Jolene has never liked doing PR work, and I figured she'd take any chance she could find to get out of it. On the other hand, Jolene's no-show left plenty of time for the kids to ask questions and to interact with the puppies and kittens Stan had brought, and nobody complained about that.

When class was dismissed, most of the students wanted to linger with the animals, but Melanie broke away from the crowd, ran up to me, and hugged me hard. "Thanks for the pictures, Raine," she said, beaming up at me. "You saved my life!"

I mean, really. Who wouldn't love that kid? I fought to keep my expression stern as I prompted, "And?"

"And I'm sorry I was bratty on the phone," she replied immediately, "and I promise to read the instructions more carefully from now on."

I smiled and tugged one of her curls. "Good deal. Now how about helping me pack up some of this stuff?"

"I will. Just a minute." She paused to give Cisco a quick hug and told him, "You did great!" Cisco panted his gratitude for the compliment and licked her face, then she walked over to Stan.

"Mr. Bixby?"

Stan, who had been packing up the extra brochures,

turned to her with a smile. "Hello."

Melanie stuck out her hand. "My name is Melanie Young."

Stan shook her hand, still smiling. "It's a pleasure to meet you, Miss Young."

"I'm doing a research project on William Stockton and Adam Bowslayer, and how Murder Creek got its name," Melanie said, "and I understand you live in the place where William Stockton first settled."

He pulled a thoughtful face. "Why, I believe you're right, Miss Young."

She looked gratified. "Raine says you know more about history than practically anybody else around," she added.

He glanced at me, amused. "Well, that's real nice of her. "

"I need to have three interviews for my project, and so far I only have two—Raine and Aunt Mart. I'd like for you to be the third, if that's okay."

"I'd be honored," he said. "To tell the truth, my specialty is more military history, but I do have a couple of books on local genealogy at home you might want to look through."

I said helpfully, "Genealogy is the study of ..."

"I know what genealogy is, Raine," she said with a small eye roll. She turned back to Stan. "Mostly, I want to hear about the feud between Mr. Bowslayer and William Stockton, and the cow and the murder."

"Well," he said. He stroked his chin in a ponderous manner, his eyes twinkling. "I wasn't here when it happened, so I don't have any direct, firsthand knowledge ..."

Melanie giggled. "I know that!"

"I'm not a native of Hanover County, you know, I just

moved here when I retired," he added. "I remember the real estate agent telling me about the old Stockton place and Murder Creek when I bought the land, though, and we did find a few arrowheads when we did the grading. Is that the kind of thing you'd be interested in?"

Her face lit up. "That's *great!*" she exclaimed. "Arrowheads, that's just what I want to hear about. And I thought while I'm there maybe we could walk around and look for the old log cabin William Stockton built," she added. "My dad looked it up on the real estate maps and said the original cabin was on your property, probably close to the creek."

I lifted an eyebrow. The log cabin, again. That explained why she had zeroed in on Stan for the interview, and not Marshal Becker or the Callanwells or anyone else who lived on that side of the creek. And so much for not helping Melanie with her homework. I made a mental note to needle Miles about that when we talked that evening.

Stan looked amused. "Well, I've got to admit, I've never seen any sign of a log cabin as long as I've lived there, but you're more than welcome to look around. I do," he added helpfully, "have a chicken coop. It looks a little like a log cabin."

"Cool!" said Melanie. "I'll bet if we look hard enough, we can find exactly where it used to be. And from there I can, you know, recreate the scene of the crime."

Now it was Stan's turn to lift an eyebrow. "Well, I'm not sure how I feel about that. As I recall, there was an ax involved."

She grinned and took out her phone. "I'm not allowed to play with sharp objects," she assured him. "So, how does tomorrow afternoon at 4:30 look for you?"

"You have a tennis lesson," I reminded her, proud of myself for remembering.

But of course she had her entire schedule on her phone, and had already factored that in. "It's over at 4:00," she said. "I'll have plenty of time."

Stan assured her that 4:30 p.m. would suit his schedule just fine, and Melanie, practically skipping with her victory, went to disassemble and pack my jumps-and-weaves kit. I couldn't help grinning as I watched her go. "Thanks, Stan," I said. "That was nice of you."

He gave a small shake of his head, smiling in return. "Boy, they sure make kids work for their education these days, don't they?"

"Melanie is a bit of an overachiever," I assured him.

I remembered suddenly that I had turned my phone off during the presentation, and I scrambled to remove it from the side pocket of my duffel. I had two missed calls, both from the same 826 number, and one message from Corny. I quickly excused myself to Stan and dialed my voice mail.

"Miss Stockton," Corny said breathlessly, "he called! Mozart's—I mean, Buzz's—owner. He said he could be here by 5:00. I gave him directions. I thought you'd want me to. He sounded very nice. He said the dog jumped out of the car when they stopped for gas and ... well. I guess I can tell you that when I see you. I just thought you'd want to know they're on their way. Bye."

I hung up the phone, grinning, just as Melanie returned with an armful of PVC weave poles. Cisco, whose leash was still tied around my waist, got up and wagged his tail furiously at the sight of her. "Good news!" I told her. "Mozart's owner is on his way to pick him up. But we've got to hustle."

174

Stan glanced over at me. "That *is* good news," he said. He seemed almost as relieved as I was. "It's not every day these stories have a happy ending."

It wasn't until he spoke that I realized the story was not exactly over. We still didn't know how Mozart had ended up in the dead man's car.

TWENTY-ONE

Gene and Marsha Callanwell arrived just as the deputies were finishing their search of the stable. Buck didn't like to look at the dread on Marsha's face as she climbed out of her truck, her horrified eyes taking in the multiple police cars, the flashing lights, even the ambulance which was standing by as per protocol whenever they made a drug-related arrest. Gene's face was drawn into bitter, resigned lines which only grew deeper as one of the deputies came forward and explained the situation to him. Marsha tried to push past the deputy, but Gene caught her arm. They were both wearing dusty jeans and logo tee shirts, and the back of the pickup was filled with bales of hay. Their lives were hard enough; now they had to deal with this.

Buck turned to Jolene as she exited the stable. "There's a bunk room where it looks like he was staying," she said. "We found the usual paraphernalia, a baggie of what will probably turn out to be heroin, some oxy, mollies, and a half-dozen fentanyl patches. The boys are cataloging it now."

"Jesus," Buck said. "It's a wonder he's not dead." He glanced at the suspect, now safely subdued in the back of a patrol car, his head lolling back, staring fixedly at nothing at all. Buck said, "What about Seconal? Secobarbital. Any sign of that?"

She shook her head, looking puzzled. "Not something you'd expect to find in a street junkie's arsenal. I'll take

Nike back in and do a final sweep after we get the evidence bagged up, but I think we got everything."

He nodded. He could hear Marsha Callanwell crying, and to avoid looking at her, he pulled his gaze back to the creek. "So you waded across the creek," he said.

"That's right."

"How far were you from the place where we found the keys when you got the call?"

She thought about that. "Maybe a hundred yards upstream. The water's shallow there, so we crossed and came up behind the building. I could see your car as soon as I started up the hill."

"And it took you, what? Four, five minutes to get here?"

"Closer to four," she said. "Do you mind if I ask ..."

He cut her off. "I don't guess you found the shell casing."

"No," she said. "But we didn't search this side of the creek. We'll do that before we leave."

"Okay, good enough," he said. "Let's get him booked. Have somebody let me know when he's sober enough to be interviewed. And get a deputy to run those car keys in and take prints and DNA. Run the prints against again Callanwell's. I'll be in the office."

Jolene said, "Is your vehicle drivable?"

Buck had already determined that the damage to his car was mostly cosmetic, but it still made him grimace to look at it. "Yeah, it'll make it to town." He walked toward the car, and then looked back. "Hey," he said. "Thanks."

She looked at him for perhaps a beat too long, her expression unreadable. "Just doing my job," she said and walked away.

Buck started to open the car door, then changed his

mind and walked a couple of dozen yards back to where Gene Callanwell was standing at the police barricade, his face sagging with the weight of all he saw. Marsha had returned to the truck and was leaning against it, staring out at the creek, smoking a cigarette with a shaking hand.

Buck said, "I'm real sorry about all this, Gene."

Gene blew out a breath. "I reckon we all knew it was just a matter of time. Breaking Marsha's heart, though. You know he tried to get clean a couple of times. The court ordered it once, and he did okay, stayed straight for over a year. It's a disease. At least that's what they tell us." His gaze wandered to Buck's car, and rested there. "He do that to your car?"

Buck said, "Yeah."

Gene pushed a hand across his balding head. "Well. We got insurance. Have to, you know. With the horses."

Buck said, "Has Daniel been working for you long?"

"If you can call it working. Most days he does okay. I don't like him around the customers, though. Not much of a personality."

"Do you know if he was around here Saturday?" Buck asked. "During the day, I mean. Say, 9:00, 10:00 in the morning?"

"Sure," said Gene. "We all were. Saturday mornings we give riding lessons. We're booked solid this time of year. Started at eight, ended at noon."

"Does Daniel give lessons, too?"

Gene shook his head. "Like I said, I don't like him around the customers. He handles the tack, grooms the horses, keeps the rings clean, that kind of thing."

Buck nodded, his eyes wandering to the creek. Four minutes across.

He said, "So if one of the horses gets sick or hurt, what do you do? Call Doc Witherspoon out here?"

"Nah. We'd be broke in no time if we paid a vet to come out every time one of the horses got a stone bruise or needed stitching. Most of the time we take care of it ourselves."

"In this stable here?"

Gene shook his head. "No, this is for our clients' animals; we're not going to keep a sick horse down here. We've got another barn up closer to the house." He released another long breath. "I reckon I'd better see about getting a lawyer, huh? Can Marsha and me drive up to the house?"

Buck said, "I think they're about done. The deputies will let you know when you can go through. We're going to take Daniel down to the jail and book him. You probably won't be able to see him until the morning."

Gene nodded slowly, heavily.

Buck clapped him lightly on the shoulder. "You take care, Gene."

Gene did not reply, and Buck walked back to his car.

The medical examiner's report was waiting in his in-box when Buck got back to the office. He had to dodge the well-wishes of the staff and the few deputies who weren't out at the Callanwell place, and he had just finished printing out the ME's report when Marshal stopped by his office. He tapped lightly on the frame of the open door.

"You okay?"

"Not even a scratch," replied Buck, spinning his chair around to take the papers from the printer. "Sorry I can't say the same about your car."

When Buck was sheriff, he would have been on the scene with the first radio call, but that was not Marshal's style. Buck was a soldier; Marshal was a general. Buck had never appreciated how important it was to know the difference until he had tried to do a job he'd never wanted and wasn't suited for.

"Hardware is replaceable," Marshal said, coming inside. "Highly trained personnel, not so much. So what's the short version?"

"The kid was high on something," Buck said, scanning the first page of the report. "Probably heroin. I stopped by to ask him about ..." His voice trailed off, then he murmured, "Well. There you go."

He looked up at Marshal. "This is the autopsy report on Jim Rutherford. It looks like we've got a homicide."

Marshal frowned sharply. "How?"

"Seconal toxicity," Buck summarized, still reading. "I thought at first it might've been suicide, but the post-mortem uncovered an injection site on the back of the neck ... not likely a man with no history of drug use would choose to start by stabbing himself in the neck—the back of the neck, no less—with a hypo full of barbiturate. Ten times the fatal dose."

"Damn," said Marshal softly. Then. "Do you need help from the state boys?"

"Yeah, probably," Buck said absently, still reading. "Let me do a little more research first."

Marshal gave a small shake of his head and turned to go. "It never rains but it pours, right? Keep me informed."

"You got it."

Marshal paused at the door. "Listen, I hope you didn't take anything I said this morning the wrong way. I'm not the kind to poke my nose into how you do your job. I was just surprised when Hank asked me the other day about an investigation I didn't even know we were running."

After all that had happened between their last conversation and this one, it took Buck a moment to realize he was talking about the Carolina Free forum. And he was still confused. "Hank?"

Marshal smiled. "Your boss? The county prosecutor?"

Of course. All the computers were on the same network in the prosecutor's office, and Jolene wasn't the only one who'd noticed his interest in tracking the forum. He hadn't worked very hard to keep it a secret, and he might have mentioned something to Hank about the forum in relationship to the federal case that was still pending against several Hanover County residents. He felt like a fool.

He said quickly, "Yeah, no problem." Except for the fact that he had really stepped in it with Jolene. Again. He added reluctantly, "Anyway, you might've had a point. I guess I still have some things to work out about everything that happened last year."

Marshal nodded. "Let me know if I can help."

And the thing was, Buck could tell he meant it. Marshal was just that kind of guy.

TWENTY-TWO

Mozart was shampooed, brushed, perfumed and pedicured within an inch of his life by the time the white minivan pulled up in front of the Dog Daze building. I confess, it was all I could do not to press my face against the window in my eagerness to see who, after all the questions and speculation, actually turned up to claim the dog. Melanie had no such inhibition.

"He looks like a schoolteacher," she reported from her position at the window. She was kneeling on a grooming stool and had her hands cupped around her face to shield against the glare of the sun on the glass. "Not like Coach Birkus but more like Mr. Potter, my music teacher. Not much hair. Real skinny."

"Melanie, get down," I scolded. "He can see you." I peered over her shoulder. "Can you see the license plate?"

"Nope, not from here. But, hey, think there's somebody else in the van. Maybe a kid." She climbed down from the stool. "I'll go tell Corny they're here."

I had asked Corny to keep Mozart in the grooming room until I had a chance to interview the person—or people—who came to claim him. I don't know what I was expecting. I wasn't even sure what I wanted to ask. But my palms were sweating a little and my chest was tight as I waited for whoever was about to come through that door.

I said, "No, wait. I want to talk to him first."

She gave a nod of approval. "Right. You can't just turn over a dog to any old body off the street. What if he's a dognapper?"

Or, I thought, staring fixedly at the door, *a kidnapper?*

But the man who opened the door a second later didn't look like either. He was probably in his early forties, clean shaven and nicely dressed in a pale peach Polo shirt and white jeans with driving moccasins. He was slender and not particularly muscular, and his light brown hair was thinning on top.

He did not look in the least familiar to me.

He took off his sunglasses and looked around, and when he saw me, he smiled uncertainly.

"Hi," he said. "I called earlier. I'm looking for ..."

"Raine Stockton," I supplied, coming forward with my hand extended. "That's me. I own this place."

He shook my hand with a warm, dry grip. "I'm Scotty Benson," he said. "I called about the Newfoundland you found. Buzz?"

Melanie looked him over suspiciously. "Can you describe him?"

I placed my hands lightly on Melanie's shoulders and said quickly, "This is Melanie. She helps out around here."

He gave Melanie the easy, warm smile of someone who has children of his own. "Well, thank you for helping take care of Buzz, Melanie," he said. "He was a lucky dog, huh? To be found by somebody who owns a boarding kennel."

"Well," I said, "we didn't *literally* find him ..."

"He was locked in a hot car," Melanie supplied. "And the man who locked him there was ..."

I clamped my hands down on Melanie's shoulders, squeezing a warning. "TMI, Melanie," I said, and added quickly to Scotty, "It's kind of a long story. Would you like to sit down?" I gestured to one of the client chairs that were stationed against the wall. "Can I get you something to drink?"

He glanced toward the door. "Actually, my daughter is in the car ..."

"Your daughter?" I might have seized on that a little too quickly. After all, most people who have dogs have kids, and at least half of those were bound to be girls. "Don't you want to bring her inside?"

"I didn't want to get her hopes up until I'd seen the dog for myself," he explained. He was starting to look anxious now. "Look, is everything okay? I mean, you still have the dog, right? And what's this about a hot car?" He glanced at Melanie and then back at me, his expression anxious. "He's all right, isn't he?"

"He's fine," I assured him, watching him carefully. "I was just wondering ... you wouldn't happen to know a man by the name of James Rutherford, would you?"

He looked thoroughly confused. "James ...? I'm sorry, I don't. Would it be okay if I had a look at the dog now? You said he had a blue collar and a name tag ..."

"Right," I agreed readily, "but we couldn't read the phone number on the tag. So how did you lose your dog, anyway?"

"Like I told the person on the phone," he said, "we're just in town for a short time. We were on our way back from Spartanburg, and we got diverted off the expressway because of an accident. I decided to just take the back roads the rest of the way, and when we stopped for gas ..."

"Oh," I interrupted, "the rest of the way where? I mean, do you have a place here, or ...?"

He gave me an odd look, and I could tell he thought my questions were getting a little pushy. "My mother," he explained patiently, albeit somewhat coolly, "had a cabin in the Rock Hill community."

I said, "Oh, sure, I know where that is. A lot of people have summer cabins up there."

"Her place has been with a management company for the past few years as a rental. But my mother died last week in a nursing home in Spartanburg and I've decided to put the cabin on the market. So I've been going back and forth between Spartanburg and here to try to get her affairs in order."

"Oh." I felt bad now. "I'm sorry."

"We were estranged for many years," he replied briefly. "But yes, it's been a stressful time. A stressful couple of years, if you want to know the truth, for both my daughter and me, and losing Buzz was just about the worst thing that could have happened after everything else. We let him out of the car when we stopped for gas and Chris was walking him in a field behind the station when he saw a rabbit or something and just took off. We searched until dark, but it was hopeless." He shook his head sadly. "It was my fault. He's such a big doofus, we never put a leash on him at home, but I should have known, in a strange place, with all the traffic and all ... I should have been paying attention. Chris hasn't stopped crying since."

I really *did* feel bad now. But still, I'm not known for my ability to let an idea—or a subject—just drop. I said, "So where did you get Buzz? In South Carolina?"

Again, he gave me a peculiar look. "No. We're from St. Louis. That's where we got him."

"From a breeder?"

"From a shelter." He seemed to be on the verge of losing patience. "Why all these questions? Are you going to let me see the dog or not?"

"We need ID," Melanie spoke up firmly before I

could. "What if you're not even his owner? We can't just give him away to anybody, you know."

Scotty looked from Melanie to me, and I gave a small, apologetic shrug. "It's policy," I said, even though it was a policy Melanie had more or less just now made up.

Scotty reached into his pocket and took out his phone. He tapped a couple of screens, and then turned the phone around to me. There was a picture of Mozart—or Buzz, as I supposed I should start calling him—snoozing on someone's sofa, taking up the whole length of it. He tapped another screen, and there he was again, sitting on a spring-green lawn with a young girl's arms stretched around his neck. There was no doubt about it, the dog in my grooming room and the dog in these photos were one and the same. I looked closer, trying to make out the child's features, but her face was turned away from the camera and I couldn't see. Fortunately, it didn't matter. The bell over the door chimed, and she walked in.

"Daddy?" she said. "Did you find Buzz yet? Where is he? Can we go?"

Again, I don't know what I was expecting, but there was nothing familiar about this child. She looked to be about Melanie's age, although a lot taller and ganglier, with short-cropped brownish hair and a pierced ear with a gold stud in it. Her eyes were hazel colored, maybe green, maybe gray, and her frame was slight. She wore denim shorts and—as though I needed further proof—a blue tee shirt with a photo-transfer picture of Mozart emblazoned across her chest.

"Hi," I said to her. "My name is Raine. What's yours?"

"Chris," she replied warily, going over to her father. "Do you have my dog?"

"I'm not sure," I said. "I hope so. How old are you,

Chris?"

"Twelve," she replied.

Kylie, had she lived, would have only been nine.

"And how long have you had your doggie?" I asked.

She reached for her father's hand, suddenly shy. "Since he was a puppy."

Scotty said, "Miss Stockton ..."

I turned to Melanie. "Melanie, go tell Corny to bring the dog out."

Melanie skipped from the room, and the three of us stood in awkward silence for a moment. Finally I said, "Look, I hope you understand ..."

At that moment Mozart burst through the swinging door with Corny at the end of the leash. Chris cried, "Buzz!" and ran toward him with arms wide.

Corny, who could subdue a wild-eyed border collie or frothing Doberman with a stern glance, never had a chance. Mozart practically flew toward the child, the leash snapping in the air behind him. I cried out and rushed to intervene, alarmed for the girl's safety, but I needn't have worried. Chris fell to her knees and Mozart skidded to a sit, and by the time I reached them Chris had her arms wrapped around the big dog while he licked away her tears of joy. "Buzz!" she cried, "Oh Buzzy-Buzz we found you! I was so worried! Don't ever run away like that again! I love you so much! Oh, Buzz, Buzz!"

Buzz—erstwhile Mozart—the big, powerful monster of a dog, laid his chin gently atop the child's head and heaved a great sigh of relief. It was the most moving display of adoration between a dog and a child I had seen since ...

Since Kylie and Mozart. And it made no sense to me whatsoever.

Scotty's features softened as he looked down at them. He went over and cupped his hand around the dog's big head, scratching his ears. "You gave us a scare, big guy," he said. "Don't do that again, okay?"

Buzz, completely absorbed in the ecstatic embrace of his human, didn't bother to respond. Scotty looked up at me, smiling. "Well, Miss Stockton," he said, "any more questions?"

I had a lot, but I didn't think he could answer any of them. I returned his smile a little weakly. "I'm glad I could help," I said. "Have a safe trip home. And," I added, gesturing, "you can keep the leash."

Scotty offered to pay me for the boarding, and I assured him there was no charge. We saw them to their car and Melanie snapped a couple of photos for her Instagram account. We waved as they drove away.

"Well," said Corny, pleased. "All's well that ends well, yes?"

"They seemed like nice people," I agreed, trying not to sound as uncertain as I felt. "And the girl was crazy about her dog."

"He was pretty crazy about her, too," Melanie said as we turned to go back to the office. "But there's no way that kid was twelve years old."

I gave her a questioning look and she explained, "She didn't even have boobs. *All* the girls in seventh grade have boobs. Say, Raine, when do you think I'll get boobs?"

"Seventh grade," I replied confidently, and over Melanie's head I saw Corny trying not to grin. I raised my eyebrows at him in a semblance of a silent shrug.

How to Raise Dogs and Kids by Raine Stockton, *Chapter Eight: Never Let Them See You Sweat.*

TWENTY-THREE

Buck pulled up in front of the neat little mission-style house on Green Street at twilight. It was an older neighborhood but nice; the kind where young families could find affordable housing and working men and women felt safe. There were bikes in some of the yards and pickup trucks in almost every driveway. Dogs barked down the street, and someone's television set could be heard through an open window, but otherwise it was quiet. Buck had observed that it was usually quiet after supper pretty much everywhere in town.

He took the flowers and the paper bag from the front seat of his truck and went up the painted concrete steps. He knocked on the front door. Light from the uncurtained window spilled onto the front porch, and Buck could see unopened boxes stacked against the wall inside the living room, trash bags filled with bubble wrap and newsprint, books and knickknacks and children's toys scattered here and there across the floor. Jolene had clearly seen him get out of the car, and she answered the door on his first knock.

Charlie Daniels Band was playing in the background. That was the first thing that surprised him. Jolene was in jeans and a tee shirt and bare feet, her hair done in a smooth braid down the back of her neck. Her toenails were painted red. That was the second thing that surprised him.

Buck said, "Charlie Daniels?"

"We don't all listen to rap, you know," she replied, with just a tinge of annoyance. "What are you doing here?"

"Housewarming present?" He offered her the flowers. "For your mother," he explained.

She took the flowers, although with some obvious reluctance. He reached into the bag and brought out a toy police car. "For Willis," he said, and added apologetically, "He probably already has one."

"He has three." But she took the car anyway.

She obviously had no intention of making this easy for him, and let him stand there searching for the next thing to say far longer than was necessary. The silence had just crossed the threshold of awkwardness when a voice called from inside, "Who's at the door, Jolene?"

Jolene returned over her shoulder, "Gentleman caller, Mama!" and that made Buck smile.

A tall, slender woman with close-cropped salt-and-pepper curls came into the living room, drying her hands on a dish towel. She wore pink-framed glasses, a crisp cotton shirt, and pink slacks. Unlike her daughter, she wore shoes, as well as a big smile.

"Well, for heaven's sake, don't keep him standing there on the stoop!" she declared. To Buck she said warmly, "Hello, I'm Eloise Smith, Jolene's mother."

Buck extended his hand across the threshold. "I'm Buck Lawson. I work with your daughter."

She clasped his hand with both of her own. "Of course you are. I've heard so much about you."

"Unfortunately," Buck replied ruefully, "it's probably

all true."

She laughed, which seemed to annoy Jolene. Jolene thrust the flowers at her mother. "He brought you these, Mama."

The other woman took the bouquet of grocery-store carnations and inhaled their fragrance deeply. "Well, aren't you sweet! Come in, come in. The place is a mess, but …"

Buck said quickly, before Jolene could, "No, ma'am, thank you. I know you all are busy and I don't mean to stay. I just stopped by to say welcome to town and …" He glanced at Jolene. "Maybe have a word with your daughter? About work," he clarified.

Jolene held his gaze for a minute, then glanced at her mother. "Mama, will you make sure Willis brushes his teeth? I'll be in in a minute."

Eloise hesitated, and then smiled. "It was nice to meet you, Buck. You stop by anytime, you hear?"

Buck said good night to her, and Jolene closed the front door. She looked at him with what could not be interpreted as anything other than an intimidating stare. "Well?" she said.

Buck reached into the paper sack and brought out the last of its contents, a six-pack of beer. "It's cold," he said.

She looked at him for another moment, then walked to the top step and sat down. Buck took a beer from the pack, twisted off the cap and sat beside her. He handed her the bottle, then opened one for himself.

He said, "I thought you went over my head to talk to Marshal about what I was doing on the forum. I was wrong. I'm sorry."

She looked at the bottle in her hand. She said, "Is this a race thing?"

"No." He took a breath, released it, and was silent for

a moment. "It's me. It's just that my head's been up my ass since … well, it doesn't matter." He took a draw from the bottle. "I screwed up, I'm sorry. You're one of the best law enforcement officers I've ever worked with. I wish we could start over. I'd like to ask you not to hold this against me, but I understand if you do."

She set Willis's toy police car on the step beside her, and she drank from the bottle. She said, "I heard about your reputation as a charmer long before I came here." She looked at him, her dark eyes flat and cool in the dim light. "You need to know, it doesn't work on me."

"Understood." Buck drank again and lowered the bottle between his knees. "I ran the prints on the key fob against Daniel Callanwell's," he said. "No match. DNA may tell us more, but it'll take a while. I checked the GPS on Rutherford's car, but the directions he plugged in were to Hansonville center, no specific address. He hadn't made any calls from his cell phone except to his wife in the past three days, so it's possible whoever he came here to see didn't know he was coming."

Jolene said flatly, "And you're telling me this at eight o'clock at night on my day off."

Buck went on, "The GPS map did show a route to the end of Old Stage Road, where the Callanwell Farm is, and then back to Murder Creek Park. James Rutherford was killed by an injection of Seconal to the back of his neck. Seconal is used as a large animal sedative. We'll have a search warrant for the rest of the Callanwell property tomorrow morning. "

Jolene said softly, "Damn. What do you make as the motive?"

Buck shook his head. "That's what gets me. Up until now, I don't see any connection between James Rutherford and Daniel Callanwell. Rutherford was investigating a series of cop killings that happened twenty-five years ago. Something in his investigation led him to Murder Creek. Somewhere in between, there's Callanwell, and a large animal sedative called Seconal."

"Did you talk to Rutherford's wife?"

He nodded unhappily. "Not my favorite part of the job. I told her we are following up on some leads. It was the best I could do."

"What about Callanwell? Did you get a chance to interview him yet?"

"Just for a minute. He claims he never heard of Rutherford, never met him, never talked to him. I'll have another go at him tomorrow, but right now we need more evidence."

Jolene said, "You think that whoever fired at Stockton this afternoon is the missing link?"

"Maybe." He lifted the bottle to his lips.

"I guess you got the report that we didn't find the shell casing."

"Yeah," Buck said. "It would've been nice if the shell had matched the ones from Daniel's rifle, but if Nike didn't find it, it wasn't there. Whoever fired that round made sure not to leave any evidence behind."

"Callanwell had a bolt-action rifle this afternoon," she pointed out. "That would've made it easy to pick up the casing."

"I don't know a hunter around here who doesn't own a thirty-aught-six bolt-action," he replied. "That doesn't prove anything."

"A minute ago you sounded sure Daniel Callanwell was our suspect," she said.

Buck took another drink from the bottle. "Yeah, well, at this point the one thing you can quote me on is I'm not sure of anything. I just wanted to give you a heads-up on the search warrant."

She said, "The Callanwells run a horse farm. Chances are, we're going to find a large animal sedative on the premises."

Buck drank again. "Right."

"I take it Callanwell doesn't have an alibi for Saturday morning."

"None to speak of. They give riding lessons on Saturdays. Lots of cars in and out, and the parents were busy. Daniel could've left and come back."

"Sounds reasonable."

"It's just ..." But he finished the sentence with a dismissive shake of his head.

She looked at him. "What?"

"I just keep coming back to the damn dog," he said.

"What, the one in Rutherford's car?"

He nodded. "How did it get there, if Rutherford didn't pick it up? And why? And, come to think of it, how did the car keys get a good half mile from the car, in the middle of the woods?"

Jolene was thoughtful. "So the working theory is that Rutherford came here to question Daniel Callanwell about a series of cop killings that happened when he was, what, maybe five years old?"

Buck said, "Him, or somebody else at the farm."

"Daniel's got a jacket, right? Maybe he met somebody in jail that Rutherford was interested in."

"Maybe. But if all Rutherford wanted was information, why would Daniel kill him?"

Neither of them had an answer for that.

Jolene said, "So Rutherford came here to interview somebody in connection with a series of cop killings that happened back in the nineties. That person was threatened enough by Rutherford to kill him rather than let him find what he came there for. Suggesting that whoever Rutherford came to see was the killer from all those years ago."

"That's the theory," admitted Buck

She glanced at him. "Could it have been the father?"

Buck said, "My gut says no. As far as I know, Gene Callanwell has never been out of Hanover County, and these killings took place all over the south. But I'm looking into it. From here on out, it's going to be a process of elimination."

"I'll assign a couple of deputies. You'll need help with the legwork."

"Maybe not." He sipped from the bottle. "I'll turn in my report to Hank in the morning and he'll probably want to send it up the ladder to the State Bureau of Investigation. If my theory proves out, they'll call in the FBI. I'm just hoping to get some more information first. I don't like the thought of a cop killer hiding out here in Hanover County."

Buck couldn't help thinking about what he had read on the forum yesterday. He had a feeling Jolene was thinking about it too. But when she spoke her tone was neutral.

"So," she said, "all we really know for sure is that somebody killed Rutherford with an injection of Seconal. If it happened at the Callanwell farm, that person would have had to drive Rutherford to the creek in Rutherford's own car, dump his body, and escape through the woods."

"Where he either dropped or tossed the car keys."

They both considered that for a moment. "I don't see where the dog fits in," Jolene said.

"Exactly," Buck said. "I can't see a killer wrestling with that big dog to get a body in the car. The dog would have escaped, or the killer would have chased him off.

Why drive him to the creek?"

"Maybe Rutherford was alive when he got into the car. Maybe he was killed at the creek."

"Possible," agreed Buck. "It still doesn't explain the dog."

Jolene said, "I saw a couple of cameras at the stable. Maybe security footage will show something."

"A lot of maybes," Buck said. "And we're not going to be able to hold Daniel forever on drug and assault charges. His folks'll make bail."

They drank their beer in silence for a while. The faint sound of music came through the windows and they just sat, listening.

He said, after a moment, "So what's with the Charlie Daniels Band?"

She shrugged. "I don't know. I like some of what they've got to say. Nothing wrong with a plain-talking country boy." She slid a glance toward him. "As long as you keep your eye on him, of course."

Buck smiled, and let it fade. The night crept in around them, dampening the warm light from the house. Far away, a dog barked, and stopped. A door slammed.

"Do you ever feel like you're living somebody else's life?" Buck said, gazing into the shadows. He glanced at her. "I mean, look at you. How the hell did you ever end up here, in a two-bit town in the middle of the Smoky Mountains, with a six-year-old kid and a mother to take care of? You could be making twice as much in Raleigh, and God knows how far you could've gone if you'd stayed with Homeland."

She was silent for a moment, turning the bottle around in her hands, watching it catch the light from the windows. Then she said, "When I asked Mama to move here, I told her she'd be the only other black woman in town, maybe in the whole county. Do you know what she said? She said, 'There's worse things.' I've been hearing that from her all my life, whenever I worried about something. There's worse things. Maybe this time, she's right." She took a sip of the beer. "At least here there's not much chance of being blown up by an IED."

"I guess."

Inside the house, the music ended. They could hear dishes clattering and a child's voice. Buck said, "I never thought it would turn out this way. I married my high school sweetheart. I thought I'd be married forever. I thought I'd come home from work every day and mow the grass and weed the garden and eat supper across the table from a familiar face, every night. Right now, today, we should be raising tomatoes and kids and golden retrievers. Somehow it all got away from me. This is not my life. And I think I'm blaming everybody for that but me. Which is why I keep going off on you. So, again, I'm sorry." He finished the beer and set the empty bottle down on the porch.

Jolene was silent for a while. She took another sip of her beer, and said, "If this is what one beer does to you, you ought never to drink."

"Good advice." He stood.

She looked down at the bottle in her hand. She said, "Willis's dad liked the Charlie Daniel's Band. He was a redneck, like you, and a Marine. He died in Afghanistan. Sometimes listening to the music makes me feel like he's still here."

Buck nodded silently in the dark. "See you at work, Jolene. And welcome to the neighborhood."

She did not reply as she watched him walk to his truck and get in.

From across the street, in a car parked several houses

down, someone else watched, tracking him through the site on his weapon, knowing he was too far away to make a clean shot. Not yet. Not yet.

Not yet.

TWENTY-FOUR

Melanie had plenty to report to her father when we called him that night, and so did I. I left the details of the school event, her upcoming interview with Stan Bixby, and even the excitement of turning Mozart over to his real owners, to Melanie. When she had bounced off to let Pepper outside and get ready for bed, I swung my feet over the top of the sofa, propped a pillow under my head, and sighed.

"Do you believe in parallel universes?" I said.

"Nope," he replied comfortably. "I have too much trouble managing the one I can see."

We had elected not to video chat tonight, because Melanie had a theory that it was too confusing for Pepper and because I didn't want to change out of my spaghetti-sauce stained tee shirt. We communicated by good old-fashioned speakerphone, which was easier on everyone. I propped the phone on my chest and Cisco crawled up onto the sofa, settling himself into the narrow space beneath my legs. I stretched out a hand, twirling the fine fur of his ear around my index finger. Mischief and Magic helped themselves to the remaining space at the end of the sofa, curling into matching balls of fur that fit just perfectly between the sofa cushion and the golden retriever. Surrounded as I was by fur and heartbeats, with the voice of someone who loved me on the other end of the telephone, you'd think it would be impossible to feel sorry for myself. Nonetheless, I managed it.

"Because," I said, "that was exactly what it was like. There was this great, big, goofy, out of control Newfie-mix, and there was this little girl who adored him, and watching them run into each other's arms was like watching Kylie and Mozart all over again. Only it wasn't Kylie, and …" I sighed again. "I guess it wasn't Mozart."

"Baby," Miles said with conviction, "there is no one in this world who's more tuned into dogs than you are. If you say it was the same animal, there's no doubt in my mind that it was."

And there, right there, is one of the many, many reasons I'm crazy about Miles. What he sees in me is anybody's guess. It's enough, I suppose, that he sees something.

I said unhappily, "I don't see how it could be. The girl said they'd had the dog since he was a puppy, and the dad said they got him from a shelter in St. Louis. Mozart was a year old and over ninety pounds when he disappeared from South Carolina. Nobody could call that a puppy."

"It'd be pretty hard to mistake a dog that big," Miles agreed. "Which brings up another point."

"Right," I said. "How did a dog that big just disappear all those years ago with every law enforcement agency in the southeast looking for him, and his picture on television and the internet and in every newspaper in the country? Even if he did end up in a shelter, in St. Louis or anywhere else, how did he get there?"

"To be fair," Miles said, "law enforcement wasn't looking for the dog. They were looking for the little girl."

"Who definitely was not this little girl," I said. "She wasn't even the right age."

Miles said, "It's a puzzle for sure. What did the sheriff have to say about this new development?"

I blinked. "Marshal? I never talk to him. And anyway,

the sheriff's office turned over the dog to me. They don't think he has anything to do with the Rutherford case." I hesitated. "Why? Do you think I should have told them before I turned the dog over to the owner?"

"Technically, no," he said. "You did exactly what you were supposed to do. But the dog was found in a dead man's car. The police might be interested in knowing who owned him."

When he put it like that, I couldn't disagree. "Great," I muttered. "Something else for Jolene to yell at me about."

"Stay the course, sweetheart," he replied, "stay the course. Listen, I'm going to be here for another couple of days, see Mom settled in with her home health care nurse. I'll probably head home Thursday afternoon. Do you need anything before then?"

"Just you," I said. I'm not usually a sentimental person, but Miles brought out the worst in me. "I really miss you. And, Miles." I paused a minute, choosing my words. "I probably don't say this enough, but thanks. For, you know, being on my side."

I could almost see his smile. He had a great smile. "My pleasure, sweetheart." He was silent for a while, and I thought he was going to say good night. Instead he said, thoughtfully, "You know, sugar, I've found that when I can't find the answer, it's usually because I'm not asking the right question. Maybe you should consider taking a different approach to this thing with the dog."

At this point, I didn't know how many approaches were left, but I appreciated his input. Miles was hardly ever wrong ... except, of course, on subjects about which we disagreed. I said, "Yeah, maybe. Thanks, Miles. Hurry home, okay?"

He said, "You bet. I love you, baby. Give Mel an extra

kiss good night for me, okay?"

We said goodbye, and I felt a little lonely when we hung up. I swung my feet back to the floor and put my phone on the coffee table. Cisco rested his chin on my knee, and the Aussie girls bounded to the floor, wiggling and wagging their way into my attention. I did my best to pet all three dogs with only two hands, hugging and scratching ears and kissing noses until Magic became distracted by a fleece tug toy that someone had left lying on the floor and sprinted over to it. Mischief wasn't far behind, and soon the two sisters were involved in a spirited game of tug. Cisco turned his head to watch them for a minute, but decided against joining the game. Instead he wiggled over on his back and showed me his silky white belly, which I obligingly rubbed.

"So, buddy," I told him, "things didn't entirely turn out the way I thought they would today, huh? You did great, though."

I heard the back door slam and the thunder of Pepper's paws and Melanie's tennis shoes as they reentered the house. Pepper did a circuit around the sofa, then raced up the stairs after Melanie. "Don't forget to brush your teeth!" I called.

"I'm not three!" she called back with an invisible eye roll in her voice.

I noticed then the light on my phone was blinking, indicating a voice mail had come in while I was talking to Miles. Cisco jumped down to join the Aussies' game of tug, and I dialed my voice mail.

"Hi, Miss Stockton, this is Jenna Lake at 4Ever Paws Newfie Rescue," the woman's voice said. She sounded uncertain, maybe even a little embarrassed. "I got your message and, well, this is going to sound so weird. I wasn't sure whether to call you or not but … that Newfie mix you found … the thing is, I think I recognize him. It's been a few years ago, but he's a hard dog to forget. The family who owned him called him Mozart. Anyway, could you call me back, please?"

I don't know how long I sat there, feeling as though I'd been sucked down a rabbit hole, staring at the phone as though it were my only lifeline out.   I even replayed the message to make sure I'd heard her right. This couldn't be happening.

One very busy summer holiday weekend, I had a full kennel of boarders, including two one-year-old golden retrievers who looked enough alike to be twins. They weren't twins, however, and when the owner of the first dog arrived to claim her pet, my kennel help accidentally brought out the wrong dog. The customer was almost out the door with a golden retriever that didn't belong to her before I realized the mistake. It was every kennel owner's nightmare, and the most humiliating moment of my professional life.

This was much, much worse.

I dialed the number she left with fingers that were, quite frankly, a little unsteady. She answered on the third ring, and after I introduced myself, there was a long pause.

"Oh, Miss Stockton," she said at last. She sounded nervous and embarrassed, and she talked really fast. "I feel silly for having bothered you. The thing is, I'm not even involved with Newfie Rescue anymore, not really, I mean. I just keep up the website and send out notices to our foster homes when a new dog comes up … I mean, it's not like I did all that much before, except I guess I'd feed the dogs and help take care of them when my neighbor was away … he's the one who really started the whole thing, you know. He used to keep the rescue dogs at his house, sometimes five or six of them at a time. Not that it was a problem, he was a CPA or something, worked at home, and the dogs never barked or anything. I adopted my first Newfie from him, and that's how I got involved, and after he left I made sure all the dogs had good homes, like I promised I would, but I guess his lease was up and ... well." She paused long enough to suck in a breath. "Anyway, I'm married now, and I barely have room for Linus—he's my dog, a Newfie, of course—and I feel bad that I can't foster so I try to help out wherever I can. Doing home visits, interviews, that kind of thing. I'm not really in charge, or anything. No one is really, I guess. We just do the best we can."

By this time I was ready to scream with frustration, and my fingers gripped the phone so tightly I thought I might break the case. I managed, "Um, you said something about the dog ..."

She took another loud breath. "Yes, well, that's the thing. About six years ago we had a breeder turn in a puppy—she called it a misbreeding because the father was a Labrador retriever. Anyway, we hardly ever get puppies, and this one was so cute—he had that one crooked ear and that white mark on his forehead, like a paint spatter—and I knew he would go fast. So I called my cousin Carol, because I knew they were looking for a puppy for their little girl. We used to be a lot closer back then, before her drinking got so bad and, well ..." Her tone briefly lost its animation. "I guess the whole family was a lot closer back then."

I said, very carefully, "Your cousin's name was Carol? Carol Goodwin? And the little girl was Kylie?"

The silence that followed was surprised, then she said, "Right. I guess the case was pretty famous."

"Also," I prompted, "because I was the one who

trained their dog. You recommended me to them."

"Did I?" There was another brief silence. "I'm sorry, I don't remember. We used to have a whole stack of business cards from trainers, pet food suppliers, boarding kennels, you know. And they went through a lot of trainers."

I said, gripping the phone hard, "I know." In my head I was thinking, over and over again, *What have I done? What have I done?*

"So what I'm saying is, it's not like I never saw the dog again after we adopted him out. I knew that dog. I mean, when they got him, Kylie was just a baby, but Jason wanted them to grow up together, and he wanted a dog big enough to protect her, but not aggressive, and what could be more perfect than a Newfie, right? And even though he did turn out to be a little hard to handle, I still think it was a good match." This time her silence was longer. "I'll never forget that dog."

Neither would I. It was all I could do not to say it out loud.

She went on in a rush, "So anyway, that's why I called. Kylie and the dog, Mozart, disappeared that night six years ago and no one ever saw or heard from them again. Then I got that picture of the dog you found and it looked so much like Mozart I started thinking, What if it *is* him? What if he's been alive all this time? And if he's alive maybe Kylie is too. So I know it's stupid but ..." Another sucked-in breath. "It would make me feel so much better just to see him. The dog, I mean. And, of course, we'll take him into rescue, even if it isn't the same dog. Which I'm sure it's not. I just need to see him."

With every word she spoke, I squeezed my eyes more tightly shut, trying to block out the dread, the confusion, the conflicting certainties. How could both of us be wrong? How *could* we?

In the end there was nothing I could do but open my eyes, take a deep breath and tell the truth as best I knew it. "The owner," I said, stumbling a little over my words, "a guy by the name of Scott … Scotty Benson …"

She interrupted, "I'm sorry, who?"

"Scotty Benson," I repeated. "He came by this afternoon to pick the dog up. He had his daughter with him. He said they were in from out of town to settle his mother's estate, and when they stopped for gas the dog ran away. If there had been any doubt in my mind about ownership," I added, and even I could hear the slight note of defensiveness in my voice, "I never would have turned the dog over, but he had pictures on his phone, and the little girl … if you could have seen the way the dog and the little girl ran to each other …"

There was nothing but silence on the other end of the phone.

I said, "Listen, if it makes you feel better, I thought the same thing at first. About Mozart, I mean. The resemblance was remarkable, and the age would have been right, but …"

She said, in an odd, almost halting tone, "Scotty Benson … that was the name of my neighbor. The one who started Newfie Rescue. He left town about a week after … after everything happened. I don't understand. It doesn't make any sense."

My head was spinning. Scotty Benson. Newfie Rescue. How could I possibly have known that? Today I deal with dozens of rescue organizations across the region, and sometimes I jot down the name of the person in charge, or sometimes he or she is listed on the website or Facebook page. But back then I worked for the Forest Service, dogs were just a hobby, and I never would have heard of a Scotty Benson who ran a rescue in South Carolina for a breed who wasn't my own ... Just like he, most likely, never would have heard my name. I used to put ads in nearby papers for obedience lessons, or leave flyers at dog events, but I never listed my name. The only connection Scotty Benson and I had was a big black dog named Mozart ... and neither of us had any way to know that.

I heard Pepper's toenails scrabbling on the stairs and then on the hardwood floor. She skidded on the throw rug and left it scrunched up in a corner as she rushed to join the game of doggie tug that was taking place near the fireplace. Cisco abandoned the two Aussies for one of his own kind, and began an enthusiastic—and vocal—game of jaw-wrestling with Pepper. I pressed a finger into my free ear, blocking out the chaos.

"Maybe ..." I said. "You said Scotty left town right after Kylie disappeared? Is there any way he might have taken Mozart with him?"

"I don't see how. Or why. He said he was moving in with his mother in North Carolina and she didn't have room for the dogs."

"He told me he was estranged from his mother," I replied. "She died in a nursing home."

Again she was silent.

"You said he left his dogs behind?" I pursued.

"No, not really." She still sounded baffled, and a little stunned. "I mean, he knew he couldn't take the dogs with him, and he had already made arrangements for them to be fostered or adopted. He just needed me to follow up, and take care of them until they were placed."

"How many were there?"

"Four, I think. Five. One came in right before he left, but he placed it really quickly. All the rest were in their new homes within a week. It's not like he abandoned them or anything."

I remembered what Jolene had said. *There are a lot of black dogs in the world, Stockton.*

I said, "Five Newfoundlands, all big and black and floppy-eared ... the only thing that distinguished Mozart was that white splotch on his forehead. And if someone blacked that out, maybe with a marker, even you might not have noticed him."

"I think I would have noticed if one of the dogs had black marker on him," she asserted. "I took good care of those guys after Scottie left. Brushed them every day, took them for walks ..."

"But Mozart might have been gone by then," I said.

Silence.

Melanie plopped down on the sofa beside me, dressed for bed in her golden-retriever shortie pajamas and floppy-eared puppy slippers. Like most girls her age, she had a tendency to overwork a fashion theme. Propping her feet up on the coffee table, she started to scroll through pages on her phone. Miles had strict limits on her screen time, but at the moment I couldn't remember what it was.

"What about his little girl?" I said suddenly. "She would have been five or six. Did she live with him back then or—"

"Scotty didn't have any kids," she interrupted. "That's the thing. He was gay. Everyone knew that. He always said the dogs were his children."

We couldn't be talking about the same man. Or dog. And yet we had to be.

"He could have adopted," I said.

"I guess." She didn't sound convinced. Neither was I. But I didn't think it was for the same reasons.

I said, "I don't suppose you have any pictures. Of Scotty, I mean. Or Scotty with Mozart."

"No," she said. "I'm sorry."

Melanie scooted around in front of me and held her phone in front of my face. I was staring at a photo of Scotty, Mozart, and the little girl Chris in my office this afternoon, preparing to take their pet home.

"I cannot believe," declared Melanie with yet another eye roll, "that you still don't follow me on Instagram."

I snatched the phone from her. "Jenna," I said, "I'm going to text you a picture. I'll call you right back."

TWENTY-FIVE

Buck thought about going home when he left Jolene's house; in fact, that was fully his intention. But what was the point? He decided to stop by the office to see if the full fingerprint report had come back on Rutherford's car or keys. Excluding Daniel had only been the first step; now the prints would be run through a general database that included prisoners, the military, schoolteachers, and anyone who'd ever applied for a security clearance. That could take a while. The report was still pending, which neither surprised nor disappointed him. Fingerprint evidence was highly overrated in a case like this, anyway. Unless the prints were already in the system, there would be nothing to match them to and he would be no further ahead than he was now. The best he could have hoped for was that Daniel Callanwell's prints would be found somewhere on the car or the keys, and even then he would have had a long way to go in building a murder case against Daniel.

Particularly since he wasn't entirely sure that Daniel Callanwell was the killer.

He sat down at his desk, woke his computer, and shuffled through the papers on his desk until he found the list of names that Rutherford's friend, Gil Monroe, had given him. Eight cops had served under Rutherford's command and had died unexpectedly within three years of each other. Three homicides, four accidents, one heart attack. All easy enough to arrange,

Monroe had said, and he was right. Especially if you had access to heavy-duty barbiturates and knew how to use a hypodermic so it didn't leave a mark.

Obviously, Daniel couldn't have committed those twenty-five-year-old murders, but Rutherford must have thought he had information about who had. Otherwise why would he have driven all the way up here to talk to him, claiming, as he had done to his wife, that he was onto a major breakthrough in the case? And what was it Rutherford had said to Gil Monroe just before he supposedly "cracked the case"? Something about instead of trying to figure out what they had in common when they died, he should have been looking at what they had in common when they were alive.

Almost absently, Buck turned back to his computer, opening the database he had abandoned in frustration earlier. This time, instead of searching for information on individuals, he typed in a search string that included all eight names Gil Monroe had given him, but excluded Jim Rutherford. The results were almost immediate, and so obvious he couldn't believe he hadn't thought of it before.

"Son of a gun," he murmured. What the eight men had in common was not Jim Rutherford. It was each other.

He dialed Gil Monroe in Jacksonville. When Buck identified himself, the other man sighed heavily and replied, "Yeah, I figured you'd be calling. I talked to Liz this afternoon. My wife is still over there with her, as a matter of fact. Homicide, huh?"

Buck repeated what the post-mortem report had said, and added, "Listen, at this point all we've got is speculation, but I've got to believe that if I can find whoever Rutherford came here to talk to—and why—it will lead me to his killer. I have a theory, but first I have to ask you something. We have a suspect in custody who might have a connection to this case. His name is Daniel Callanwell. Does that name sound familiar to you? Did Rutherford ever mention it?"

"No," replied the other man thoughtfully. "I have Jim's laptop here. Hold on, I can search his documents for the name. Spell it."

Buck did, and after a moment Monroe said regretfully, "No, nothing here. It doesn't look like his computer is going to be as much help as I'd hoped it would. It's not like he wrote up reports on the old cases he was working on. Most of it was online research, and it'll take weeks— and probably somebody a lot smarter than I am—to go through his browsing history. Seeing as how this'll probably become evidence in a homicide case now, I'm not that comfortable going any further than I already have with this. So what's your theory?"

"Those eight cops who died," Buck said, "yeah, they all came up through the ranks and worked for Rutherford in Major Crimes at one time or another in their careers. But that wasn't the main thing they had in common. For three years they all worked together under the command of Major Donald Gleason, Special Weapons and Tactical. And Gleason was …"

"The first to die," supplied Monroe. "And …" His voice deepened with thought, or perhaps reluctance. "He was also one of the most incompetent jackasses in the department at the time. One of those overzealous idiots who never should've become a cop. The city was sued more times over his screw-ups than I can even remember. The union wouldn't let us fire him, but the word was he was about to be transferred when he had the heart attack."

"One of the effects of Seconal is cardio-respiratory failure," Buck said. "I don't suppose there was an autopsy?"

"Not that I recall. There probably wouldn't have been. He was a big guy, ate like a lumberjack, high blood pressure, the works. He collapsed at his kid's soccer game, softball game, something like that, on one of those days when it was 100 degrees in the shade. There were probably two hundred people in the stands, nothing suspicious about it. Somebody tried to do CPR but he was pronounced on the scene."

"Just like Rutherford," Buck said.

"Yeah." Monroe was silent for a time, processing this. "So you're thinking that something that happened while all those men worked in SWAT with Gleason is at the bottom of all this. Like revenge, or maybe some kind of professional hit."

"I think it's a place to start," Buck said. "I was hoping you could get me a list of all the operations the team was assigned during those three years. I could go through channels, but it will take a while."

"Yeah, I can probably get you a list of the targets. Pulling the records is going to take an official request."

"Maybe start with the lawsuits," suggested Buck.

"Hell, that's easy," replied the other man. "That'd be in the city's public records. I can e-mail you a link as soon as we get off the phone."

"I appreciate it," Buck said. He was contemplative for a moment. "I want to wrap this up," he said, "for the sake of the Rutherford family. But I've got to tell you, this is one theory that I hope doesn't pan out."

"I don't follow," said Monroe. "It's a good theory, a solid lead. Why don't you want it to work out?"

"Because," Buck said, "if I'm right, that means there's

a serial killer living right here in Hanover County. And nobody even noticed."

Buck waited for the link to come in from Monroe, absently scrolling through the forum posts to pass the time. Nothing much had happened since that morning. A lot of posts on the thread Deke had started about the dog, but Deke himself was strangely silent—which probably just meant he was too drunk to read.

His computer dinged with a new e-mail, and he switched pages to retrieve it. The links Monroe had sent were to half a dozen separate cases filed in superior court in which the Jacksonville Police Department and the City of Jacksonville were codefendants. It took him a while to go through them. Some were the usual nuisance suits: a police car had dinged another vehicle, a civilian claimed excessive force resulting in permanent low-back pain during his arrest for drug trafficking, a couple of false arrests suits that had been awarded damages. On two occasions, Gleason's SWAT team had been called in as witnesses. The name of the plaintiff on the second case made Buck sit up straight.

He recognized that name.

His cell phone rang, and he glanced at it quickly before rejecting the call. Raine. He scanned the details of the court case quickly, but there wasn't much he could learn from a summary sheet. The team, under the leadership of Gleason, was found negligent in the death of the plaintiff's wife and dog and was awarded a $1,000,000 judgement. That didn't seem like a lot for a negligence case that had resulted in a death.

The dog. It all came back to the dog. Somewhere, in the back of his mind, a story was starting to come together.

Buck switched over to the forum again.

MountainMan904. He looked at his own cell phone, and the last number he had dialed. Nine oh four was the area code. Jacksonville, Florida. He couldn't believe it had taken him this long to make the connection.

His phone rang in his hand and he answered impatiently. "Are you okay?" he demanded.

Raine answered, "Yes, but—"

"Is anybody bleeding?"

"No, but—"

"Then I'll have to call you back. I'm in the middle of something."

He was about to hang up when she said, sounding more than a little irritated herself, now, "I have some information about the dog's owner. The dog who was found in Rutherford's car. I think it's important. Since you're the county's chief investigator, I thought you might be interested. But if I'm bothering you …"

Buck rubbed his forehead, pressing out the stress. He said, "Look, I'm sorry. I'm still at work, but I'll stop by on my way home if it's not too late. There's actually something else you might be able to help me with, and I do want to hear about the dog."

She did not sound in the least mollified as she replied, "I'm not going to wait up all night. It's a school night."

For a moment he didn't understand what she was talking about, but then he remembered. The little girl. Miles Young's daughter.

He said, "Right." As he spoke, he had been typing a search string, and now the page came up. "Talk to you later."

He disconnected and, without glancing at the phone again, sat back to read.

Local Man Files Ten-Million-Dollar Lawsuit in Swat-Team Killing.

It was past 11:00 when Buck looked at his watch and swore softly. The things he had learned over the past couple of hours were deeply disturbing, and virtually undeniable. Nonetheless, if he tried to wake a judge to get a search warrant at this hour of the night with what he had, he would most likely make an enemy for life. There was nothing he could do but wait for the fingerprint report, even though he knew what it was going to say.

He printed out his research, created a file folder, and tucked it into the top drawer of his desk. Then he shut down the computer, locked up, and headed home.

He was halfway there when he realized he was starving, and all he had in his refrigerator at home was half a container of expired coffee creamer. He was too wound up to sleep, so he swung into the convenience store and picked up a frozen pizza. And not until he got to his car did he remember Raine.

He suppressed a groan and took out his phone. She was going to be mad, but the least he could do was text an apology. Leaning against the car door in the light of a mercury vapor lamp, he started to tap out a message.

And that was when the shooter, concealed behind the dumpster fifteen feet away, finally squeezed the trigger.

TWENTY-SIX

I texted the photo of Scotty, Chris and Mozart to Jenna and waited for a reply. When I got none after five minutes, I called her back. Her line was busy. Deciding to take no chances, I e-mailed a copy of the photo to the only address I had for her, which was the rescue site. I texted her: *Did you get it?*

Nothing. Nothing. Nothing. Finally, she replied, *Got it.*

I typed back, *Well? Is it him?*

I waited. And waited. Finally she replied, *I'll call tomorrow.*

By now, it was long past Melanie's bedtime. I got her settled with Pepper in the guest room, which was now crowded with Pepper's princess bed, Melanie's stuffed animals, her entire wardrobe, electronic devices, and a wicker laundry basket filled with Pepper's toys. I went back downstairs and let my own dogs out into the yard for their evening toilet break. While I waited for them, I went to Melanie's Instagram page and brought up the pictures she had taken of the happy reunion this afternoon.

No way that kid is twelve, she had said.

The more I looked at her, the more I tended to agree. She was tall, and she was skinny, but she did not look like a child on the verge of her teenage years. Could she be closer to ten years old—or even nine—than twelve? Could the girl Scotty Benson had called Chris actually be Kylie Goodwin?

She had been three-going-on-four the last time I had seen her. Dogs were one thing, but kids? I barely even noticed the ones I liked. There was no way I could tell for sure. And as for Kylie, the last time she had been here Dog Daze hadn't existed. She and Mozart had practiced their exercises in a grassy yard behind my barn. Would she remember me, a stranger she had met when she was three? Did little kids even remember things when they were that young?

Did she remember who she used to be?

I didn't have all the answers, or even most of them, but I had already begun to piece together the story in my head. Miles had said I was asking the wrong questions, and he was right. Instead of trying to figure out how Mozart ended up in a locked car at Murder Creek, I should have been asking how he had disappeared in the first place. And the answer was: he hadn't.

That was when I called Buck.

I waited for him to stop by, or at least to call with an excuse, until past 11:00, and I've got to say I was more than a little annoyed when I finally gave up and went to bed. First Jenna, then Buck. This appeared to be my night to be ignored.

I was so wired I didn't think I'd sleep at all. When I finally fell into a restless slumber it was filled with dreams of big black dogs who turned into bears and camouflaged themselves as trees in the woods.

I was awakened by a persistent buzzing mere seconds—or at least that how it seemed—after closing my eyes. I hit the snooze switch on the alarm clock, but the buzzing didn't stop. I squinted through the dark, trying to locate the source of the sound. Cisco yawned loudly, stretched and curled his tail over his back, then plopped back down in his duck-printed dog bed, chin on his paws. That was when I noticed the blue light of my phone, pulsating with each buzz. I picked it up and stabbed the answer icon. "Jenna?" I said. I don't know why I thought it was her; I just did.

"Stockton, wake up."

The voice on the other end was crisp and businesslike, but also oddly strained. It made me sit up in bed, my heart beating palpably.

"This is Jolene Smith," she said. "I'm at the hospital. There's been a shooting. You need to come." She paused, and it seemed like forever that I waited to hear the next words, although I think I've been waiting to hear them my whole adult life. "It's Buck," she said. "And it's bad."

I'm not entirely sure how I got to the hospital. I arrived clutching my keys and breathing in short, irregular breaths through my nose, looking around wildly for direction. I had pulled a pair of jeans over my pajamas. I didn't have my purse, or my phone. Later I'd realize I was wearing two different sneakers. There were deputies in the lobby with grim, angry faces, and they parted for me in the way they might for a head of state ... or the widow of one. One of them said something to me and pushed an elevator button. I got inside.

There were more deputies in the waiting room on the surgical floor, huddled in knots, talking in low, rumbling tones. Everything had that eerie, late-night hospital fluorescent glow that makes you feel like you're walking underwater. Marshal came over and took my arm, leading me to a chair. He was wearing a gray sweat suit and I almost didn't recognize him. I'd never seen him so casually dressed before.

"He's in surgery," he told me quietly. "We don't know much about what happened yet. He was at the convenience store on West Juniper Street around 11:30. He was shot twice. Once in the torso and once in the leg. The store clerk called 911 and ran out to help, but the bullet nicked the femoral artery and he lost a lot of blood. From what I understand, there may be some damage to the lung."

You know that moment when you realize that the thing you're certain can't possibly be happening just might, in fact, be happening after all? I hovered on the brink of that moment for the longest time, then let myself plunge over. I dropped my head between my knees and took several long, shaky breaths. Marshal rested his hand on my shoulder, and he didn't say anything stupid. I appreciated that.

I straightened up with one final breath. "Okay," I whispered, and Marshal dropped his hand.

One of the deputies came over to me with a bottle of water. I wrapped my hands around it but didn't open it. After what seemed like a long time—because that was the speed at which my brain was working—it occurred to me to ask, "Why?" My voice sounded small and querulous, and I looked at Marshal helplessly.

The lines around his mouth tightened. "We're working on it. The shooter was out of range of the store's surveillance cameras, and there were no witnesses. We'll check all the security footage from the businesses in that area, but there were no cameras within range of the store. It's not always as easy as it looks on TV."

Jolene came over to us. She was in full uniform, crisp and pressed and ready for work. I wondered vaguely, irrelevantly, if she ever wasn't working.

But I was glad she was here now.

She spoked to Marshal. "I sent a couple of deputies out to Deke Williams's house. He wasn't there. His mother said she hadn't seen him since yesterday morning. I left the team there in case he comes back, and we've got a BOLO on his car."

I said uncertainly, "Deke? What does he have to do with anything?"

Jolene glanced at me. "He threatened Major Lawson yesterday at Meg's Diner in front of thirty witnesses. Right now he's our prime suspect."

Major Lawson. It took me a minute to realize she meant Buck. And then I remembered she had mentioned something about that yesterday at Murder Creek. I had been in such a hurry to get home I'd barely paid attention. Yesterday was a lifetime ago.

Jolene turned back to Marshal. "I'm calling in D shift to give blood, and four men from A shift to help with extra patrols."

Marshal said, "When word gets out, they'll all come in." He sounded weary, but also proud. "We've got a good team."

"Yes, sir," Jolene agreed.

"But make sure nobody gives blood who has to work the next shift," Marshal added. "We need everybody alert if we're going to catch this bastard."

I started to surge to my feet. "I should give blood," I said.

Marshal placed a calming hand on my knee before I could stand. "Maybe wait," he said.

Jolene looked at me, started to say something, then turned back to Marshal. "What do you want to do about the Callanwells?" she said. "We have a search warrant for evidence in a homicide, their son is in jail for assault with a deadly weapon, and the officer he assaulted is currently undergoing surgery for gunshot wounds sustained by an unknown assailant. I call that probable cause."

Marshal nodded curtly. "Expand the search warrant to include all security camera footage for the past week. I want video evidence of the whereabouts of everybody on that farm between 10:00 and midnight tonight, and I want it within the hour."

"Yes, sir." Jolene spun on her heel and went off to bark her orders to the waiting deputies. I watched her go with a dull, unfocused gaze, and then turned on Marshal. "What is she talking about?" I demanded hoarsely. "You should be out there trying to find out who shot Buck, not … what is she talking about? What do the Callanwells have to do with anything?"

Marshal explained gently, "Daniel Callanwell took a shot at Buck this afternoon when he went to question him about what happened to you in the woods. Several shots, actually. He was high. Buck thinks he might know something about what happened to Mr. Rutherford."

I stared at him blankly for a moment, then said, "I didn't know." There was so much I didn't know.

Marshal frowned a little. "Raine, given the fact that Deke Williams is still at large and we're not sure what involvement the Callanwells have in this, I've assigned extra patrols to your house. Somebody took a shot at you this afternoon, and until I get some answers, I'm not going to assume anything. I know you've got Miles Young's little girl staying with you, and …"

It was as though someone had hit me with a sheet of ice. I literally felt the cold shock of fear burst through the muscles of my face and down into my fingertips, and I staggered to my feet, gasping for air. "Oh, my God," I whispered.

I frantically patted my pockets for my phone, couldn't find it, turned in a frantic full circle with the room strobing around me until I spotted a red patient phone on the console table at the far end of the room. Marshal said something to me, touching my arm, but I bolted across the room and snatched up the receiver. I dialed Corny's number with shaking fingers.

"I am so sorry!" I burst out when his groggy voice answered. "There's been an emergency. I had to leave the house. I'm at the hospital. I'm okay. Corny, I need you to go to the house and stay with Melanie. You know where the key is to the back door, right? I don't know how long I'll be here. Just go, please. Can you do that?"

His quick and reassuring, "yes ma'am" and "don't worry" and "no problem" punctuated every sentence I spoke until, gradually, my breathing resumed an almost normal pace. "Thank you, Corny," I managed finally. "She probably won't even know I'm gone, but just ... if you can be there when she wakes up, okay?" I shot a quick glance at Marshal and added, "And there might be a deputy watching the house." Marshal nodded his reassurance. "It's just a precaution. Don't worry. I can't talk about it right now but ... thank you. I'll be home as soon as I can. Just ... thank you."

I hung up the phone, pushing out a long, slow shuddering breath. I leaned my forehead against the wall briefly, trying to compose myself.

Marshal came over to me and I straightened up to look at him. His face softened with compassion. "Do you want me to call Ro and Mart? I wasn't sure if we should."

Slowly, I shook my head. "Let's wait until we know something. Uncle Ro will be mad, but ... he has a heart condition and ... let's wait."

And so we waited. Medical personnel came and went. So did deputies. Marshal left, and came back. So did Jolene.

Someone in surgical scrubs came and told us that Buck was out of surgery but in guarded condition. The surgeon would be out to talk to us soon. I could not unknot my muscles.

Jolene sat beside me. She had two paper cups of coffee in her hand. She offered one to me. I didn't want it, but I took it anyway.

She said, "According to his phone, you were the last person he talked to last night. What did you talk about?"

I just stared at her for a moment. I gave a single disbelieving shake of my head. "God, Jolene. Not now."

"Now," she insisted. "You called him at 9:48 p.m. Why?"

I pushed my hand through my tangled curls. "The dog," I said. "I wanted to tell him I found the dog's owner. He came by to pick him up today. I had a theory I wanted to run by Buck. It sounded good at the time, but now …" Again, I shook my head. "It doesn't matter."

"Is that it?" she insisted. "What did he say?"

"Nothing. He said he was busy. He didn't have time to talk."

"What was he busy with? Did he say?"

"No." And then I hesitated, trying to remember. "He said he'd stop by on his way home. He said I might be able to help him with something."

"He didn't say what?"

I shook my head. "He never …" My throat clutched unexpectedly, choking off the words. It was a moment before I could go on. "He didn't come by."

She took a sip of her coffee, nodded, and started to rise. "Okay, Stockton, stop by the office tomorrow and give a statement."

"Wait a minute." I caught her arm. "What have you found out? Did you get Deke? Why would he want to hurt Buck? They were friends! And what about the Callanwells? Did you find out anything?"

She looked pointedly at my fingers on her arm. "Need to know, Stockton," she said coolly. "And hands off."

"How *dare* you!" The words came out as a low, furious roar, and instead of obeying her order, I tightened my grip on her arm briefly, then let go with a snap. I felt heat blaze in my chest, and in my face. "The man was my husband for ten years and he might be dying, and you're treating me like a—like a witness! Like a bystander on the street! How dare you!"

Out of the corner of my eye, I saw Marshal start toward us, but a small gesture from Jolene made him hesitate. She kept her gaze on me, calm and unblinking, until I managed to bring my breathing under control. I felt like a fool, which didn't make me any less angry.

In a moment she said, "This is exactly why we don't discuss ongoing investigations with family members. They tend to get hysterical in public places."

"I'm not—"

She said, "Deke Williams was picked up yesterday afternoon in Clancy for DUI. He's still in jail. We've got video and witnesses to suggest he might have been stalking Buck, maybe even planning mischief, but he wasn't the shooter. Security footage of the Callanwell Farm shows nobody leaving or entering after 6:00 p.m. So we're fresh out of leads."

"That's why you were asking me what Buck said on

the phone," I said quietly. "You think this might have something to do with the Rutherford case."

She nodded. "It's possible. He was getting close to something. Rutherford was here investigating a series of cop killings that happened twenty-five years ago, all of them on the Jacksonville police force. He went to the Callanwell Farm, according to his car's navigation system, and ended up being killed by an injection of a barbiturate called Seconal to the back of the neck. Buck's theory was that whoever he met there was involved somehow in the killings, and that he killed Rutherford and dumped his body in the creek."

I said, "Not necessarily."

She looked at me sharply.

I said, "Whoever Rutherford met wasn't necessarily at the Callanwells' place. Once you get past the pavement on Old Stage Road, it's too narrow to make the turn to go back to the highway without running into a ditch in most places. So people just go to the end of the road and turn around in front of the Callanwells' place, where there's a wide spot." I gave a small shrug. "That property belonged to my family a long time ago," I explained. "We used to have picnics and things by the creek when I was a kid."

Her eyes narrowed thoughtfully, but she said nothing.

I looked down at the coffee cup in my hand, it's contents still untouched. I knew I should stay quiet, and I knew the time for staying quiet was over. This time I couldn't let it go. I said, "Why don't you like me?"

She returned a mildly incredulous and completely impatient look. "What are you talking about?"

I don't know why it mattered, nor why it seemed as though now, after all this time of sparring with each other, it seemed vital to have the answer. But it did. I said, "What have I ever done to you? I want to know."

She shook her head, the impatient frown deepening. "I don't have time for this."

Again, she started to rise, but I insisted, "I'm serious. Tell me."

She released a puff of breath, and looked at me with a mixture of reluctance and what might very well have been pity. "It has nothing to do with liking you," she said. "It's just hard to respect a woman who doesn't respect herself."

I stared at her, astonished. "What?"

Her lips pressed together briefly, and she shook her head. "This isn't the time."

"What?" I repeated with a low ferocity in my voice that once again caused a few glances to turn our way. "What are you talking about?"

She looked at me for another moment, and she took a sip of her coffee. "You kept coming back," she said.

I looked at her blankly, and she sighed.

"Look," she said, "this has nothing to do with your ex. He's a nice guy, and I like him. Everybody does, and God knows he's the last person any of us wanted to see something like this happen to. But he cheated on you, more than once. And you kept coming back." She shook her head again, gaze straight ahead, jaw muscles tightening. She looked very much as though she wished she'd never spoken. "It's none of my business. But you asked."

I didn't know what to say. I didn't even know what to think. After a moment my shock turned to bafflement and I said, "But you called me tonight. Why?"

Now she looked at me. "Because," she answered simply, "you're all he's got."

She turned her gaze away. There was a long and heavy

silence. She took a sip of her coffee.

There was a stirring in the room and both of us got to our feet as a bearded man in a white lab coat came in and introduced himself as the surgeon who had operated on Buck. He told us his name, but I wasn't interested. All I wanted to hear was that Buck was going to be okay.

"We gave him ten units of blood," he reported, "and repaired the damage to his lung, which wasn't as severe as we had feared. The leg was a little trickier. We were able to repair the artery, but we had to deal with some tissue damage caused by bone fragments. I don't anticipate any permanent disability from either injury, though, as long as he keeps up with his physical therapy. We'll keep him on the ventilator in ICU for another twelve hours, but that's routine after this kind of surgery."

Marshal said, "When will he be able to talk to us?"

The doctor shook his head. "Maybe twenty-four hours. I know how important it is for you to get as much information as you can, Sheriff, but it's just not going to happen today."

I spoke up. "What about family members?"

The doctor looked at me sympathetically. "Come back at 11:00 in the morning. The nurses will let you see him for a minute then. Until then ..." He swept a gaze around the room. "There's really nothing any of you can do for him here."

He started to go, but I spoke up again. "He's going to be okay, right?" I insisted. "You're sure?"

The doctor smiled at me reassuringly. "We expect a full recovery," he said.

I knew doctors only said that when they were sure. That's what the doctors had said about Miles's mother, and about my knee when I had ACL surgery. I felt those muscles that I thought would never unknot slowly begin to unwind. He was going to make a full recovery.

"Thank you," I said, and it seemed to take every last ounce of strength I had to utter those words. "Thank you."

Wearily, I walked toward the elevator.

It was barely sunrise when I pulled into the driveway. There was a patrol car parked on the shoulder of the road across from my house, and the driver flashed his blue lights at me once in acknowledgement. That was good. That meant everything was okay.

Although there was an hour left before Melanie had to get ready for school, the kitchen light was on. I could see Corny through the window, his frizzy orange hair even more disheveled than usual, sitting at the kitchen table in a screen-print tee shirt with a Pomeranian playing in a rose garden on the front, and pawprint sweatpants that weren't that different from the pajamas Melanie wore. She sat across the table from him, a glass of milk untouched before her, shredding a tissue and looking disconsolate.

Both golden retrievers bounded to the door when they heard my footsteps; the Australian shepherds started barking in their crates. I opened the door and Melanie knocked over her chair in her haste to run to me. "You left me!" she cried. "I woke up and you were gone and I thought you were dead! You left me!"

I swept her into my arms. Both goldens jumped on me, knocking me to my knees, but I held on to Melanie. She was sobbing.

Corny said anxiously, "Miss Stockton, I'm so sorry. I got here the minute after you called, but ..."

"I woke up and Cisco was here, but you weren't, and I looked but I couldn't find you, so I thought you were kidnapped!"

Her arms were so tight around my waist that they hurt, and her tears wet my pajama top. I kissed her curly hair. I whispered, "I'm sorry. I'm so sorry ..."

"I tried to tell her everything was okay," Corny said helplessly, "but I didn't know what to tell her, exactly. We tried to call you, but your phone ..."

My phone was on the nightstand where I had left it when I ran out of the house, blind with the kind of fear Melanie was experiencing now. Only hers was worse, because the one person she had trusted to protect her had abandoned her, and she was left all alone.

"My m-mom died," she said, choking on the words, "and G-grandma almost died, and I thought ... I thought you were dead!" She burst into sobs again. "There were p-policemen outside! You left Cisco. You would never leave Cisco! And you wouldn't forget me! You had to be dead! Raine, why did you leave me?"

I held her and rocked her, whispering "I'm sorry" over and over again, my heart breaking. I looked to Corny for aid, but all I saw in his eyes was helplessness. This was not his job. It was mine.

How to Raise Dogs and Kids by Raine Stockton, *Chapter Nine.*

I've got nothing.

Nothing at all.

TWENTY-SEVEN

In typical Melanie fashion, she was fine by the time I dropped her off at school. At least I thought she was fine. What did I know?

I explained to her what had happened to Buck, though I downplayed the violence as much as I could. Still, the fact that there was a shooting seemed to distract her from her own ordeal, and she pumped me for details. She always likes being in possession of information no one else has. She reminded me that she had an appointment to interview Stan Bixby that afternoon, and I was glad. I had completely forgotten.

Aunt Mart was already at the hospital when I got there, along with a knot of off-duty deputies dressed in full uniform to show solidarity for their fallen brother. It reminded me so much of the night Uncle Ro had had his heart attack that it was all I could do to keep from bursting into tears at the sight of them. Aunt Mart brought me up to date with her usual calm efficiency: he'd had a good night, they were taking him down to a patient room shortly, and the prognosis was good. Uncle Ro had already been and gone, and was now at the sheriff's office consulting with Marshal. Somehow, even in the middle of this nightmare, just having Aunt Mart here made everything seem normal.

I texted Miles. It took me almost an hour to get the words right, to keep the balance between honesty and reassurance. *Buck is in the hospital*, I decided on. *He'll be ok. Staying with him until Mel gets out of school. Everything ok.*

Don't worry. I added, *Phone off. Hospital rules. Don't worry.*

Those were not, in fact, hospital rules, but I turned my phone off anyway. I couldn't talk to Miles. I couldn't tell him how I'd abandoned Melanie in the middle of the night, how I'd *forgotten* about his daughter and left her alone in the house with a killer on the loose. I just couldn't do it. Not now, not yet.

And the worst part was that now, in one of the darkest moments of my life, I had never needed Miles more.

A little before noon, I went in to see Buck. The nurses told me he was still heavily sedated, and might not know I was there, but I went in anyway. I almost wished I hadn't. His skin was ash-white, and he looked like he'd lost twenty pounds. There were dark bruises under his eyes and tubes and IVs everywhere. I held his hand, and after a while, his eyes fluttered open. He tried to smile. So as hard as it was seeing him like that, it was worth it.

When I went back out into the waiting room, Jolene was there, and she had a big basket of baked goods in her hands. I thought I was hallucinating. Aunt Mart made a fuss over her and helped her unpack the trays of cookies and muffins, napkins and paper plates, breakfast breads and butter. Hungry deputies descended on the feast like a swarm of bees.

"Mama sent them," she explained when she saw me just standing there staring. "Buck brought her flowers."

I almost smiled. "Of course he did."

"How is he?"

"He's off the ventilator," I said, "but they're keeping him sedated."

"Can he answer questions?"

I shook my head. "Not yet." I added, "But you can see him in another hour. Maybe by then."

Aunt Mart brought me a poppyseed muffin on a paper

napkin. "Here, honey, eat this. Do you want me to get you some juice from the machine? How about some coffee?"

I could tell by the way Jolene lingered that she hadn't come by just to deliver muffins, so I smiled at Aunt Mart and said, "Thanks. Orange juice would be good, if they have it."

When she was gone, Jolene turned back to me. "CCTV at the courthouse shows a dark blue Chevy Tahoe leaving the parking lot across the street last night when Buck did, appearing to follow him until they were out of range of the camera. A similar vehicle was caught on the security camera at Kimbel's jewelry store last night at 11:36, going east on Main Street."

"That's a block from the convenience store," I said.

She nodded. "Neither camera showed us the license plate," she said, "but we think it belonged to the shooter."

I said helplessly, "Everybody in the county drives either an SUV or a pickup, and every single one of them is a Ford or a Chevy. And you don't even know that it was somebody local. It could take weeks to track down that SUV."

"Which is why they call it work," she answered evenly, and went on. "I spent the morning going through his phone. One of the calls he made last night was to a former Jacksonville police captain by the name of Gil Monroe. He worked with James Rutherford and was helping Buck with some background. He said the last thing they talked about was a theory Buck had that all the cops I told you about who were killed were members of the same SWAT team, and that the killings were some kind of vendetta. Buck thought Rutherford found the killer here in Hanover County, and when he confronted him, he was murdered. My guess is that's what Buck was working on last night so late. What I don't know is whether he learned anything that could have gotten him shot."

I nodded slowly, trying to take it all in. "Did you check his computer?"

"I've got someone on it now," she said. "And the sheriff put in a call to the SBI for help. They're sending down an investigator this afternoon. Maybe Buck will be able to talk to us by then." She hesitated. "There's something else. He was monitoring this online discussion group of radical right-wingers that he thought might be connected to the terrorist group we broke up last summer. There was a lot of talk about cop killing, and yesterday a thread started about dogs, and about how killing is too good for anybody who hurts one. Yesterday Buck kept saying, 'It all comes back to the dog.' Does any of this ring a bell for you?"

I shook my head in fierce certainty. "Buck would never hurt a dog."

"Maybe he confronted someone who had."

Desperately, I racked my brain. "I don't know. He didn't say anything to me. And I haven't heard any reports of animal abuse ... I don't know. I'm seeing Stan Bixby this afternoon, he's our shelter manager. I could ask him."

She nodded. "Okay. Let me know what you find out. And ..." She glanced down the corridor toward Buck's room. "Let me know if there's any change. Every minute that we don't catch this SOB ..."

"I know," I said. Every minute that passed without an arrest in a case like this lessened the chances there would ever be one.

She turned to go but I said suddenly, "Wait." The

curtain of fog that trauma and sleeplessness had drawn around my brain parted abruptly, and I said, "The dog. Buck was talking about Mozart, right? The Newfoundland in Rutherford's car. That's what he meant when he said, 'It all comes back to the dog.'"

She nodded cautiously.

"The dog's owner came to get him yesterday," I said. "It turns out he used to be in charge of the rescue group that the Goodwins adopted their dog from. He knew them. He had a little girl with him who was close to Kylie's age, and the way she was with that dog ... the only other time I've seen something like that was with Kylie Goodwin and Mozart. I don't know how any of this ties in, but that's what I called Buck about last night. Carol Goodwin's cousin got in touch with me. She thought she recognized Mozart too. I sent her a picture of the man who came to get him, Scotty Benson, but she never called me back."

Jolene listened to all this with a thoughtful frown on her face, and then she took out her notebook. "Okay, give me details again."

I gave her the names, and the details I could remember, and I looked up Jenna's number on my phone. Jolene wrote it all down, and told me she would look into it. For the first time since all this started, I actually thought she might be taking me seriously.

She hesitated as she tucked away her notebook, and then glanced briefly around the room before settling her gaze on me again. "Stockton," she said, "I'm sorry about what I said last night. It was out of line."

"Yes," I agreed steadily, "it was. And you were wrong. It has nothing to do with self-respect. When you love somebody, you give him a second chance. And a third. And you keep giving until you have nothing left. It's what you do."

She didn't say anything, but I thought her expression softened a little as she nodded an acknowledgement. "Keep me informed," she said, and left.

TWENTY-EIGHT

I went home, showered and changed, and impulsively decided to put Cisco and Pepper in the car before I left to pick up Melanie. Melanie wasn't the only one who'd been neglected during this crisis, and I figured the dogs would enjoy a walk along the creek bank while Melanie did her interview with Stan.

I felt a little better about leaving the hospital when, the last time I went in to see Buck, he opened his eyes groggily and said, in a hoarse, scratchy voice that required many breaths, "If you ... don't stop looking at me ... like that ... I'll call the ... coroner ... myself."

I responded with a grin and a thumbs-up. He was going to be okay.

That's what I told Melanie when she climbed into the car and dropped her backpack onto the floorboard of front seat. She squealed with delight and made a fuss over both dogs, who panted and strained against their seat belts as they tried to lick her face. I was glad I'd brought them.

"We should take Cisco to go see Sheriff Buck," she said, when all three of them had finished their greeting ritual, and she settled down to fasten her seat belt. "I mean," she corrected herself, "Just Plain Old Buck." That made me smile. "We learned in Human and Environmental Studies that petting a dog can lower blood pressure and relieve stress."

"That's right," I said. "That's why we take therapy dogs to the hospital. But we have to ask the doctor first."

"When Pepper passes her therapy dog test, we're going to visit disaster areas," she informed me casually. "You know, to relieve stress in first responders. I was reading about it online."

There was no way I was going to tell her that there was a minimum age requirement for the human partner in a disaster-relief therapy dog team. Fortunately, she didn't wait for a response, but went on, "Dad called at lunch. He said your phone was off."

"Right," I told her. "I was at the hospital all morning." I wondered if she had told her father about waking up alone in the house last night. And why shouldn't she? She told Miles everything, and I was a coward for letting her do it before I had to.

But she went on easily, "He wanted to know if everything is okay, and I told him it was. Like you said ..." She shot a quick glance at me. "He has a lot on his mind. I didn't want to worry him."

I felt my heart twist in my chest. "Melanie ..."

But she interrupted, "Say, I found out some real interesting things about Mr. Bixby today. We're supposed to write a paragraph of background on all the people we interview, so I looked him up on online." She dug her iPad out of her backpack and brought up her notes. "He's pretty famous. He used to be a medic in the Marines."

I smiled weakly. "Is that right?"

"Of course," she went on chattily, "I already know all about you, how you used to be a forest ranger and have like a hundred dog titles ..."

"Well," I began modestly.

"What I really need is more background on Aunt Mart," she went on. "She's kind of the star of the story, since she remembers practically everything about it."

"I don't think she actually remembers it," I felt compelled to point out, but it was so good to hear her chattering along that I was glad to let a few factual inaccuracies slip. Kids, I decided, were amazing.

Stan Bixby's house was a low, lodge-like structure with dark-stained shingle siding and a wraparound front porch. It was secluded from the road by a long dirt driveway that sloped downhill to a flat, wooded, creek-side lot. There was a tin-roofed carport and a barn, as well as a fenced chicken coop, currently unused, that did in fact look a little like a log cabin. A row of chain-link kennels along the side of the house where he usually kept his rescue dogs was empty. I'd been here a couple of times before, and each time I'd been greeted by the raucous sound of barking dogs. It was odd not to see a single one today. Not even Regis.

Melanie looked around eagerly, unfastening her seat belt. "So, where do you think it happened, Raine?" She opened the door and hopped out, going around to the back door to let the dogs out. "The murder," she went on. "The log cabin was on the creek bank, you said. Can I go down there and look?"

"No," I replied firmly. I dug in my purse for some dog treats. I thought I could trust Cisco to behave, but Pepper was a puppy and sometimes forgot her manners. "You're not going down to the creek without me. You're going to go up to the front door and knock politely. I'll get the dogs out of the car and be right behind you."

"Okay," she responded easily, skipping toward the front steps. "Don't forget Pepper!"

She was halfway to the house before I noticed she had left her tablet on the front seat. I picked it up and started to call after her, but then stopped. The screen had come alive in my hand, and it was filled with what appeared to be a newspaper photograph of a much younger Stan Bixby standing with his arm around a woman I presumed to be his wife. A happy-looking, shiny-coated black Lab sat in front of them. The headline read, *Local Man Files Ten-Million-Dollar Lawsuit in Swat-Team Killing.*

I couldn't stop reading.

On the night of June 17, Stanley Bixby and his wife Alice watched the 11:00 news, as they always did, and went to bed. Their three-year-old Labrador retriever, Rio, curled up at the foot of their bed, as she always did. Stanley, who was a former medic in the US Marine Corps, slept with a loaded pistol in the drawer of his bedside table. That was because of his military training, though, not because of any real fear for his safety. The Bixbys lived in a nice neighborhood.

At 1:54 a.m. the front door of the Bixby home was broken open by a battering ram, and a flood of assailants in tactical gear carrying automatic weapons burst in. Rio, barking, ran toward the disturbance. She was shot twice in the head at the front door. Stanley grabbed his gun and ran to the top of the stairs, opening fire. His wife, Alice, recovering from a recent heart surgery, heard the gunfire and ran out of the bedroom, armed only with the telephone with which she was trying to call for help. She collapsed at the top of the stairs and her husband, dropping his weapon, rushed to her aid. He was shot in the shoulder as he attempted to give CPR. Alice Bixby was pronounced dead at the scene by paramedics when they arrived fifteen minutes later.

This was not a gang shooting, nor was it a ruthlessly planned home invasion executed by hardened criminals. The invaders were members of the Jacksonville Police Department's highly trained SWAT team, and they had the wrong address.

"Oh, my God," I whispered.

"He's not there," Melanie said over my shoulder. There was a definite pout of disappointment in her voice. She startled me so badly that I dropped the tablet. "Do you think he forgot? His car is in the carport."

My gaze went to the carport. The back end of a blue Chevy Tahoe could be seen parked inside.

I said hoarsely, "Melanie, get in the car."

"But—"

"Get in the car!" I fumbled in my purse for my phone, dragged it out, pushed the button to unlock it. Nothing happened. I had forgotten it was turned off.

Melanie still hadn't moved. She stood at my open door, a stubborn look on her face. "What about Cisco?" she demanded.

I swung my gaze to the backseat. Pepper was lying on the bench seat like a perfect lady, safely secured in her seatbelt, paws crossed, eyes on Melanie. Cisco's seat was empty.

I swiveled back to Melanie. "You unfastened his seat belt?" There was just the faintest note of hysterical accusation in my voice. "You let him out?"

She replied defensively, "You said you were right behind me!"

I looked wildly around the yard, but my heart didn't stop pounding in my chest until I spotted Cisco's gold-and-white tail feathers trotting confidently into the barn. I grabbed a leash from the glove compartment and climbed out of the car.

"Get in," I told Melanie. "Lock the doors. I'll be right back."

But panic flashed in her eyes. She grabbed my arm. "You're not going to leave me?"

There was real desperation in her voice, and it stabbed

at my heart. No, I was not going to leave her. How could I leave her?

I grabbed her hand. "Come on," I said.

We moved quickly across the yard; Melanie running, me trotting. I held on to her hand as tightly as I knew how, and my heart was pounding in my throat. All I could hear was the hiss of my own breath rushing in my ears. Even the rumbling of the creek was muted.

But when we entered the barn, all was calm. The sunshine slanting through the open doors showed dust motes and spider webs, nursery pots and bags of mulch. There were the usual garden tools, a lawn mower, some neatly stacked pieces of lumber in the corner. A couple of dog crates were lined up against the wall, and there was a grooming table in the center of the room. Cisco, with his infallible tracking instincts, had gone straight to the smell of other dogs.

"Cisco," I called, and he turned to grin at me with a companionable wag of his tail. It was my fault. I had meant to sound commanding, but the word was barely above a gasp.

He trotted over to a workbench that was attached to the wall and started sniffing the floor around it. As soon as I reached him I saw why. There was a bag of dog treats on the bench, and I suspected some crumbs had scattered on the floor. Cisco noticed the treats as soon as I did and put his paws up on the bench. I quickly snapped the leash on his collar.

"Hey," said Melanie, looking around. "Pretty cool. He has a lot more stuff than you do at Dog Daze, Raine."

She was referring to the shelves above the workbench that held veterinary supplies—most of them, I guessed, taken home from the animal shelter. There was nothing wrong with that; the shelter regularly shared supplies and medications with foster homes and rescue groups when we had excess, and Stan wouldn't even have had to ask. There were boxes of heartworm pills and flea and tick preventatives, medicated shampoos and vitamin supplements. There were cartons of gauze and vet wrap bandages, as well as first-aid sprays and ointments. There was also a box of hypodermic needles, and several small vials of injectable medications. I saw Ivermectin, a common dewormer; acepromazine, a sedative for anxious animals; Adequan for arthritis, and secobarbital. Seconal.

I picked the vial up, staring at it as though the mere act of holding it could give me the answers. It couldn't, but that didn't matter. I already had all the answers I needed.

Ours is not a no-kill shelter. We use Seconal, also known as secobarbital, to euthanize those animals who are too sick or temperamentally unsound to be adopted. I know this because I am on the board of directors and twice a year approve expenses for a list of medications including, unfortunately, euthanasia drugs. Stan, our shelter manager, is trained in the procedure and therefore responsible for euthanizing the unadoptable dogs. I knew he had also humanely put down some of his senior rescue dogs when the time came. There was no reason for him not to have this drug on hand. None at all.

"Raine?"

I whirled guiltily at the sound of the voice behind me. Cisco, always ready to say hello, spun away from the workbench and scrambled to greet the newcomer. I tightened the leash and pulled Cisco back to my side. Stan Bixby stood at the door of the barn in knee-high mud boots over his cotton work khakis. Regis, panting from the exertions of age, was beside him. Stan's long-sleeved shirt was open over a faded green tee shirt with an etching of a Labrador retriever on it, but I saw the shape of a gun holster beneath his shirttails.

I closed my hand over the bottle of Seconal in my hand, trying to hide it, but too late. Stan's eyes flickered to the gesture, and then to the shelf where the bottle had been. He looked at me, and I know he saw the truth in my eyes. I know it because there was a moment—just a moment—when his own gaze flooded with sadness. And then it was gone.

He said, "Sorry I didn't hear you drive up. I was down at the creek."

Melanie said, "We were looking for you. Say, are you wearing a gun?"

He smiled at her. His expression was pleasant, but there was something distant about that smile. "Lots of copperheads this time of year, sweetheart. I killed two last week. You be careful when you're out walking in the woods." He turned his gaze to me, and there was no mistaking it now. His smile did not reach his eyes. "You, too."

I said, "We have to go." Melanie swiveled her head to look up at me incredulously, but I plowed on. "There's been an emergency. At home. I just stopped by to let you know. We can't stay. I'm sorry."

Melanie objected, "But Raine ..."

I put the bottle of Seconal on the table. I had to, so that I could grasp Melanie's shoulder. "We have to go," I repeated   firmly.

Stan came into the room, moving toward us. Regis looked as though he might follow him, then changed his mind and plopped down in a patch of sun outside the door. I wound another loop in Cisco's leash around my wrist, and I couldn't help it—my hand tightened on Melanie's shoulder until she squirmed.

"Raine!" she complained, and then turned to Stan. "Mr. Bixby, it'll only take a minute, I promise, and I'll be careful of copperheads. If you'll just show me where …"

"No," I said. Even I could tell that what I had intended to be firmness in my tone sounded like desperation. "No, we can't stay. Melanie, you go to the car. I'll be there in a minute."

"But—"

"You know," said Stan easily, "I'll bet that's what that shooting was about yesterday." He was very close to us now, and I took a step back. "You know, the one Buck Lawson asked me about? Somebody shooting snakes."

"Yeah," I managed. "That was probably it."

"And if a shot went wild," he suggested, "maybe crossed the creek, it would've just been a warning. About snakes."

I nodded, swallowing hard. "Right."

He was right in front of us now. I took another step back and dropped my hand from Melanie's shoulder to wrap it around her chest, pulling her close to me. She twisted around to look at me again with an outraged look, but something about my face must have stopped her from speaking. Cisco, sensing the tension through the leash, plopped down into a sit at my feet, panting hard.

Stan picked up the bottle of Seconal, turning it over in his hand. His expression grew regretful as he looked at it. "Regis doesn't have much longer. Sometimes I have to carry him outside at night. That's no way for a dog to live. But I wanted him to have one more chance to show off for the kids, and he sure did that at the school yesterday, didn't he?"

I swallowed hard. "He did great," I said. "Everybody loved him."

Melanie clutched my arm with both hands, and I

realized my grip had tightened. I loosened it.

"Melanie needs to go to the car," I said, pleading. "She left her dog there. She needs to go check on Pepper. It's okay if she goes, right?"

Stan swung a sharp look on me, his eyes hot. "I was a Marine," he barked at me. "I don't hurt kids. Or dogs."

Melanie must have understood then that something was wrong. Her eyes were worried when she looked up at me, and she gripped the hand that crossed her chest.

I said on a breath, "I know that, Stan. Only someone who loves dogs the way you do would have stopped that day and picked up the lost Newfie. Even though ..." My heart was pounding in my ears, almost drowning out my words. "Even though you had more important things to do."

He scowled abruptly, remembering. "This never should have happened. All of that ... that ugliness, it belonged in another life. It was finished. Why couldn't Rutherford leave well enough alone? I put it all behind me, tried to make something out of my life. I used the settlement money to build this place, start the Lab rescue, to be the kind of man my wife would have wanted. It should have been over."

He let a silence fall, long and heavy, lost in his thoughts. I looked at Cisco, who was panting nervously at my side, his gaze moving from Melanie to me. I slipped my hand into my pocket, trying not to rattle the dog treat bag.

Stan went on abruptly, "And then Rutherford came strolling in here, knowing too much, asking too many questions, bringing it all back to life again. What choice did I have? He surprised me here in the barn and I knew I had to stop him. He left me no choice. I knew if I made it look like he was just a tourist who went for a hike and drowned in the creek, no one would question. And it almost worked. I put him in his own car and drove it to the park ..."

He shook his head briefly. "And then the dog. The damn thing ran right out in front of me. I thought I'd hit him. What was I supposed to do? But when I got out to check, he jumped right in the open door. What was I supposed to do?" He looked at me with eyes filled with sorrow. "I meant to be right back. I never would have left the dog there in the car. I dragged Rutherford down to the creek, but before I could get back I heard your car drive up. I climbed up the hill and watched you from the woods until you got him out. And then ..." He gave a short, wry shake of his head. "Both the dogs took off up the creek and I thought for sure they'd lead you straight to me. Especially Cisco. But then I remembered the car keys, and I threw them, and that distracted Cisco long enough for me to get down the hill and across the creek to my house. It wasn't until later that I realized how stupid that had been. The keys had my prints all over them. It's a wonder Cisco didn't lead you right to them that day."

I said simply, "He probably would have, if we had known what to look for. But we didn't."

"I can't tell you how many hours I spent looking for them," Stan said. His tone was almost ruminating. "There was no way to guess where they'd landed. But then you came back. Cisco's a good dog, great nose. I knew the minute I saw you there from across the creek, I knew what you were looking for. And I knew you'd find them."

He turned to the workbench, his back to us, and reached for the box of hypodermics on the shelf.

I took Melanie's hand and carefully unwound her

fingers from mine. I dropped Cisco's leash. I bent down and whispered fiercely into her ear, "Run! Get Cisco and *run!*"

At the same moment I withdrew from my pocket a wad of smushed-up liver treats and I tossed it toward the door with all my power. Cisco immediately bolted after it. I cried in what I hoped was a good imitation of surprise, "Oh!"

Melanie cried, "I'll get him!" and she took off at a run.

Stan whirled from the workbench with an uncapped hypodermic in his hand. I took advantage of his moment of distraction to lunge toward the bench, hoping to knock the bottle of Seconal out of his reach. But I wasn't fast enough. He took a quick step toward me, blocking my way, and I threw up my hands in a gesture of surrender, breathing hard.

Out of the corner of my eye I saw Melanie scoop up Cisco's leash and keep running. Stan saw it too, but he did nothing to stop them. Regis lumbered to his feet and gave a single bark of acknowledgement, then lost interest. He plopped back down into his patch of sunny ground.

Stan looked at me with sad eyes. "You didn't have to do that," he said quietly. "I wasn't going to hurt her. And Cisco ... you know me better than that, Raine."

He turned back to the workbench, this time positioning himself between me and the door. I shot a quick desperate glance toward that square of open sunlight, calculating my chances of making it past him. But he had a gun. What were the odds of making it to the car without drawing his fire, and how could I risk Melanie accidentally being caught in that gunfire?

I concentrated on relaxing my shoulders, breathing evenly, trying to appear calm. After a moment, my heart stopped pounding in my throat long enough for me to speak.

"Stan," I said, "what happened to your wife—and your dog—was unforgiveable. The SWAT team was wrong. If I had my way, the people responsible would all go to jail. But the men you killed ... most of them were just following orders. They had families too. And James Rutherford, he had a wife, a son, grandchildren."

Stan's back was still to me. He focused on what he was doing at the workbench. "Here's something interesting," he said. His voice was almost casual. "The justice system uses actuarial tables to decide what a life is worth. Because my Alice had a preexisting heart condition, they decided her life was only worth $1,000,000. Do you know what a dog's life is worth? Nothing." He was silent for a moment, contemplating this. Then he said, "I could have killed them all that night, you know, when they broke into my house. It would have been self-defense. But when Alice collapsed ... well. I had to make a choice, didn't I?"

He turned then and looked at me. He had the hypodermic in his hand, filled with liquid. He said, "I want you to know I've got nothing against Lawson. I just needed to slow him down. He was getting too close, and after you found the keys ..."

I swallowed hard. "You shot Buck ... because I told you about finding the keys in the woods?"

"My fingerprints are in the system," he said. "I was in the military and ..." There might even have been a small smile in his voice. "I had to be fingerprinted to volunteer at the school. How about that for irony? Still, I thought if I could slow down the investigation, just a little, it would give me a chance to figure out what to do. Maybe give Regis a few more good days. But I was wrong. I'm out of options. There's no place left to run."

"What," I said hoarsely, "are you going to do?"

"Nothing," said a sharp voice from the door. It was Jolene, and she was flanked by two deputies. All of them had their weapons drawn. "He's not going to do anything. Drop the syringe, Mr. Bixby, and put your hands over your head."

Something flickered across Stan's eyes—regret, perhaps, or simple resignation. He said to me, "You'll take care of Regis, won't you?"

Jolene's voice grew more forceful. "Sir! I won't tell you again! Drop the syringe and put your hands over your head. Do it now!"

He moved his hand downward, as though to drop the hypodermic on the floor. He said to me again, "Won't you?"

"Yes," I managed, watching him. "Of course I will."

He plunged the syringe into his thigh.

TWENTY-NINE

Stan was still alive when they loaded him into the ambulance, but the looks on the EMTs' faces were grim. Jolene and I had both worked on him, giving CPR until the paramedics got there, and it looked as though he might not have gotten the full dose of Seconal. But there was genuine doubt whether he would ever be able to testify in his own defense.

"How did you get here so fast?" I asked Jolene as we watched the ambulance drive away. A moment later I realized it was a stupid question.

"We were on our way when Miss Young's 911 call came in," she said. She glanced over at Melanie, who sat cross-legged in the open cargo area of my SUV, an arm around each of the golden retrievers, watching the activity alertly. Jolene added, clearly enough so that Melanie could hear, "Good thing she called, though. She let us know there was a gun, otherwise we might have walked in blind."

Melanie looked pleased with herself, but also a little worried. I gave her an encouraging smile, even though smiling was the last thing I felt like doing.

Jolene walked a few steps away, gesturing with a nod that I should follow.

"We found a freshly dug grave down by the creek," she said quietly. "It looks like he planned to put the dog down, and then commit suicide. He knew we were closing in."

I nodded slowly, suppressing a shudder. "How did ... how did you figure out it was him?"

"I didn't," she admitted. "Buck did. The notes were in his desk, and the fingerprint report came back. Bixby's prints were all over Rutherford's car, and the keys. Buck was able to talk to me for a little while this afternoon. He said he figured out that one of the people on that radical forum I was telling you about was Bixby. Mountain Man 904. He said some pretty incriminating things. Buck sent him a direct message last night, asking him to come in for an interview this morning. Looks like that's what probably got him shot."

I blew out a shaky breath. "I thought ... it was because of me. Because I told him about the investigation, and about finding the keys."

She replied dryly, "Not everything is about you, Stockton."

My eyes wandered across the yard. There were uniforms everywhere, securing the scene, collecting evidence. Every now and then, one of the deputies would pause to scratch Regis's ears or give him a belly rub. The power of a therapy dog at work.

"I promised to take care of his dog," I said. "Do you think—would it be possible to get one of the deputies to drop him off later? I need to get Melanie home."

She followed my gaze to Regis, who had found his patch of sun again, and two deputies who knelt to pet him. "I don't think that will be a problem," she said. "Matter of fact, I wouldn't be surprised if one of these boys decided to take him home himself."

I hoped so. Despite what Stan said, I thought Regis still had a lot of good days left.

Melanie was thoughtful on the way home. "Raine," she asked finally, turning a troubled gaze on me. "Was Mr. Bixby a bad man?"

I was careful about my answer. "I don't think so," I said. "Mr. Bixby had some bad things happen to him, and people don't always know how to deal with that. It's like you said, remember? Sometimes the good guys get it wrong."

"Yeah." She sighed. "I don't know what I'm going to do about my essay, though."

I reached across the seat and squeezed her hand. "Hey, you did great today," I told her. "You heard what Deputy Smith said. You saved the day by telling the 911 dispatcher about the gun. You might even get some kind of medal of valor or something."

She brightened. "Hey, yeah. I might. That'd be something, huh?"

I made up my mind right then that she would in fact get a medal, if I had to make it myself.

I have never been so glad in my life to see the familiar SUV parked in my driveway … or so sorry. Melanie cried, "Dad!" and unbuckled her seat belt before the car even stopped moving. Miles came down from the front porch with his arms outstretched and she ran into them.

"Dad, you're home! Boy, you won't believe what happened! Just wait 'til you hear!"

He swept her up into his arms and swung her around, making a big show of kissing her face all over, and she squealed and scrunched up her face and pretended to slap him away, giggling all the while. "Dad, I'm serious! Wait 'til you hear! I was a hero!"

"You're always my hero, sweetheart."

He set her on her feet and his eyes met mine, smiling, across the hood of the car. By this time I had released the dogs from the backseat, and they both scampered forward to join the party. Miles rewarded them with dog biscuits and ear scratches, and then told Melanie, "Go get your things together for school tomorrow, and you can tell me all about your big day over dinner at that Italian place on the highway. It looks like you and Raine could both use a night out."

"Cool," she agreed readily. "They're the ones that put your pizza on a cake stand, just like that place we used to go to in New York, remember, Dad? You'll like it, Raine!" She raced off to the house, with both dogs trying to outdo themselves to beat her there.

Miles's smile gentled with compassion as he opened his arms to me. I walked into them, melting into his embrace, pressing my face against the rock-solid strength of his chest. I wrapped my arms around him and for the longest time I just held on to him, my anchor in a rocking sea. I squeezed my eyes shut against the furious blur of hot tears and I held on, for as long as I could. "You came," I managed finally. "You came."

He kissed my hair. "Of course I did, sugar. I left as soon as I got your text this morning."

"But your mom …"

"She's fine." He stroked my back. "She's got more personal health-care workers taking care of her than the queen of England, and besides, she was a little too eager to see me go." There was a hint of a rueful smile in his voice. "I think I might have been getting on her nerves."

"Miles, I …"

He took my face in his hands and he kissed me. That was all I'd ever wanted, and more than I would ever deserve. I stepped away, my heart aching. "Miles …"

"Marshal gave me the details," he said. "I was worried when I couldn't reach you. The latest update is that Buck is going to be fine. But you don't need to be going through this alone. And ..." He smiled as he wiped a tear from the corner of my eye with his thumb. "No offense, but you look a little rough. Why don't you go shower and change for dinner? I'll help Melanie pack."

I moved back, lowering my arms to my sides and closing my fists for courage. I said, as steadily as I could, "I have to tell you something. I screwed up. Last night ... last night when I got the call about Buck, I was in such a panic ... I forgot about Melanie. I left the house and I forgot about her, I left her alone. It's like, it's like they always say about those parents who forget and leave their kids in the car, when something breaks your routine ... I left her alone and there could have been a fire or a break-in or ..." I drew a ragged breath. "I called Corny to come stay with her, and Marshal sent a deputy to watch the house, and I thought she'd be okay. I thought she wouldn't even miss me. But I was wrong. She woke up alone and she was terrified, Miles. When I got home, she was practically hysterical, and I know it was the worst thing I could do, the worst possible thing I could do to a child who's just lost her mother, and ..." I sucked in a choked breath. "I'm so sorry, but I don't think I can do this. I wasn't meant to be a parent. I'm no good at it. I just ... I can't do this."

With every word I spoke I saw his eyes grow more distant, his face grow tighter. I saw his muscles tense and his breath slow. Eventually, he looked away from me. He said into the distance, "You left her. For Buck."

There was absolutely nothing I could say. Nothing.

When he looked back at me, there was such sorrow in his eyes, such disappointment and regret, that it was almost more than I could bear. "Raine Stockton," he said quietly. He caressed my cheek, briefly cupping the side of my face, and then let his hand drop. "I always knew you'd break my heart someday."

He went into the house to help Melanie pack, and he did not speak to me again.

THIRTY

It's funny, how when everything is going right in your life, the things you love fade into the background. You take them for granted. Your friends. Your family. Your dogs. But when your life starts to come apart at the seams, suddenly those are the only things that matter. I'd barely noticed Cisco over the past week, I'd been so consumed with Melanie and Mozart and the myriad of things that surrounded them, all of them pecking at my brain. But over the next twenty-four hours all I wanted to do was hug Cisco, and his fur was wet with my tears.

That's the great thing about dogs. They're there when you need them, and even when you don't.

Buck was going to be okay. I knew this because, when I teased him about toddling from the hospital bed to the chair with his walker, he flipped me off. It made me laugh. And made me cry.

Stan Bixby was still in a coma, his condition guarded. But Regis had in fact found a home with one of the deputies, a single guy who understood that while his time with the old dog might not be long, it would be rich. I guess that's all any of us can ask for.

Two days after Buck's shooting, I returned home from visiting him in the hospital to find two police cars parked in front of Dog Daze. One had the familiar insignia of the Hanover County Sheriff's Office on it. The other was a black cruiser with gold lettering on the door that read, Hampton Crossing Police Department. When I went inside the building I was surprised to see Sheriff Marshal

Becker there, rubbing Cisco's ears and making a fuss over him, along with Jolene. A woman in jeans and a ponytail was petting the two Aussie girls, while another woman— pale, blonde, and tense looking—stood by awkwardly. With them was a middle-aged man in a dark blue police uniform who looked vaguely familiar to me. Corny, behind the counter, gave me a helpless, confused look and said, "Um, Miss Stockton. These people just got here."

The man in the policeman's uniform stepped forward and offered his hand. "Miss Stockton, you probably don't remember me. I'm Lin Booker, Hampton Crossing Police Chief. I worked with you on the Kylie Goodwin search some years back. I was on street patrol back then, but I remember you and your dog well, and how generous it was of you to come all the way to South Carolina to help out."

I shook his hand, beginning to put the pieces together. Marshal straightened up from petting Cisco and Cisco bounded over to me. "We probably should have called first, Raine," Marshal said, "but all things considered, it seemed faster to let these people explain the situation to you themselves."

The woman who'd been playing with the Aussies came over to me, offering her hand. "I'm Jenna," she said. "We talked on the phone. And this is my cousin Carol."

"Carol Goodwin," I said slowly, turning to her.

She nodded and forced a smile that quickly faded. "I remember this place," she said. "It looked different back then, and of course I..." she swallowed hard. "I was different back then. But I came for the puppy's graduation, remember?"

I nodded dumbly.

Jenna spoke up quickly. "I didn't know what to do

when I saw that photo you sent. That was definitely Scotty, and that was definitely Mozart, but kids ... they change so much. How could I be sure? Finally I decided to send the picture to Carol ..."

"It's her," Carol said tightly. She crossed her arms over her chest and squeezed her elbows until her knuckles were white, as though trying to restrain the emotions that threatened to burst through. "It's her eyes, her cheekbones ... You said he called her Chris, right? Kylie's middle name was Christina. Her father used to call her that sometimes. Kylie Christina. It's my baby, I know it. It's my fault she's gone, I take responsibility for that, but if there's even a chance of getting her back, even after all these years ..."

I said uncertainly, "Your fault?"

She drew in a breath and straightened her shoulders, but did not let go of her arms. "I'm an alcoholic," she said, "recovering now and clean for five years. But back then ... I was drinking so heavily that I would lose whole days. Jason threatened to take Kylie and leave so many times, but I told him I'd make sure he never got custody and he knew I could do it, too. My father had money, influence, and he would never have let Jason take Kylie. I kept telling the police, when Kylie disappeared, that it was Jason, but they thought I meant he had hurt her, not taken her. And I was so messed up ... I was hardly even conscious most of the time. I couldn't think, I couldn't remember ... and nobody ever thought that Jason might have hidden her away somewhere. Or that he had an accomplice."

I said carefully, "Did you know about Scotty?"

She hesitated, her eyes filling with weary sadness. "Not him, specifically. I don't think I ever would have guessed it was him. I suppose I must have known on some level that Jason was gay, but something like that ... it's so hard to come to terms with. I knew he was in love with someone else, but it was easier to believe it was a woman. Everything from those days is such a blur. If I'd only paid attention, if I'd only been able to think, I might have been able to point the police in the right direction. But if it hadn't been for my drinking, Jason never would have been forced to do what he did ... to protect Kylie from me."

I wonder if she knew her ex-husband was now dead. But it wasn't up to me to tell her.

Desperation crept back into Carol Goodwin's eyes. "Please, Miss Stockton. I know it's her in that photograph. I know it's Kylie. You've got to tell us where she is."

"I told her we should go to the police," Jenna said. "And so ..." She cast her gaze toward the police chief.

"It seemed worth an interview," the police chief said, "and we have a court order for a DNA sample."

"Deputy Smith said the gentleman told you they were staying somewhere here in the county," Marshal said. "And that you might recognize the vehicle."

I nodded. "He said he was cleaning out his mother's cabin in Rock Hill, to get it ready for sale. I could take you up there."

Marshal gestured toward the front door. "Let's go."

I rode in the sheriff's office car with Marshal and Jolene, and the other police car followed. The truth is, they probably could have found the place just as quickly without me. The first clue was the big black dog, barking from behind the railing of the cabin's front porch. The second clue was the young girl swinging on the tire swing that hung from an oak tree a few feet away.

We got out of the car, one at a time, poised with

expectancy, looking around. The little girl jumped down from the swing and called, "Buzzy! Quiet!" The big dog stopped barking, licked his chops restlessly, and settled into a sit.

The child started toward us, then stopped, her eyes growing big when she saw the gun on Jolene's belt and the uniform she wore. She called, "Daddy! Daddy, people are here!"

In a moment the door opened, and Scotty came out. He looked at me first in confusion, and then to Jenna in startled recognition. Then his eyes fell on Carol, who stood with her hand at her throat, her bright gaze fixed on the child. Understanding settled onto Scotty's face, along with a measure of quiet inevitability.

"Carol," he said. He smiled tiredly. "So you figured it out."

"It turns out that Jason Goodwin got his cancer diagnosis a few months before Kylie disappeared," I explained to Buck that night when I visited him. "That's when he knew he had to get Kylie away from Carol, and he and Scotty came up with the plan."

Interestingly enough, my visit to Buck had coincided with Jolene's, and she hadn't left when I came in. Perhaps even more interesting, Jolene was wearing jeans and sandals and a casual cotton shirt, with earrings and a baseball cap. I'd never seen her in civvies before.

She picked up the story. "Apparently they kept them both at Scotty Benson's house for the first couple of days. The girl couldn't be separated from her dog, and they figured the only place a big black dog wouldn't be noticed was in a yard filled with other big black dogs. When the

261

police found the child's pajamas in the lake and turned their attention to interrogating Jason Goodwin, Scotty moved the dog and the child here, to his mother's cabin."

"It was winter by then," I reminded Buck, "and Rock Hill would've been deserted. No one would even think to look for them there."

"They were taking a hell of a chance," Buck said. His voice was still raspy and his breathing labored, and he tired easily. But he grew stronger and more alert each time I saw him. "The police were ready to arrest Goodwin. He would have lost everything."

"The sheriff said the same thing," Jolene agreed. "The plan was that if Jason was arrested, Kylie would simply reappear. A failed kidnapping with no suspect."

Buck shook his head slowly against the pillow. "A bad plan."

"But it worked," Jolene pointed out.

"Over the winter," I went on, "Scotty took Kylie and Mozart to Missouri. The police had no leads and the case was growing cold. Jason divorced Carol and followed Scotty. They bought a farm close enough to Kansas City for Jason to get his treatments, but far enough out in the country so that they could keep to themselves. They changed Kylie's name, and hair color, and even her age. They changed Mozart's name. Jason worked a bunch of low-profile jobs, just enough to keep his health insurance going, and Scotty ran his CPA business from home so that he could home-school Kylie."

"Kids are pretty impressionable at that age," Jolene said. "Pretty soon she forgot all about the life she used to have, and the woman who used to be her mother. As far as Kylie knew, she was just a girl with two daddies, like a lot of kids these days."

"But I think Scotty must've known they weren't going

to be able to keep up the lie after Jason died," I said. "Eventually Kylie would have to go to school, or college, or get a job, and that means a social security number and all kinds of other legal paperwork. I think Scotty loves Kylie, but he seemed relieved to have it all out in the open."

"What will happen to her?" Buck asked.

"That's the sad part," Jolene said. "She's in foster care until they unravel this whole mess. Benson will probably be charged with kidnapping. And in the end, custody of the child will be awarded to a mother she doesn't even know."

"But," I put in hopefully, "Carol Goodwin did take Mozart home with her. When Kylie comes home, it'll make the transition easier."

Again, Buck shook his head, this time in disbelief. "And to think," he said, "if Stan Bixby, a stone-cold cop killer, hadn't stopped to pick up that dog on his way to dispose of a body, none of this would have ever happened. That child never would have been reunited with her mother, and Carol Goodwin never would have known what happened to her little girl. Life is funny, huh?"

We talked for a little while longer, but we both could see that Buck was getting tired. We said good night, and Jolene and I walked to the elevators together. The silence was awkward for a moment, and then I said, "It was nice of you to come see him."

She pushed the elevator button. "The sheriff wanted me to keep him up to date on the cases," she said. "And," she added as we waited for the elevator to arrive, "my mama would have had my hide if I hadn't. She likes him."

I smiled a little. "Everybody likes Buck."

The elevator dinged and the door slid open. We got inside.

"It's good to have family around," Jolene said, "to remind you of who you're supposed to be. How you're supposed to act."

I think that was the closest thing to something personal Jolene had ever said to me. I literally did not know how to respond.

The elevator opened in the lobby and we got out. "Nice working with you, Stockton," she said. "See you in church."

I stood still, staring at her. "Wh-what?" I managed.

But she just grinned and sauntered away.

THIRTY-ONE

Miles called several times over the next couple of days, but I did not pick up. There would be plenty of time for that agonizing goodbye, the gut-wrenching words, the regrets, the sorrow. The returning of the ring. I was a coward. I wasn't ready. I knew it was coming, but I couldn't face it. So I didn't pick up.

I put on a cheerful voice for Melanie when she called to read me her essay. It was a story about brave pioneers and the legacy of the land, with slightly less emphasis on the murder than I had expected. According to her, history often makes judgments based on one side of the story or the other, while the truth usually lies somewhere in between. I could see her father's deft hand in that last, and it made my heart twist with pride … and yearning.

"I sure do wish you and Dad would get over your fight," she said, just before she hung up. "It's starting to get on my nerves."

That did make me laugh, but as soon as we hung up, the laughter turned to tears.

I did not see Jolene at church that Sunday, but I did see Melanie, who waved gaily to me from the portico before turning to Aunt Mart, eagerly showing off something made of construction paper and beads. Aunt Mart waved to me and beamed beneficently, and the two of them turned to go inside.

I had decided to put in an appearance partly for Aunt Mart's sake, but mostly because, after everything that had happened over the past week, I felt that church was where I needed to be. I wondered whether I'd made the right decision when I looked across the yard and saw Miles, looking like something I'd dreamed up in a light-colored sports jacket and a yellow shirt, standing with Uncle Ro and Marshal and a couple of the other community leaders, talking to them and chuckling with them as though he had been doing so all his life. He saw me standing there awkwardly on the sidewalk, excused himself to the others, and came over to me. My heart was pounding like a high-school girl who was hoping to be asked to the prom by the most popular guy in town— and who was terrified she wouldn't be.

His eyes were crinkled against the morning sun as he looked at me, making it difficult to read his expression. He said, "I was hoping you'd be here." And then he smiled. "I understand it's not always a regular thing with you."

I didn't answer. I was too busy waiting for the anvil to fall.

He touched my arm. "We've got a few minutes before the service starts. Can we talk?"

We walked over to a low stone wall that bordered a wildflower garden and sat down. People dressed in their Sunday best, clutching the hands of toddlers or chatting companionably with their spouses, passed in front of us. I smiled at the ones I knew, which was almost everyone.

"So," Miles said, "you're a hard person to get hold of."

I determinedly looked anywhere but at him. I said tightly, "It's been a long week, Miles."

He fixed his gaze on something across the parking lot: a toddler in a pretty spring dress chasing after her big brother. He said, "You'll admit I had a right to be upset."

I didn't even try to argue.

"I know there's a part of you that will always love Buck," he went on. "I came to terms with that a long time ago, and in a way it's one of the things I admire most about you. That doesn't mean I don't get to act like a fool now and then when I think he's coming between us." Now he looked at me. "But you chose me. You said yes to me. I know you didn't do that lightly. I just wish you'd remember that a little more often."

I said quickly, "Miles, I—"

He held up a staying hand. "You had every right to go to Buck's side when he needed you. You would have done the same for me, even if you'd had to fly halfway across the world to do it. I don't doubt that for a minute."

He was right. I would have. Somehow hearing him say it filled me with a wild surge of hope … hope that was all but dashed with his next words.

"Raine," he said, "I wasn't hurt by what you did, but what you said. You're like a rabbit in the woods, poised to bolt every time you hear a twig crack, and how do you think that makes me feel?"

I objected, "I don't mean to—"

He went on, "You'll walk into gunfire, lead an expedition through a blizzard, rescue a child lost in the woods, face down a killer … but every time things get a little complicated between us, you throw up your hands and walk away."

Again, I protested, "I don't—"

"That's exactly what you do," he returned firmly, "and I need you to stop it."

I said helplessly, "Miles, I never …"

He took my chin between his thumb and forefinger

and turned my face toward him. There was nothing I could do but look into those quiet, sincere, brutally honest eyes. He said gently, "Are you in this with me or not, Raine Stockton? I need to hear it."

I said without hesitation, "Yes. I am. But Miles …"

He placed his index finger across my lips. "There's nothing that comes after that," he told me firmly. "Nothing."

He dropped his fingers from my face, and I looked away, trying to compose myself.

"Melanie told me about all your adventures," he said. "How you protected her from Stan Bixby and tricked Cisco into running away so that she could escape and call 911. How you stayed behind and kept him talking even though he had a gun. You know the one thing she didn't tell me about?"

He was silent for so long that I had to look at him again. "She didn't tell me," he said deliberately, "about waking up scared and alone at your house the night you went to the hospital. When I finally asked her about it, she told me she didn't say anything because she didn't want me to be mad at you. That's how much she loves you."

I swallowed hard. "That doesn't change the fact that I …"

"Made a mistake? Yes, you did," he said. "Fortunately, Melanie has one parent who's never done that in his life."

I looked at him in surprise, and his expression gentled. "Honey, I've been a full-time dad for less than two years. God knows I've made enough mistakes in that time to keep Melanie in therapy until she's middle-aged. We're both learning. We'll both screw up. But I told you when I made you Mel's guardian that I'd never separate you two.

We're all in this together. And I'm sorry if the way I reacted the other day made you think differently."

I looked at him. My throat was so tight, my heart was so full, I didn't think I could speak. But I did. "You keep coming back," I said. "I keep giving you reasons to leave, I keep expecting you to leave … and you keep coming back."

He took my hand, lacing his fingers through mine. "And I always will," he said. "You should know that about me by now." He looked down at my hand, tracing the stones of my ring with his fingertip—first the bright solitaire, then the dark chocolate diamonds. "Light and dark," he reminded me. "Through good and bad, thick and thin … That's what you do when you love someone. Right?"

I brushed away the burning in my eyes with an impatient fist. I didn't want to miss a minute of what I saw in his eyes, and what I saw made me smile. "Right," I said.

He brought my fingers to his lips and kissed them lightly. "So," he said, "you should probably know I'm in negotiations with Mom about moving down here."

I caught a breath of surprise and delight. "Miles, seriously?"

He lifted a cautionary finger. "Nothing's been settled yet, but talks are ongoing. You and I have big, complicated lives. So does Mel, if it comes to that, and so does Mom. But I think it'll be easier for all of us to manage if we're together. And you know what you were asking the other day, about where we're going to live when we get married. I think I have a plan. It might take a little engineering, but the possibility for a family compound exists, you know. We have three houses between us, and a network of trails connecting them. No one's life or business has to be disrupted. I know that's what you were worried about. We can make this work, sugar. All we have to do is want to."

I didn't even have to think about that. I said simply, "I want to."

I drew in a deep, glorious breath. The entire world suddenly smelled like sunshine and wildflowers. I turned to him. "I was thinking October," I said. "The leaves will be gorgeous from your deck, and we can see the waterfall. Melanie and Pepper will be the flower girls, and Cisco will be the ring bearer."

"Naturally." He smiled.

"Just family," I cautioned. "Nothing fancy."

"Maybe a string quartet," he put in, because he always has to be a little contrary, mostly just to see if I'll notice.

This time I surprised him. "Maybe," I said.

He added, "I could probably get Elton John to perform."

I slanted him a look. "Don't push it."

"Nick Jonas, then."

I said, "Maybe Jenny from the church choir."

He kissed my fingers lightly. "Whatever you want."

We sat there for a long moment, smiling at each other in a perfectly ridiculous, completely comfortable way, and I was aware that, for as long I was looking at him, I wanted nothing else in this world.

As though on cue, the church bells began to ring. I stood. "Let's go in," I said. "I've got a lot of thanking to do today."

We moved to the sidewalk with the other families who were strolling toward the sanctuary. "Me too, sugar," he said. "Me too."

And so, hand-in-hand, we walked into the church.

EPILOGUE

July

I walked with Melanie up the dirt path from Buck's garden toward the house. Melanie struggled with the weight of a wicker basket filled with tomatoes, while I carried a similar basket of zucchini and yellow squash. I could feel the flush of the sun on my bare shoulders and sweat had soaked my hair beneath my straw hat. Cisco and Pepper, the smartest members of our garden committee, had deserted us for the shade of the porch fifteen minutes into our vegetable-picking enterprise, and now lay panting and watching as we mounted the steps.

"Thanks for the help, boys," I said, addressing both canines and humans as I set my basket on the porch floor with a thump. Cisco and Pepper, tails wagging, got up to inspect the produce.

Buck lifted the cane that was propped against his chair. "Hey, I have an excuse."

"Me, too," said Uncle Ro, pouring me a glass of lemonade from the pitcher by his chair. "It's too blasted hot." He handed me the glass with a twinkle in his eye.

I swept off my hat, blotted my forehead with my arm, and chugged the lemonade. Melanie came up behind me and Uncle Ro got up to help her with the basket.

"Boy, you sure do have a lot of tomatoes," Melanie declared. "What're you going to do with them all?"

"Give them to you," Buck replied. "After all, I wouldn't even have a garden if it hadn't been for you."

The truth was, just about everyone in the community

had come together to help with Buck's garden, resulting in one of the lushest, most abundant crops in the county. He had already supplied two church suppers and a Rotary Club dinner with fresh produce, and harvest season had barely begun.

Melanie wrinkled up her nose. "I don't like tomatoes."

Buck pretended to be disturbed. "Oh-oh," he said. "I guess you should've planted licorice then."

Melanie giggled. "You're funny." She looked at me. "Can I go cool off with the hose?"

"There's lemonade," I pointed out.

"In a minute." She looked at me, pleading. "Please?"

The child had two swimming pools at home, but her favorite thing was to stand fully clothed under the spray of the hose, preferably with a dog or two dancing in the water beside her.

"Okay," I said. "But don't let the dogs get muddy." That last fell on mostly deaf ears as she bounded down the steps, two golden retrievers racing after her.

"Well." Uncle Ro pushed to his feet. "I reckon I'd better get going. You need anything from town, Buck?"

"Thanks, I'm good," Buck replied, "but you're not leaving me with all these vegetables."

Ro looked woefully at the two baskets. "Martie will kill me."

"I heard her say she was putting up soup this weekend," I supplied helpfully. "Here, I'll help you carry them to the car."

I tucked the two baskets into the backseat of Uncle Ro's car, and we hugged goodbye before he drove away. When I returned to the porch, Melanie had the hose going and the two golden retrievers barking and trying to catch the water stream with their teeth while she squealed with delight. Buck and I watched the show for a minute, chuckling at their antics.

"I should go too," I said, "before she turns your yard into a mudhole."

"Ah, she's fine," Buck said, smiling. "Remember when we used to play under the hose like that? Hard to believe we were ever that young."

"Speak for yourself." I sat down on the top step, leaning against the rail so that I could keep an eye on Melanie and still see Buck.

He said, serious now, "I guess you heard about Stan Bixby."

I nodded. Stan had died earlier that week without ever regaining consciousness. I wasn't entirely sure how I felt about that.

Buck said, "Ro's been helping me coordinate with the Jacksonville Police Department to try to wind up all those old murder cases. What a mess. It could take years to get all the paperwork straightened out."

I said, "Are you back at work full time, then?"

"Nah, just a couple of days a week for now. I heard you were over in South Carolina, giving testimony in the Goodwin case."

"It was just a preliminary hearing," I said. "I think Scotty's lawyer is trying to go with some legal theory about Jason being a custodial parent and Scotty acting on his instructions ..." I shrugged. "Who knows? It might work. Kylie and Mozart are home with Carol Goodwin now, but I didn't see them."

Melanie squealed as Cisco almost succeeded in grabbing the hose from her hand, and Buck and I turned our attention to the play for a moment. Both she and the dogs were soaked now. Good thing I kept dog towels in the car precisely for moments like these.

When I glanced up at Buck, he had an odd look on his face—not quite smiling but not sad either. "You know," he said, "when something like this happens"—he gestured vaguely to his injured leg—"it changes things, and being laid up like this, I've had a lot of time to think." He looked at me, somber now. "The day that I was shot, it was like my number was up. Three men tried to kill me. Crazy Deke ..." He gave a disgusted shake of his head. "They caught him on surveillance cameras two different times, pointing a gun at me and pretending to fire. God knows what he was thinking. Then Daniel Callanwell, going on his drugged-out shooting spree. Any one of those bullets could've taken me out. And finally, Stan Bixby." He was silent for a moment. "I should have died that day, but I didn't."

Melanie's laughter and the barking of happy dogs faded far, far into the background as Buck turned his gaze on me. That same almost-sad-but-not-quite smile was in his eyes. "You know you're the only woman I've ever loved, Raine," he said. "But I can't go on like this. I think I've known that for a while now. It just took a couple of bullets to make me admit it."

His gaze moved to Melanie and lingered there for a moment. "You've got a great life lined up, Raine," he said, "but I can't be a part of it anymore. I never thought I'd hear myself say that, but you know something? I'm okay with it." He looked back at me. "Are you?"

It took a moment before I could meet his eyes, but when I did, it was with a smile. "Yeah," I said. I reached up and snagged his pinky finger with my own, swinging it briefly like we'd done when we were kids, and then letting go. "I am."

Cisco shook off his coat, water droplets sparkling in the sun. Melanie screeched and jumped away as Pepper did the same, spraying her with water. She was, of course, already soaking wet.

"Melanie," I called, "time to go!"

"I'll get the towels!" She turned off the water and ran to the car. The two dogs loped beside her, trailing mud from their paws and their belly fur.

Buck smiled as he watched them, and then he looked back to me. "Things are going to change," he said. "I'm not sure how yet, but they have to."

I smiled back at him and got to my feet. "Change is good," I said.

And most of the time, it was.

ABOUT THE AUTHOR

Donna Ball is the author of over a hundred novels under several different pseudonyms in a variety of genres that include romance, mystery, suspense, paranormal, western adventure, historical and women's fiction. Recent popular series include the Ladybug Farm series, The Hummingbird House series, The Dogleg Island Mystery series, and the Raine Stockton Dog Mystery series. Donna is an avid dog lover and her dogs have won numerous titles for agility, obedience and canine musical freestyle. She lives in a restored Victorian barn in the heart of the Blue Ridge Mountains with a variety of four-footed companions. You can contact her at

www.donnaball.net.

Made in the USA
Monee, IL
23 May 2021

69347123R00164